Michelle Kenney is a firm believer in magic, and that doorways to other worlds can always be found if we look hard enough. She is also a hopeless scribbleholic and when left to her own devices, likes nothing better than to daydream about these worlds in the back of a dog-eared notebook. When not scribbling, Michelle can usually be found beachcombing with her family or rescuing Ted, their loopy Labrador, from himself. Michelle is the author of the bestselling Book of Fire trilogy, and a graduate of the Curtis Brown Writing for Children Novel Course 2015. She also has a LLB (Hons) Degree in Law, an APD in Public Relations, and an unhealthy obsession with all things Regency - Doctors say they're unlikely to find a cure any time soon.

facebook.com/BookofFireMK
x.com/MKenneyPR
instagram.com/mich_kenneybooks
tiktok.com/@michkenneyauthor

Also by Michelle Kenney

The Fairfax Sisters
The Mismatch of the Season

The Scandal of the Season

The Book of Fire
Storm of Ash

City of Dust

Book of Fire

THE SCANDAL OF THE SEASON

MICHELLE KENNEY

One More Chapter
a division of HarperCollins*Publishers* Ltd
1 London Bridge Street
London SE1 9GF
www.harpercollins.co.uk
HarperCollins*Publishers*
Macken House, 39/40 Mayor Street Upper,
Dublin 1, D01 C9W8, Ireland

This paperback edition 2025
1
First published in Great Britain in ebook format
by HarperCollins*Publishers* 2025
Copyright © Michelle Kenney 2025
Michelle Kenney asserts the moral right to
be identified as the author of this work

A catalogue record of this book is available from the British Library
ISBN: 978-0-00-868492-1

This novel is a work of fiction. Any references to real people, places and events are used fictitiously. All other names, characters and incidents portrayed are a work of the author's imagination and any resemblance to actual persons, living or dead, events or localities is entirely coincidental.

Printed and bound in the UK using 100% Renewable Electricity
by CPI Group (UK) Ltd

All rights reserved. No part of this publication may be reproduced, stored in a retrieval system, or transmitted, in any form or by any means, electronic, mechanical, photocopying, recording or otherwise, without the prior permission of the publishers.

Without limiting the author's and publisher's exclusive rights, any unauthorised use of this publication to train generative artificial intelligence (AI) technologies is expressly prohibited. HarperCollins also exercise their rights under Article 4(3) of the Digital Single Market Directive 2019/790 and expressly reserve this publication from the text and data mining exception.

*For my parents,
who started it all*

Chapter One

A BROTHEL, SOMEWHERE IN LONDON

February 1821

Lord Dominic Hugo Rotherby withdrew from his entanglement with unusual regret. It wasn't that his fair companions were difficult to leave, all such pleasures came to an end after all, but he was to trade their peachy skin and dulcet tones for a much less agreeable task, and he wasn't in the mood for murder.

Thoughtfully, he surveyed his sleeping companions, their limbs entwined like sirens, wondering where to hide their fee so neither had the chance to abscond with the whole. He'd been burned before, and had no desire for that curmudgeon, Johns, to be sending demands any time soon. His noble lips twitched as he recalled the last time one of Johns's surly henchmen tried to gain admittance to his townhouse, only to be confronted by his fiercely protective household who sent him on his way with the aid of a poker and a sharp reprimand.

Benson, his elderly butler, and Mrs Farleigh, his housekeeper, were still a force to be reckoned with, even in their dotage – though it didn't stop them worrying their young master was dicing with the devil.

Suppressing a smile, he leaned low over the copper-headed beauty to graze the rise of her pale breast, before crossing the floor to slip four shillings into their discarded stockings. He liked to be generous where he could and tonight he had appreciated their company more than usual.

'Thank you, Rotherby darling,' her sable-haired friend murmured, before drifting back to sleep.

He nodded as he picked up his pocket watch, its tiny archaic arms glinting back in the moonlight. It was a poignant reminder and his gaze narrowed briefly before he retrieved the rest of his scattered clothing, and dressed with the same careless grace that always made his tetchy tiger grin.

Horace, the most talented and exceptionally ill-humoured member of his household staff, was just a grubby orphan when Dominic chanced upon his skill with his precious team of chestnuts. Yet in less than a few months, he was managing the entirety of *his guvnor's* stable with the kind of canny acumen that made his lordship the envy of the ton. He was also the only member of his lordship's domestic staff with courage enough to tell him exactly *what* he thought, precisely *when* he thought it, and his guvnor's relaxed Corinthian style had long been a source of great amusement to him.

Wryly, Lord Rotherby recalled the many times he'd flown some lady's lodging in a state of complete disarray, only for Horace to spend the greater part of the homeward journey mopping up tears of laughter. This brutal honesty, coupled with an unerring ability to know a *high-stepper* from a *rum 'un* while remaining singularly unimpressed by any amount of devilish driving, had established him most firmly in his lordship's affections. And now he was his guvnor's most valued member of staff, with strict instructions to revert immediately should any of his less-than-noble friends attempt to poach him – which they had, on numerous occasions.

Lord Rotherby sat down to pull on his spotless Hessian boots – his only fashionable quirk – before casting a final, rueful glance back at the most agreeable hour he'd spent all week. Perhaps, with hindsight, he should have stuck to the opera house these past few months and not compromised his usual rule that his interests should be married and bored, or widowed and free.

He wouldn't make that mistake again.

Exhaling softly, he made his way from the room and down the rickety backstairs of the old theatre where Augusta, Johns's eagle-eyed wife, was keeping vigil in her usual chair. He nodded. He might enjoy the crime, but he didn't have to court the villains.

'I trust you enjoyed your company, m'Lor'?' Augusta asked, her sly words rasping inside her rotten teeth.

'Our opera girls have quite the reputation to uphold!'

Then she laughed in the way that always grated his nerves.

'Indeed,' he returned smoothly.

'Their falsetto was sublime!'

'Which is why you'll understand that I've paid them directly, Augusta, so that they might nurture their talents.'

Her laughter died away as he stepped past her into London's crisp and starry night with a faint smile. It might be hypocritical, but Augusta and Johns were the worst of their kind, and if it weren't for their monopoly, he'd never cross their threshold at all.

Briefly he paused to fasten his great-coat and assemble his thoughts, most of which related to a growing regret at having disposed of his tiger's services, given the bone-cold night. In fairness, Horace had been considerably unimpressed when he suggested he might walk back to Grosvenor Square.

'Y'sure y'ain't still in your cups, guvnor?'

It had taken all Rotherby's efforts to assure his cantankerous tiger that he was, in fact, quite sober and, while it had elicited a monologue of fluent cursing that won even his lordship's admiration, he had conceded in the end. And now Lord Rotherby wished he hadn't bothered.

The night had taken an unusual turn and rather than a leisurely midnight walk, his mind was focused on more practical considerations, such as whether *The Rotherby Lady*, his luxury yacht, could be readied imminently for a Channel crossing. The weather wasn't ideal, but his crew had enjoyed generous leave this year, and they were all reliable. Then there was his Grosvenor Square household to consider, and the fact that he'd fully intended to withdraw for a shooting party in the late spring. He exhaled as a myriad of seasonal commitments and half-formed plans competed for attention. Yet the night was still young, and while this whole matter was an entirely unforeseen nuisance, there was time.

Whistling softly, he pulled a hip flask from the pocket of his coat and took a deep draught. Brandy was his usual defence against the cold and briefly he congratulated himself, whisky would have had only half the desired effect. Then he set off in the direction of Park Lane, the toniest of all addresses, appearing to all who might see him to be the most carefree bachelor in town.

In truth, at a heady eight-and-twenty years, he really was quite content that ambitious mothers only ever eyed him with two questions in mind: the first related entirely to their unmarried daughters and, when they'd mourned the possibility of a dazzling match long enough, the second only to themselves. He was also quite certain that the advantages of remaining a black sheep on the marriage mart far outweighed any short-lived wedded bliss. Not only was he invited to the grandest balls, the most select hunting parties and desirable of soirees, their hostesses knew far better than to ask him to do anything but enjoy himself. Indeed, he'd discovered that so long as he kept to a few basic rules, and never *ever* talked of love, his wild reputation ensured two more important things: firstly, a steady line of worshipful bucks trying to be him, and secondly an even longer line of seasoned ladies determined to bed him. And, while this happy adoration perpetuated his myth as a *nonpareil* amongst the gentleman, and an *archfiend* amongst the ladies, his glinting eyes and cavalier grace ensured he remained the regret of every matriarch of the ton. In short, it was safe to say that Lord Dominic Hugo Rotherby – daring gambler, devilish dueller and notorious rake – was excessively content with life, and his place in it.

Which only made this evening's turn of events an irritation, to say the least.

He sighed as he pulled off his silk cravat, tied in a swift

Georgian knot, before loosening his high shirt collar to reveal a golden throat many a young lady had eyed over her ratafia.

'For I'll be damned if I spend any last night trussed up like a roast bird,' he muttered to himself, wondering if he might just as well finish the brandy.

His dawn assignation was creeping closer, and he had no desire to duel sober; he was a crack shot either way, but the consequences were far less troubling when he was fortified.

Frowning, he thought back to the point at which his evening had taken a decidedly unwelcome turn. The challenge had come over the faro table, and just when his luck had changed too. Quite why Sir George Weston had chosen that exact moment to demand satisfaction was a mystery, to say the least. The ton may have noticed Sir Weston's pretty sister making cow eyes at him, but he couldn't be responsible for every debutante's flight of fancy, and the heat of his challenge was most curious for a gentleman who usually presented in sensible coats and a quiet manner.

Even if they did have history.

Lord Rotherby's eyelids sank lower as he recalled the moment he suggested it might be Miss Weston's fanciful nature that required a challenge, rather than his good self, and that anyone who knew him knew his rules too.

With hindsight, his suggestion that Sir Weston might guess he wouldn't look for the attentions of a silly chit who was not only prone to fits of the vapours, but also possessed a 'braying laugh that could wake an entire neighbourhood', might have been a little sharp. But the more he thought on it, the more he was convinced it wasn't his fault the girl had a tendency towards theatricals – much less so that she'd invented an entire fanciful romance with him playing the role of chief villain. All of which had led to the ruin of the best hand of cards he'd had in a while.

Lord Rotherby sighed. It really was excessively inconvenient, especially since the season had just begun and he'd backed some real sweet runners at Cheltenham. But as any real gentleman knew, he had little choice but to see the matter through. A challenge, once issued, was a matter of honour and even if there hadn't been several witnesses present, he'd still be duty-bound to meet sensible Sir George Weston at dawn, with his affairs fully in order.

He slowed as he reached the wide steps of Rotherby House, the grand Grosvenor Square home he'd inherited upon the passing of his parents, and turned to gaze out at the moonlit park. It was his favourite time of day, when the whole neighbourhood was quiet, and illuminated only by the handful of lanterns left to burn overnight. Tonight though, a strange and melancholic mist hung over the silhouetted silver oaks, almost as though they sensed that he might have to leave for a while.

Briefly, he considered the options that lay before him once again. He couldn't rely on Sir Weston being a terrible shot; he'd hunted with him on a number of occasions and he could hold a pistol like any man. It was more that a Rotherby never missed.

His father's faded face reached through his thoughts as he gazed at the shadowed park, ignoring an old twist deep inside. As a boy, he would often sleep fitfully, dreaming of the glass-eyed stags his father felled and imagining their escape instead, but the cold light of day would only ever confirm his fears. And when he grew old enough to refuse to join the hunt, his father labelled him 'a coward, unworthy of his bloodline' – words to which he'd grown hardened after discovering his betrayal.

His mother's face followed, and Lord Rotherby closed his eyes, recalling the way her gentle tone had always soothed him whenever he was distressed. She'd been his one saving grace, and her untimely death the very reason he would never marry or have children or his own.

'Do you require a nightcap, my lord?'

The large front door creaked inwards, revealing an elderly gentleman bearing a candle and a kindly smile.

Lord Rotherby regarded the proud retainer, who'd been his butler for as long as he could recall, with real affection. He really needed to put his domestic affairs in order as a matter of priority; they all depended on him after all.

'No, I thank you, Benson. And shouldn't you be abed this hour? What have I said about waiting up for me?'

His tone was short but Benson merely inclined his head, unabashed.

'I beg your pardon, my lord, but I had some personal correspondence to finish.'

Rotherby nodded, though they both knew the truth.

'I have also left a fire burning in the library, my lord, just as you like.'

'Thank you,' Rotherby returned in a milder tone. 'Though you know you need only ask if you need time off, Benson. No one should be writing letters at one o'clock in the morning!'

'Thank you, my lord. I am in need of no extra time. Will that be all, my lord?'

'Yes… That is to say…'

The butler paused his withdrawal, as his young master frowned.

'It is likely … *highly* likely that I will need to leave town tomorrow … for a few weeks. I'll send word as soon as I can but, in the interim, I'd be grateful if you and Mrs Farleigh could oversee the closure of Rotherby House – as my mother would have wished?'

He paused to consider the damnable speed at which gossip travelled through the ton.

'Also, it's probably best not to mention this to anyone – at least not until I send word.'

Lord Rotherby rarely mentioned his parents, save to those long-standing members of his household who remembered them, and even then only when absolutely necessary. In truth, he was quite aware that collectively, they could claim many more memories than he, and suspected most of their enduring loyalty was out of love for his mother, who'd bewitched them all in her short, bright lifetime, rather than his father who'd done little but instil fear.

Yet their marriage had resulted in one note of hope: a quiet boy who adored his mother with all his heart until the day she and his unborn sister died, when he swore his father's violent blood would end with him. Thankfully, his father had outlived his mother by only a few months and, by the time an eccentric aunt had filled the breach, he was quite used to being thought an orphan. She'd arrived with three trunks of books and a glaring parrot, maintaining that she would guide him only until he came of age and, true to her word, she'd left for Europe the morning of his twenty-first birthday, advising him to look for her only if he 'made a real mess of things'.

Tonight was the first time he felt he might have come close.

'As you wish, my lord,' Benson said with a nod, the tiny crease between his eyes the only sign that he was at all surprised. 'Although, might I suggest you peruse the contents of the letter that arrived ten minutes ago before making any … permanent arrangements? I've put it on your desk, my lord.'

Lord Rotherby frowned.

'Thank you, Benson. That will be all.' He nodded briskly before making his way through the grand hallway of Rotherby House in the direction of his library. Benson was discreet, but the last thing he needed was for Mrs Farleigh and the rest of his overprotective household to get wind of his impending duel. They all worried enough as it was.

Swiftly, he strode across the warm room to pick up the new missive. The lettering was clearly written in haste, and he broke open the Weston seal with a sigh of exasperation. Whatever the coxcomb said now had better not add insult to injury, for he was quite out of patience.

Lord Rotherby,

>*I write in haste to withdraw my challenge. At the time of issue, I had good reason to believe you'd acted dishonourably, but my sister has since assured me that your attentions were only ever courteous and noble.*
>
>*In light of this new information, I find myself satisfied there has been no improper conduct, and therefore no impeachment of honour.*
>
>*I trust this letter will find you in good time, and you will have no objection to considering the matter concluded.*

Yours respectfully,
Sir George Weston

Lord Rotherby screwed up the letter with a gleam of contempt.

'Infernal popinjay!' he cursed, tossing it onto the fire.

He'd always known Weston disliked him but had never thought him a troublemaker before. Indeed, he was less than persuaded by his reference to *new information* and would have to be vigilant in the future. Not only did they share history, it seemed a few of his close friends thought him entirely capable of seducing a chit scarcely out of the schoolroom too. They hadn't said as much, but he had seen the doubt on their faces, which meant he must accept Weston's apology lest they think any truth to it.

Rotherby cursed again, his eyelids lowering lazily as he watched the flames dance in the hearth. Perhaps pretty, doe-eyed Sylvia Weston really had intervened on his behalf, or perhaps one of Weston's bourgeois friends had warned him about Rotherby's record with a single-shot flintlock. Either way, he was sure his main consideration should be for the fact that his honour was still intact, and there were no unsightly bodies to explain away.

Fortified by the thought that the evening had taken a much more encouraging turn without him having to lift even one murderous finger, Lord Rotherby exhaled. The night was yet young, White's was always open to its patrons, and he had a taste for drink poured by a fairer hand than his own.

Seconds later, he pulled on his great-coat and headed back out into the hallway, now lit by a lone, flickering candelabra. It was one of Benson's traditions, left over from the time when his young master might climb out of bed because he couldn't sleep. He smiled faintly before extinguishing the flames.

Tomorrow, he would put his household in order, just in case, but right now he had one thought uppermost and that was to celebrate his reprieve the only way a notorious rake knew how.

Chapter Two

KNIGHTSWOOD MANOR, DEVON

February 1821

'The trouble with notorious rakes is that they cannot *bear* anyone else behaving notoriously!'

Sophie smiled primly as she pulled a ringlet free from her golden locks that were dressed *à la Sévigné*, and paused to inspect the effect.

'You mean like *pigwidgeoned dunderheads*?!' Matilda asked, rolling herself up inside Sophie's coverlet, roly-poly pudding style.

'Matilda!' Sophie scolded as Josephine stuffed another of Cook's infamous shortbreads into her mouth and tried not to snort.

'What have I told you about listening to Billy Briggs and the village boys! Thomas will stop your pin money for a month, and you're already on your best behaviour after the pig-race debacle.'

'That wasn't just me!' Matilda protested.

'Edward and Henry placed actual bets, and I heard Phoebe say—'

'I don't want to know what Edward and Henry did. Or what Phoebe said!' Sophie exclaimed.

'And a *pigwidgeoned dunderhead* isn't what I meant anyway!'

She returned her attention to her ringlets and a new velvet ribbon.

'Harriet gave me a coming-out talk,' she clarified, rolling her eyes, 'and specifically warned me against notorious rakes, who "behave scandalously, and get away with it" because they're so charming? She also said the moment anyone tries to 'play them at their game' they lose interest, because they cannot bear a threat.'

'Oh! You mean, like a libertine?' Matilda frowned. 'What game?'

'Matilda Fairfax, what on earth do you know about libertines at the grand old age of thirteen!' Sophie admonished.

There was a muffled giggle before the youngest Fairfax emerged from the coverlet, wearing her most indignant expression.

'Actually, I overheard Harriet telling Cook, that Mama said Thomas might end up an *awful libertine* if he didn't find himself a wife by the extremely old age of thirty!

'Though Blackbeard the fearsome pirate also fought for libertines, I think?' Matilda added, wrinkling her nose.

'Blackbeard the fearsome pirate fought for *liberty*!' Josephine corrected, dissolving into peals of laughter.

'And really, dearest,' Sophie exhaled, as though in pain, 'it's probably best you don't go around repeating unsavoury gossip, especially if it concerns members of your own family!'

'But if Mama said it…' Matilda began, before catching the warning light in her sister's eye. 'Oh well, what game anyway?' she grumbled, retreating inside the bedding.

'Why, the season of course!' Sophie returned, dabbing a small amount of homemade lavender perfume on her wrists and neck. 'Otherwise known as the marriage mart, or entertainment of the ton, while gentlemen sit in Parliament and make all the important decisions about our lives.'

'You're beginning to sound like Phoebe!' Josephine accused with a grin.

'I've never disputed that the female mind is vastly underappreciated,' Sophie retorted. 'Only that *real* change requires a little more ingenuity than swapping our corsets for pantaloons and calling ourselves heroines. Not that I wouldn't look extremely fetching in a pair of fitted riding breeches, of course,' she murmured, side-eyeing her reflection.

'Of course!' Josephine chimed in, still grinning.

'For I do believe,' Sophie mused, 'and I say this entirely without prejudice, that I have a better leg than most gentlemen…

'Anyway, Harriet says the game or season is a 'vicious place for any debutante', for while mamas and their offspring vie for the biggest prize, there is always 'a pack of notorious rakes waiting in the wings'!'

She mimicked their old nurse perfectly, while bringing her new Prussian parasol to her shoulder, musket-style, and eyeing her youngest sister with suspicion.

'They *prowl* the market,' she growled, stalking the bed and making Matilda shriek and retreat back inside the coverlet. 'Hunting the finest *trophies*, before using every last ounce of their wit and charm for the kill! And woe betide anyone who gets in their way'—she paused to take aim at Matilda's giggling, padded form—'for they are *pigwidgeoned dunderheads* indeed!'

'Sophie!' Matilda wailed as her sister dropped the parasol and began tickling her mercilessly instead.

'Trophies like Arabella Huntingdon?' Josephine sniffed, immersed in a library copy of Lord Byron's *Childe Harold's Pilgrimage*.

'Yes, just like Arabella Huntingdon,' Sophie sighed, finally taking pity on her sister and returning to her toilette. 'Though how she didn't guess Lord Sutcliffe was a cad remains a total mystery to me. She agreed to a clandestine elopement, thus compromising her reputation, and for what good reason? She is never to be seen anywhere *in* town, while he is rarely to be seen out. It was truly a marriage of contrivance, and how she ever thought it would end otherwise was the greatest piece of folly.' She pulled a small pair of lace day gloves from her dressing table drawer.

'Phoebe is happy and she nearly eloped,' Josephine said with a frown.

'Well, yes, but she didn't actually marry the brother she planned to elope with!' Sophie replied drily. 'And Phoebe and the viscount are an exception anyway,' she added.

'They were not only lucky enough to find love, but also to make a perfectly respectable match that the ton has embraced. It is the best and most fortunate of outcomes! Can you imagine actually *desiring* to spend time with the person you've married, rather than planning your happiness around their absence? It has to be most satisfying – a meeting of both hearts and minds...' she tailed off wistfully.

'Phoebe and the viscount never agree,' Matilda scowled. 'They'd argue over breakfast eggs, given half the chance!'

There was a brief silence before they all started to laugh.

'That's very true,' Sophie conceded. 'In fact, sometimes I'm not sure who's more disagreeable of the two!' she added, making them laugh harder.

'And yet ... they do seem to *love* being perfectly disagreeable together. It's the oddest sort of happiness I've ever seen,' Sophie sighed, wiping her eyes. 'But then, perhaps that's the secret. Perhaps real, enduring love is only to be found with someone similar enough in nature, and yet confident enough in spirit *not* to concede their opinion every five minutes? Perhaps the combination keeps both interest and affection alive?'

'Like Titania and Oberon!' Josephine exclaimed, her eyes shining. 'Or Romeo and Juliet, or Hermia and Lysander ... or—'

'Yes, yes we get the picture, dearest,' Sophie assured rapidly, before Josephine recited her entire list of favourite fictional lovers.

'Is that what you want though, Sophie?' Matilda asked, frowning. 'To find someone you can be perfectly disagreeable with? Because I think it a terrible idea. You'll be forever enacting a Cheltenham tragedy!'

'Moi? A Cheltenham tragedy?' Sophie repeated, throwing up her hands in mock horror. 'Though you may be right,' she smiled after a beat. 'And, disagreements and tragedies aside, I fully intend to make an advantageous love match this season!'

She paused to flick open her new ivory brisé fan with practiced ease.

'For why shouldn't it be possible for modern debutantes, who know their own mind?'

She peered coyly over the edge of the fan.

'You really do sound like Phoebe!' Matilda declared, grinning.

'Phoebe didn't want to marry at all,' Sophie replied, 'whereas I can't imagine not marrying! But that doesn't mean I'll settle for just anything either. I know it seems that only gentlemen can be ambitious or have aspirations in this life, while we are required to play a much milder role, but I wish for as much success with my husband's heart as I do his situation. And if it is not to be that I am woken up with violent protestations of love and devotion every day, I shall move to Paris and become a famous modiste instead!'

'Good grief!' Josephine exclaimed, pushing her loose spectacles up her snub nose. 'Does Thomas know about your ambitions in the fashion industry? And surely all that devotion, violent or otherwise, is going to get very wearisome after a while? I mean, I'm happy you're my sisters of course, but some days I could quite easily go without seeing any of you.'

'Charmed, I'm sure!' Sophie glared at her sister.

'Ditto!' Matilda called in a muffled voice. 'And I'm most definitely *not* going to marry anyone disagreeable, or violently in love, or anything in the middle if I can help it.'

'Why? Who are you going to marry then?' Josephine quizzed. 'Or are you going to be an old maid, like Harriet?'

'Harriet seems perfectly happy to me!' Matilda flashed.

'And Phoebe says we should have as much choice as our brothers so if I can't marry Misty I'm not going to marry anyone. I shall simply play the game until I'm much too old and toothless for anyone to want to marry me,' she added, finally rolling out of her hiding place.

'Hush Matty!' Sophie said, laughing in a scandalised tone. 'I think marrying a Dartmoor pony might be a stretch, even for you,' she continued, 'and young ladies don't get to play the game. We *are* the game.'

'All the more reason to change the rules then!' Matilda retorted.

Sophie sighed.

'Who knows, perhaps one day we will, but for now we must content ourselves with ensuring that those who seek only to trifle with our affections do not succeed.'

'How?' Matilda challenged.

'Ah well that, dearest,' Sophie said reassuringly, 'is where you are fortunate to be a Fairfax, with more than your fair share of fearsome sisters to help you navigate the marriage mart. Although, in practice I do believe it is not at all difficult to know a true gentleman from a cad. Take Sir George Weston, for example. He has a respectable title, good connections and the last time we saw him he tipped his hat at me – twice! Perfectly gentlemanly behaviour.'

'It was windy,' Josephine qualified, readjusting her spectacles. 'It looked as though he was struggling to hang on to it. Though, I do believe there *is* something of a Mr Bingley about him, is there not?'

Sophie glanced at her bookish sister and was surprised to see a faint blush stealing into her pale cheeks.

'He has the most sensible countenance,' Josephine continued, unaware of her sister's continued study, 'and appears to have avoided the silly, foppish ways most gentlemen adopt. He also has a quiet air of authority that neither seeks attention nor shies away from it, and his manner always suits the occasion. He neither tries too hard, nor not hard enough, and always knows just what to say too... In truth, he seems to me to be to be *exactly* what a real gentleman should be!'

She looked up then to find Sophie regarding her with such an owlish expression, while Matilda feigned vomiting, that she flushed and hid behind her book.

'Now *you're* the pigwidgeoned dunderhead!' Matilda declared, snorting with laughter. 'Any gentleman who ties his cravat in the mathematical style is a veritable fop. Alex said so, so it must be true!'

'Matilda!' her sisters chimed in protest.

'You really mustn't call Viscount Damerel Alex!' Sophie remonstrated. 'It's so improper even if we are family – and no, it wouldn't make any difference if you were a pirate either!'

'Well, it *was* windy the day we saw Sir Weston, because I almost lost my bonnet too,' Matilda returned mulishly. 'Also, I think appearances can be very deceptive! Alex says he was considered a rake before he married Phoebe, which just goes to prove you can never be sure what gentlemen are really like until you've known them for a quadrillion years!'

It was Josephine's turn to snort.

'That's a pretty long engagement by anyone's standards, and Harriet says a lady shouldn't keep any gentleman waiting too long for anything.'

'Pah! Well, this is where *my* generation will be different!' Matilda declared, snatching up Sophie's parasol and lunging at the curtains.

'We won't be afraid of offending a few old cronies at Almack's, just because we've no desire to be a trophy for some fortune-hunting rake!'

Sophie threw her gaze to the ceiling as Matilda proceeded to make short work of the thick, chintz folds.

'Heavens dearest, I shall find you donning Fred's breeches and heading to a London theatre next!' she exclaimed.

'Though you need not concern yourself too greatly,' she added. 'Thirteen is still a little young to be attracting the rakes and libertines of Georgian London. And in truth, I fully intend this season's triumph to be mine and mine alone.'

She flicked open her brise fan and brought it to her face with her most determined smile. 'Without a single, pigwidgeoned dunderhead in sight!'

Chapter Three

ALMACK'S ASSEMBLY ROOMS, ST JAMES' SQUARE, LONDON

Two weeks later

'I think almost everyone is afraid of the old cronies of Almacks,' Phoebe whispered as she waited for the footman to take her card, 'but I find they're a bit like homemade puddings: once they've let off a little steam, they really are quite squidgy on the inside.'

Sophie suppressed a chuckle as she adjusted her pink satin gloves for the hundredth time since exiting the Damerel carriage.

'Thank you, dearest sister. Now I'm going to conjure up an image of boiled suet whenever I'm introduced to any of the important matrons and patronesses!' she remonstrated.

Phoebe grinned as she attempted to smooth out a crumple in her new oyster silk ballgown.

'That's not such a bad idea. It will make you wary, and wary is good in London society.'

'Lord and Lady Amesbury of Amesbury Hall!'

The receiving line moved forwards, as the tones of the bulging-eyed footman rose above the drone of esteemed personages present.

'The Viscountess Damerel of Damerel House, Miss Sophie Fairfax of Knightswood Manor!' he pronounced hoarsely.

'So how *does* it feel to be introduced as "The Viscountess Damerel"?' Sophie asked curiously as they passed through the doors and into the crush of the main ballroom.

'Honestly?' Phoebe quizzed, accepting a glass of lemonade from a passing footman.

'No, fancifully, what do you think?' Sophie replied, with a laugh.

'Well … a touch fussy!' her sister returned after a sip.

'But, you have to enjoy it a little?' Sophie persisted, side-eyeing her sister. 'After all, you barely waited four months before waltzing down the aisle with the viscount!' She smiled dreamily. 'I don't think I'll ever forget the flurry of snow as you left Knightswood's Chapel in your ivory velvet pelisse, Phoebs – the one you promised to let me borrow, remember? It really was quite magical,' she added with a sigh.

Sophie then had the long-awaited satisfaction of watching her fiercely independent sister flush the exact shade of rowan berries, just as an elegant couple paused to offer their felicitations. The result was an even rosier hue that Phoebe attempted to hide in the bottom of her lemonade.

'First of all, calling my husband "the viscount" really does sound as though we're still plotting his downfall beneath my coverlet,' Phoebe replied when she could. 'Just call him Alex, like Matilda!

'And, as far as our wedding was concerned, it just didn't

make any sense to wait. Josephine had made such a good recovery, Aurelia had gone abroad with her parents and...'

She tailed off as a surge of deeper colour undermined her defence entirely.

'You know, watching you marry for love has been the very best tonic,' Sophie murmured wickedly.

'Tonic for what?' her sister challenged.

'For putting up with years of declarations about how you would so much rather embrace a life of heroic adventure than marry any man, let alone for love!'

'But I *am* living a life of adventure!' Phoebe protested. 'Just with rather more husband than I anticipated, which, I hasten to add, hasn't been what I expected at all! In truth, I think Fred would call marriage 'a right leveller'.' She paused to tug on a length of escaped hair, and grin ruefully. 'And yes, I do still worship the ground Mary Wollstonecraft walked upon – I just didn't realise it was possible to be a happily married feminist!'

Sophie laughed, and placed her hand over Phoebe's.

'No one who's ever known you would question your principles, dearest, and to be honest, I aspire to being a happily married *feminine-nanist*!'

'A feminine-a-what? I'm not sure that's quite the same...'

'It's better!' Sophie grinned. 'I'm a firm believer in both femininity and feminism, and that they can complement each other, so why not a happy marriage of the two?!' She leaned closer with a mischievous twinkle. 'And do tell me if there any particular aspects of matrimony you'd care to highlight as being *particularly levelling*, Viscountess Damerel.'

'Sophie!' Phoebe returned in a scandalised tone. She chuckled as Sophie fluttered her eyelashes.

'You know I can't!' Phoebe continued. 'Thomas will actually murder me if he finds out I've told you anything, plus you know you can't keep a secret for love nor money!'

'Please? I'll return your primrose muslin,' Sophie persisted, undeterred by the threat of their eldest brother.

'No, and you can keep it,' Phoebe insisted, her eyes dancing. 'All I can say is that matrimony holds a number of surprises and some of them are even better than ... macaroons!'

For a few seconds they eyed one another stubbornly, before dissolving into a fit of silent giggles that threatened to undo all their efforts to appear like sophisticated ladies of the ton. Then Phoebe caught the eye of one of the matrons and was forced to recall that while she was happily married, her sister had yet to share the same advantage.

'I must tell you, Alexander and I received the most generous letter from Dr Kapool this morning,' she tried, rapidly changing the subject. 'He wrote that his research will allow him to join us at Ebcott Place in the late spring. Isn't that wonderful? Josephine and Florence will be the first to benefit from an education under the watchful eye of a doctor in residence!'

'Mary Wollstonecraft really would approve,' Sophie returned, her voice still wobbling.

'I like to think so,' Phoebe said. 'And to claim credit too, but of course none of it would have happened without Alexander.'

'But of course!' Sophie agreed.

'Who'd have thought that the haughty old viscount would turn out to be such a staunch feminist? Or that he'd offer up his country house for the furtherance of female education generally?'

'Well, he really is neither haughty nor old,' Phoebe began indignantly.

'There you go again!' Sophie retorted with a chuckle, 'but please don't change anything for me. It's so refreshing for a society wife to be madly in love with her own husband. It gives me hope for the same.'

Phoebe rolled her eyes as Sophie took a sip of lemonade, wondering if her sister was also recalling a certain dancing-eyed Captain Damerel. Once he'd threatened to divide them, though, while Sophie had always suspected Phoebe of withholding some of the truth, it was months ago now.

'When will you and Alexander take your honeymoon?' she asked, as Marchioness Cholmondeley, one of the peacock-styled patronesses, passed by.

They both sank into a swift, respectful curtsey.

'In a week or so,' Phoebe replied, relieved to be back on safer ground. 'Alex is determined we'll see Florence and Tuscany in April – something about the Ponte Vecchio in the spring apparently – so we make for Paris first, and travel on from there. 'Hopefully we'll also see Vienna and perhaps the Alps too, but it will all depend on how long we can be away from Ebcott Place.'

'You always wanted to go on a Grand Tour,' Sophie smiled wistfully.

'Well, it's not touring as an actor, or riding bareback across windswept clifftops,' Phoebe mused with a rueful smile, 'but, I think I can put up with a tour of Europe without too many regrets.'

'Spoken like a true Fairfax!' Sophie replied, laughing. 'And now you're somewhat annoyingly happily married, perhaps you can stop filling Matilda's head with all your old notions? She really does believe she can marry Misty and become a pirate!'

'Misty, as in my fifteen-year-old Dartmoor pony?' Phoebe quizzed.

'Yes!'

'Excellent!' Phoebe chuckled, raising her glass.

'Of all of us, I wager she'll be the Fairfax to do it!'

'Oh don't encourage her, Phoebs. I—'

'Ladies laying a wager? Now there's something you don't overhear too often in Almack's.'

Startled, the sisters turned to face the tall, enigmatic gentleman who'd paused beside the lemonade table behind them.

'But please, do accept my sincere apologies for interrupting such a lively discourse!' He smiled disarmingly. 'I'm not really in the habit of doing such a thing, particularly when the ladies are so very fair, but you took me by surprise you see, and I'm not generally surprised by much these days.'

'Not at all, Mr…?' Phoebe curtsied politely, as the gentleman made a very elegant leg to them both.

'Lord Dominic Rotherby, at your service. I believe I have the pleasure of addressing Viscountess Damerel? And the delightful Miss Sophie Fairfax too?' Sophie flushed as the striking gentleman in a Sardinian evening coat bestowed the most dazzling smile on her, before returning his gaze to her sister. 'What a pleasure it is to meet the lady who has finally made an honest man of Damerel. I salute you, Viscountess.

Though why he has abandoned you to the veritable wilds of Almack's so soon is beyond my comprehension. I'm not sure I would be so complacent.'

Sophie watched curiously as Lord Rotherby lifted Phoebe's hand to his lips with practised ease. His moss-green eyes were alight with humour, but also distinctly sincere, and she suppressed a qualm. Harriet had suggested some bachelors of the ton considered married ladies fair game once their position was settled, but surely none would have such effrontery in Almack's.

'It's a pleasure to meet you too, Lord Rotherby,' Phoebe replied with a faint frown, 'but my husband is neither my keeper nor my gaoler, and I believe myself quite equal to the task of chaperoning my younger sister, without falling prey to too many villains and predators.'

Rotherby's lips twitched, while Sophie watched.

'Oh I'm sure there's no need to be cross, Phoebe,' she interjected. 'Lord Rotherby was only jesting, as all gentlemen are wont to do. You should know better than to pay my sister a compliment, sir. She's pinked a man for less!'

'Sophie!' Phoebe objected, glaring at her sister.

'But how intriguing!' Rotherby drawled.

His eyelids lowered lazily as he took a pinch of snuff from an elaborate snuff box and smiled at Sophie's guilty, dancing eyes.

'Pray do tell all, Miss Fairfax. Is this a family trait, perchance?'

'Dear Lord!' Phoebe muttered, closing her eyes.

'What a notion, my lord!' Sophie chided with an even rosier hue. 'It's more a family expression for a set-down. Phoebe is quite famous for them! And my youngest sister is much the same, though Josephine and I tend to prefer a rather less *spirited* approach.'

'Is that so?' Lord Rotherby replied, his forest greens alight with amusement.

'And Miss Josephine is another of the refreshing Fairfaxes, I take it?' he added. 'Have I had the pleasure?'

At this, Sophie felt the heat of Phoebe's gaze and looked pointedly at her lemonade. There was a strict dry rule enforced at Almack's, and no opportunity to indulge the way her sister had with Devil's Brew.

'Miss Josephine Fairfax is not yet out, sir, and not likely to be for some time to come,' Phoebe replied pithily. 'And now, if you will excuse us—'

'A pity! Still, I hope you are both finding London society to your taste? Aside from impertinent gentlemen who ask too many questions of course – though I imagine the refreshing Fairfaxes must take it all in their stride!'

His eyes glinted roguishly as he took another pinch of snuff with a distinct flick of his wrist.

'You really must excuse any frankness on our part, sir,' Phoebe returned with a frown. 'Fairfaxes aren't exactly known for their fragility or meekness.

'But, as to the rest, the season is yet young, and I'm certain my sister will continue to enjoy all the *appropriate* distractions and *suitable* company that London society has to offer,' she added carefully.

'But of course, and I'm certain the ton will be clamouring to become better acquainted with the Fairfaxes,' he replied, with an amused smile. 'Though it may be useful to recall that, in the midst of all the prestigious balls and select soirees of the season, it is usually the *unsuitable* company who make it the most fun!'

Phoebe shot Lord Rotherby a hard glance, as Sophie smothered a chuckle.

'But isn't that always the case, Lord Rotherby?!' she exclaimed impulsively. 'It's all very well being primped and preened like a peahen for debutante balls, but no one says anything above how well one looks, or how daring Miss-so-and-so is for wearing the very latest French fashion…'— Phoebe eyeballed her sister despairingly—'That is to say, we don't look for *unsuitable* company, of course,' she added swiftly. 'Only that everyone seems to behave so particularly in town that one barely talks about anything real at all. And it's not that I'm *not* enjoying all the balls and races and musical soirees, and the shopping, of course, for I am partial to a pelisse and have been designing my own for some time now … but there's just that feeling that if everyone could relax their hems a little it would be so much more—'

'Oh look, I do believe that's Lady Worthing! Look Sophie, Lady Worthing!' Phoebe interrupted, before Sophie could commit every crime known to polite society.

'Fun?' Lord Rotherby offered seamlessly.

'Exactly so!' Sophie replied, sparkling. She studiously ignored the sharp tug on her sleeve. 'At home, we know everyone well enough to talk about real things, but here in town, one's conversation is so restricted that you can't get to know anyone, not really, and then there's this feeling that beneath it all the debutantes might actually be *the*…'

'Fun?' Lord Rotherby repeated, chuckling.

'Yes! That's it exactly!'

'That's because you *are*,' he whispered theatrically.

'Lord Rotherby!' Phoebe gasped.

'Miss Fairfax, I'll let you in on a little secret which took me some time to fathom,' he continued, unabashed. 'While this year's debutantes are whispering about the most handsome gentlemen with the fastest barouches and biggest estates, the very same gentlemen are placing wagers on the prettiest debutantes with the finest connections and largest dowries.

'So, the London season really is a game, and you gentlemen are no better off than us,' Sophie sighed.

'On the contrary, Miss Fairfax,' he replied languidly, 'I believe gentlemen are *much* worse off – you at least have female intuition on your side.'

'Well, at least you know gentlemen aren't alone in their love of a wager anyway!' Sophie replied with a wide smile. 'And on that, Phoebe taught me most everything I know.'

'How edifying,' Lord Rotherby replied, eyeing Phoebe with amusement. 'The viscountess appears to be a veritable connoisseur of so many matters. Tell me, what wagers have you made recently, that are not bound by oaths of secrecy?'

Sophie's eyes danced, knowing she was being baited, while Phoebe gritted her teeth.

'Well, last week I wagered Isabella Hampton that she was too polite to refuse to stand up with Lord Endercott – the gentleman over there with dubious facial whiskers – and I was right!' she offered with a note of triumph. 'She said they only danced a boring old cotillion towards the end of the evening, but that's *still* a dance, as well we all know.'

'But of course it is,' Lord Rotherby agreed, his lips

twitching. 'And dubious facial whiskers you say? I can't say I'd noticed, but now you've mentioned them, I can't see anything else. Poor, unfortunate Lord Endercott!'

'Lord Rotherby,' Phoebe enunciated carefully, 'I've just seen one of the patrons to whom we owe an introduction and I believe—'

'But of course, Viscountess,' Lord Rotherby said assuringly, 'such matters should never be delayed. But before you go, I should like to propose a small wager of my own, in full and open acknowledgement of Fairfax family prowess when it comes to wagers.' He paused while Sophie chuckled delightedly. 'I wager that you will both find your dance cards overflowing this evening, which is why I'd like to claim one from each of you before they reach that perilous stage. And if that is not appropriate for Miss Sophie Fairfax, then I trust you would have no objection, Viscountess, as you are already quite immune to the villains and predators of Almack's?'

'My sister does not manage my dance card, sir,' Sophie replied swiftly, 'and I should be delighted!'

She sank into her prettiest curtsey, while her sister met the amused rake's gaze with exasperation. Sophie watched curiously. Lord Rotherby was one of few people she'd ever known to meet her sister's challenge squarely, and he undoubtedly knew what was *appropriate* despite any pretence otherwise. He was also ridiculously handsome with enviable cheekbones, thick, satirical eyebrows and dark, velvet eyes – which he knew exactly how to use to his advantage – and yet, despite all this charm, she was convinced he intended no real mischief at all.

'I am honoured, Miss Fairfax. Viscountess?' Lord Rotherby queried, his eyes glinting with amusement.

Phoebe inclined her head abruptly, though Sophie could tell she was torn between not wishing to start any gossip and itching to give him a blazing set-down.

'I consider myself most fortunate, and before you think me the dullest bachelor in the room, I would like to propose one last wager,' he added.

'No one could ever think you dull, Lord Rotherby!' Sophie reassured swiftly.

'I am most relieved to hear it,' he replied with a smile. 'And my wager is this, Miss Sophie of the refreshingly forthright Fairfaxes: you shall have a dozen suitors fighting over your hand before the month is out!'

She chuckled delightedly.

'Oh, my lord, you are truly incorrigible! But you know I can't accept *that* wager for I am determined to make a love match, and nothing else shall suffice.'

'A love match! *Quelle surprise!*' Lord Rotherby replied curiously. 'For they are quite rare on the marriage mart. Your own fabled circumstances are quite the exception, of course, Viscountess Damerel.'

Phoebe's eyes darkened suspiciously. 'Indeed, if the tale of your whirlwind engagement and marriage was not doing the rounds,' he pressed on, 'I'd be quite inclined to say such a thing does not exist at all.'

'Oh, but of course it exists!' Sophie exclaimed, ignoring her sister's pained expression.

'How else do you explain music or poetry or … or the

happiness of those fortunate enough to experience it? It's so real that it's visible!'

'Well then,' Lord Rotherby replied with a faint smile, 'I'll amend my wager to this Miss Fairfax: I wager you'll choose to marry for any reason *other than love* by the end of the season! And the reason I'm wagering this,' he continued, despite Sophie's protest, 'is that while the ambition you describe may seem noble, even the strongest of attachments rarely last a lifetime. Far better you spend your time pursuing a title and land for, unlike love, they are likely to yield a much more profitable return.'

'Lord Rotherby!' Phoebe and Sophie protested in unison.

'Wager accepted!' Sophie added furiously. 'I said I'll make a love match, and I will.'

He smiled and inclined his head. 'Well then, we'll consider our wager sealed, and I look forward to your endeavours on the marriage mart. I have no doubt you will be a sparkling success, Miss Fairfax, whomever you settle upon. Until the cotillion, and perhaps the Strauss, Viscountess?' he concluded, his noble lips pressed into a faint smile.

Then before either of them could respond, he turned and disappeared through the crush.

'Sophie!' Phoebe hissed, the moment he was out of earshot.

'We've barely been here above five minutes, and you've broken just about every debutante rule that exists!'

'I was only enjoying myself,' Sophie returned defensively. 'The last time I checked, that was still permissible. And anyway, you didn't refuse to dance!'

'How could I, after you'd accepted?' Phoebe retorted. 'And I'm certain his *wager* would be considered fast too!'

She groaned and seized another lemonade from a passing footman.

'Really, Phoebe!' Sophie glared, 'I'm so surprised at you. Whatever happened to forgetting the rules and running away to find your inner heroine?! At least I've not stolen Fred's breeches, or drunk too much, or found myself in a duel with a common highwayman!'

'That was different!' Phoebe countered, much to the interest of three young ladies nearby.

'Stuff and nonsense! How?'

Phoebe eyeballed her sister fiercely. 'That was me, and this is you – the girl who wants to make an advantageous love match? And anyway, I never ran away.'

Sophie threw her eyes heavenwards. 'And this is why I was reluctant to let you chaperone me in the first place,' she fumed. 'You were always *far* too protective, and now you've actually turned into Mama! Conversation is expected in Almack's, and an invitation to dance is perfectly respectable. I'm not a little girl anymore, Phoebe, and I won't be told I can't enjoy myself. The sister I once knew would say we ladies have few enough privileges as it is.'

'That's still true,' Phoebe fired back, 'but Lord knows—'

'Good! Because I may be your sister but, as you said yourself, a Fairfax is neither fragile nor meek, and above all, we *never* turn down a wager! I have four months to prove Lord Rotherby wrong, and I am quite determined to do it.'

'That,' Phoebe groaned, closing her eyes, 'is exactly what I was afraid you might say.'

Chapter Four

DAMEREL HOUSE

One week later

'I thought you said we had until the Newmarket Races!' Sophie exclaimed, stepping through the Fairfax crested trunks littering her sister's hallway.

She and Phoebe had just returned from their morning walk through Mayfair, discussing the week's round of balls, soirees and social visits.

'Oh, I suspect Thomas got fed up with playing nursemaid a little sooner than expected,' Phoebe replied ruefully, counting the luggage. 'And I do believe we have the added delight of the twins too!' she added as a door burst open and their harassed butler appeared, holding a large wriggling toad between his thumb and forefinger.

'This is the third *amphibian* I have discovered in the lilac salon, Viscountess Damerel,' he enunciated with visible control. 'Do you wish me to accommodate our *additional* guests in any particular room?'

Sophie's lips twitched, as her sister sought to placate the proud steward.

'Oh it's quite all right, Hargreaves,' Phoebe soothed. 'I'm sure my younger brothers have brought suitable ... *accommodation* with them, haven't you Edward?'

'Duke Wellington!' a ruddy-cheeked youth with copper hair exclaimed, as he emerged from the same salon. 'How did you get there? I was worried the furious French cook might have added you to the soup! Thank you!'

A gurgle of laughter threatened to escape Sophie as her youngest brother prised the giant, fat toad from the bewildered butler's fingers and popped him in his pocket.

'He has a very adventurous spirit, you see,' he added, as Hargreaves's eyes bulged almost as much as Wellington's. 'Loves to travel!'

'My apologies, Hargreaves.' Viscount Damerel's low tone resonated from the doorway of the library.

'I invited the viscountess's family to stay when I last met with Sir Fairfax, and should have given you fair warning of their arrival, together with their distinguished friends of course,' the viscount said, nodding at Edward, who positively beamed in gratitude.

Sophie was conscious of a swift pang of envy as she watched Phoebe smile at her tall, impeccably dressed husband. She would never wish for a husband like the acerbic Viscount Damerel, but she did admire their relationship. There was a tangible warmth between them that always made Sophie feel as though she were intruding, even in a crowded hallway.

'I said he'd hopped behind the atlas!' Matilda cried, running from the saloon with one of her brothers' sashes tied around her forehead. 'He was deploying his ships in readiness for Little Boney!'

'Matilda, dearest, give Henry back his trouser sash lest his buttons give way,' Sophie said with a sigh. 'No one wishes for him to be running around in his smalls! And I'm certain you shouldn't be referring to Napoleon Bonaparte in such a manner either. He was a French General after all.'

'Pooh! Fred called him Little Boney so I can too!' Matilda replied, laughing and dancing back as an indignant Henry attempted to reclaim his clothing.

But the youngest Fairfax was swifter and she was up the marble staircase with her brothers on her heels before Sophie could remonstrate further.

'I did suggest there probably weren't *too* many pirates at the Battle of Waterloo,' Josephine offered, emerging from the salon clutching the infamous atlas, 'but she was insistent.'

'Wonderful to see you too, Jo,' Sophie grinned and embraced her sister.

'I suppose piracy is a step up from marrying Misty at least.'

'Well, that all depends on the pirate!' Josephine smiled, making her way to the stairs.

'A tea tray is waiting in the drawing room, your ladyship,' Hargreaves boomed, in a final bid to retrieve his dignity.

'Thank you so much, Hargreaves,' Phoebe replied gratefully, ushering her sister towards the drawing room and closing the door.

'In truth, I'm not sure who's looking forward to Aunt Higglestone's arrival more, Hargreaves or my *furious French cook*!' She added with a chuckle.

Yet Sophie was far too distracted by the impressive receiving room to give Phoebe an answer.

'Oh gracious, Phoebe!' Sophie gasped, darting forward to inspect the floral displays crowding every available surface.

'Gracious indeed!' Phoebe returned admiringly, 'Hargreaves mentioned some deliveries but I certainly didn't expect Kew Gardens.'

'Congratulations dearest, I thought your dance card filled quickly at the Beaumont Ball!'

Sophie whirled to face her sister, her eyes aglow with excitement.

'Yes, but *all* the debutantes had full dance cards! I guess this just means that…'

'Yours filled fastest?' Phoebe laughed, walking forward to pick up the nearest calling card.

'The Covent Garden Flower Sellers extend their compliments to the "newest toast of the season"!' she read aloud, before leaning forwards to sniff some pale pink tulips.

'They're so very beautiful!' Sophie exclaimed rapturously, darting forward to pick up another of the accompanying cards.

'My goodness, there must be fifty ivory rose stems in this vase alone! "With the compliments of Lord Endercott",' she read aloud, before pulling a face.

'It *is* very generous,' Phoebe reminded her.

'That may be, but Isabella says he spends every weekend at prizefights, with rarely a win to show for it.' Sophie wrinkled her nose. 'And he has dubious whiskers,' she added. 'But just look, Phoebe,' she said, before her sister found some other redeeming feature to promote. 'Surely *one* of these must wish for a real love match? I can't believe that all these blooms indicate is a desire to marry sensibly – though many could be forgiven for thinking that is all a Fairfax requires with Thomas at the helm.'

'Dearest, you know a Fairfax can look—'

'I must write and tell Aunt Higglestone at once!' Sophie declared, interrupting her sister's ready list of reasons why a Fairfax could marry anyone at all. And wouldn't Mama be in rhapsodies?!'

'With the flowers, or your talent for hypnotising their senders?' Phoebe smiled in defeat.

She settled on her favourite window seat, and placed a small pile of post on her silk lavender skirts.

'In truth, Mama would have expected nothing less. She always said you couldn't have been "born so pretty without good reason".' Phoebe imitated their mama's indulgent tone perfectly, and they both started to laugh.

'Though I'm certain Aunt Higglestone will be beside herself, when she hears of your success,' she added kindly. 'In truth, I had no idea there were *quite* so many hopeful bachelors in London, although only one, it appears, with the sense to pick a flower that actually blooms in March!'

Phoebe leaned forward to pick a card out of the most modest affair in the room; a pretty arrangement of budding daffodils, tied with a matching ribbon. '"For the flower that puts these in the shade, Sir George Weston",' she read aloud, her brow wrinkling. 'I will never understand the need for such laboured sentiment though. When will gentlemen learn we are no more flowers or songbirds than they are?'

'Well, I happen to think it's romantic,' Sophie replied with a smile, taking a seat on a gold jacquard chaise longue.

'And you haven't so much as a milk stool to stand upon anyway. I've seen the nauseating notes Alexander leaves for you.' Sophie paused to clutch her hands to the corset of her pink muslin dress overlaid with flounces of pale chiffon that complemented her fair complexion perfectly. '"I'm counting the hours … no minutes—in fact, make that seconds my love—until I can gaze upon you—Actually, why is there always so much gazing in love? We were always taught it's rude to stare!'

'Sophie!' Phoebe squeaked, throwing a cushion embroidered with a peacock at her laughing sister. 'Need I remind you that anything addressed to me is *private*? My letters and notes aren't for your eyes – or anyone else's, especially considering you're…'

'A debutante?' Sophie finished, rolling her eyes.

'Need I remind *you* that you've only been married for a few short weeks yourself Phoebe Fairfax, so don't go acting like an old married lady of the ton with me! Besides, what am I supposed to do when the pair of you carry on like lovelorn heroes in your very own novel?' She tucked the cushion beneath her with a long sigh. 'An advantageous love match, fine houses in the town and country, a high-perch phaeton with lavender seats *and* a ridiculously romantic husband… Quite frankly Phoebe, if you weren't my sister, I might have disowned you already!'

'Promises!' Phoebe retorted.

'And you still haven't shared any particularly *levelling* aspects of matrimony with me either.'

Phoebe sighed at her persistent sister. As the eldest Fairfax girl, she was certainly no prude, but she also drew a line at describing the intimacies of marriage to an inquisitive sister who was not long out in society.

'Sophie,' she tried to reason. 'You know it's not appropriate for me to say, and besides, you're about as reliable as a parasol in winter!'

'But if you don't tell me, who will?' Sophie grumbled. 'I can't ask anyone else.'

Phoebe flushed faintly, searching for words that might satisfy her inquisitive sister.

'To be honest, dearest,' she began slowly, glancing down at her post, 'I do believe you will much prefer to discover the … mysteries of marital relations within the … precious union of—'

'Oh, enough already!' Sophie exclaimed, throwing her eyes to the ceiling. 'I cannot bear it when you start talking like an encyclopaedia! I swear you are the oddest sister in the world,' she chastised. 'Fiercely independent for yourself, while wrapping the rest of us up in so many layers we can barely breathe.'

'Well I am the eldest—' Phoebe began.

'And I am barely two years younger than you, and quite ready for the world, thank you very much!' Sophie retorted.

'I know,' her sister replied with a faint smile.

'Speaking of which, there's a letter here for you,' she added in a brighter tone.

She pulled a pretty cream envelope from the pile of post on her skirt and waved it. 'It bears the Hampton seal.'

'Isabella or Ursula!' Sophie predicted, jumping up to grab the missive from her sister's outstretched hand.

'And,' Phoebe continued, picking up an open letter, 'it

looks as though our darling eldest brother did actually have the forethought to ask if the tribe could stay while he investigates his *sweet runners* for the Newmarket races.'

She frowned, turning the letter round and round in an effort to decipher her brother's crossed scrawl.

'Did he actually send the letter with them?' Sophie asked incredulously. 'How very considerate of him, given the fact you're about ready to take off on honeymoon.'

'I'm just impressed he remembered to ask at all,' Phoebe replied, chuckling. 'He must have his eye on some rank outsider who's going to restore the Fairfax family fortune.'

'I thought the viscount had done that already?'

'Sophie!' Phoebe chastised.

Sophie clamped her hand to her mouth, her eyes dancing. Phoebe had shared the viscount's dowry-waiver in a moment of sisterly confidence before her wedding and, in truth, it had only made Sophie respect her brother-in-law more.

What more evidence of true love could there be?

'You know Knightswood is still heavily encumbered,' Phoebe continued, 'and Thomas is convinced his Monstrous Marriage Masterplan will ensure its survival.'

'I know,' Sophie replied, rolling her eyes, 'and we all have our part to play.'

'All I was saying was that it's frustrating to see our eldest brother is still offloading his responsibilities. I mean, you're barely married and I'm only just out. Damerel House really shouldn't be a dumping ground for all Fairfax waifs and strays! What must the viscount think for goodness' sake?'

Phoebe chuckled. 'He doesn't mind because I don't mind,' she replied.

'I love it when we're all under the same roof, it makes me feel as though we might be back at Knightswood,' she added. 'And as you say, Alexander and I leave for our honeymoon at the end of the week so what difference does it really make? You're the only one I worry about,' she finished, popping a cream macaroon into her mouth.

'Me? I'm the one most able to take care of myself!' Sophie replied indignantly.

'And also the one making inappropriate wagers with rakish bachelors of the ton!' Phoebe retorted. Sophie scowled as Phoebe reached for another macaroon. 'Anyway, Aunt Higglestone has agreed to come up a little earlier than planned. She's both *highly flattered and excessively excited* about escorting you to all the *glamorous balls and soirees* until I'm back,' she added with a grin.

'Thanks so much!' Sophie groaned. 'She'll be forever telling me to straighten my shoulders and mind there's no mention of mud.'

They eyed each other briefly, before the reference to their chaotic stay in Bath with their aunt saw them descend into fits of laughter.

'Just promise me you won't fall in love while I'm gone,' Phoebe managed to say, wiping her eyes. 'At least, not with anyone wholly inappropriate.' There was a moment's silence while they both acknowledged the small void that still existed between them, even though Captain Damerel had been gone for months. 'In truth, I really wish I could be here,' she added.

'No, you don't!' Sophie returned crossly. 'For you are to skip off to the continent on your long-awaited dream of a honeymoon, leaving me stuck in Aunt Higglestone's exceedingly respectable bourgeois lodgings, being harried and tormented by our younger siblings. Undoubtedly, I shall end up marrying any old country squire just to escape boggle-eyed toads and all my best bloomers being used as kites!'

'Sophie!' Phoebe gasped, using a cushion to muffle her gasps.

'What? I don't think Harriet will ever recover from the sight of my best smalls sailing over Knightswood lake and attaching themselves to the topmost branches of the old oak. Or the sight of yours as you climbed the tree to retrieve them!'

'Oh hush!' Phoebe retorted, dabbing at her eyes again. 'Whatever will Hargreaves think? He thinks I'm a respectable viscountess!'

'More fool him then,' her sister said, grinning. 'And given the tribe's arrival, I'm sure he's starting to revise his good opinion!'

'Look,' Phoebe managed finally, 'I know the timing of my honeymoon isn't ideal, especially since this is your debut season, but my going away shouldn't really affect anything. And I've suggested to Aunt and Uncle that you all stay here at Damerel Place while we're away. There's more than enough room, and they are helping us out after all.'

'You know Aunt won't do it,' Sophie replied with a sigh. 'She considers you far above us mere mortals now, Phoebs, and no matter how much I try to convince her you're still the same old trouser-wearing oddity, just elevated to the lofty heights of Viscountess, she won't have it.'

'"Wood Lodge has always been good enough for your dear uncle and me",' she mimicked. '"And I just wouldn't feel like plain old Penelope Higglestone with a fancy phaeton and pair, let alone a grand Mayfair address!"'

'Sophie!' Phoebe begged, her cheeks aching.

'Which leaves me with Aunt's bourgeois lodgings, being tormented, and marrying any old country squire!' she concluded grumpily.

'I'm sure it could be worse,' Phoebe replied, her eyes dancing, 'but what news from the Hamptons anyway?'

'Well, they've invited us to an archery party next week, which I suppose I'll be attending alone, dear sister, since you will undoubtedly be very busy *gazing*—'

'An archery party, how lovely!' Phoebe exclaimed swiftly, 'Who will be there?'

'Oh, the usual young crowd,' Sophie replied with a grin. 'Isabella and Ursula, Lady Harriet Wakeley, the Farrington twins, Lady Aurelia and a few gentlemen of the ton too – Lord Endercott, I expect, simpering Lord Riley and perhaps Sir Weston… You know what Lady Hampton is like.'

'Lord Rotherby?' Phoebe quizzed.

'Lord Rotherby?' Sophie frowned. 'I doubt it, but how should I know? I'm not in charge of the invitation list. However, if he *is* there, I shall simply remind him that while I am a *fearless Fairfax*, it is only the beginning of the season!'

'Sophie, please remember Lord Rotherby is—'

'A notorious rake and entirely unsuitable company for a debutante looking to make an advantageous love match,' she finished, rolling her eyes, 'I'm not a ninny-hammer, Phoebe! Though what real offence he has committed other than possessing a lively wit and charming disposition, I'm sure I don't know. And from what I recall, Alexander wasn't half as gallant when you were gallivanting around Bath pretending to be a seasoned actress…'

She tailed off as Phoebe shot her a dangerous look.

'Anyway, I'm not about to fall for someone who doesn't believe an advantageous love match is even possible,' she huffed. 'We just have this silly wager, as you know!'

'Yes, well I'm sure Thomas wouldn't be happy with you having a silly wager with anyone, least of all a rakish bachelor of the ton,' Phoebe retorted. There was a moment while each observed the other stubbornly before Phoebe exhaled in exasperation. 'Lord Rotherby is only interested in mischief and distraction. You must see that?'

'Of course I do,' Sophie snapped. 'I'm not a simpleton!'

'Then why bother with the wager at all? Just treat it with the contempt it deserves.'

'I can't,' Sophie replied crossly. 'He spoke as though love should be the very *last* consideration in a marriage, and that exasperates me beyond anything.' She paused to scowl. 'And while I know I should place no stock in his opinions at all, I cannot help but feel a burning desire to prove him entirely wrong!'

Sophie paused to eyeball her sister.

'But that is precisely why you *should* ignore him,' Phoebe reasoned carefully.

'Easier said than done when he's entirely determined to prove he is right! After all, why else did he read Lord Byron at the Carlisles's soiree last week?'

She rolled her eyes dramatically.

Phoebe took a deep breath. 'I think I recall that, but why should his reading Byron mean anything at all, dearest?'

'Did you not notice how Aurelia changed seats so she could be quite clearly seen by all?' Sophie replied. 'Simpering and fluttering her eyelids as though he read for her alone? Harriet says she has enjoyed a flood of new suitors since, and the marchioness is delighted. I suppose she must have all but given up hope of a decent match after her daughter informed the duke he was a pompous purple peagoose!'

'Well, he is purple,' Phoebe conceded, momentarily distracted.

'Extremely so,' Sophie agreed readily. 'But he was trying to prove, of course, that the language of love is useful only to garner attention, and little else.'

'Really? I rather think Lord Rotherby may have been proving his own popularity,' Phoebe replied drily.

Sophie scowled at her perceptive sister, aware she sounded irrational, and yet with too much disquiet threading her veins to do much else. She also knew she was stubborn when it came to wagers, and that Lord Rotherby was a known and established rake of the ton, but for some inexplicable reason he bothered her more than she could put into words.

'Dearest, you know Aurelia plays a very fast game, and that the gentlemen know it too,' Phoebe said with a faint frown. 'I shouldn't spare a second thought for her flood of suitors when you have Kew Gardens at your fingertips.'

'Lord, Phoebs!' Sophie exclaimed, throwing her eyes to the heavens. 'You sound like Mama, Harriet and Aunt Higglestone all rolled into one now! This isn't about Aurelia at all. It's just that Lord Rotherby clearly believes love is a tool, or a commodity, or something to be *used*, when you and I both know such feelings—'

'Are not always within our control?' Phoebe finished quietly, recalling the moment she glimpsed the viscount and Captain Damerel fighting in Sydney Park.

'Exactly so. And isn't it the very definition of rakish behaviour to behave otherwise? Thank heavens there are gentlemen like Sir George Weston in the world. Jo and I believe he is the very epitome of a well-mannered gentleman with a title, respectable estate *and* good connections. In fact, the last time I saw him, he—'

'Tipped his hat at you. Twice. I know.'

'Well, he did! And he is such a handsome gentleman too, though we don't tend to notice because he's so sensible – don't you think?'

'Possibly,' Phoebe agreed, her lips twitching.

'Anyway, I just can't imagine someone like him using any kind of false means to engage affections, can you?'

'No, I can't,' Phoebe replied. 'And his manners and flowers do much to recommend him too, dearest, but he is a trifle quiet and serious for you, surely?'

'And why should I not be an excellent match for someone quiet and serious?' Sophie challenged. 'I have as much of an enquiring mind and independent will as you.'

'You do,' her sister nodded sagely. 'Together with a very lively and vivacious disposition that I cannot help but think would be wasted on someone like Sir Weston.'

'Oh.' Sophie paused uncertainly.

'Well I was only going to say that I could no more think myself into loving Sir Weston for his sense, than I could into loving Lord Rotherby for his wit and charm. Such strong feelings have to come from another place altogether, don't you think?'

'I do,' Phoebe agreed with a smile, 'and I'm quite relieved to hear you say it.'

'And in the meantime we must look to our own interests instead.'

'Absolutely,' Phoebe nodded.

'Which is why I need to attend the new exhibition at The British Institution.'

'Pardon?' Phoebe paused, wondering if she'd misheard her wilful sister.

'The British Institution,' Sophie replied brightly. 'At the Carlisle dinner, I heard there is to be an exhibition of Parisian ladies' fashion there. All sorts of ladies' clothing will be featured: pelisses, gowns, corsets, chemises, plus the newest fabrics and patterns. Just imagine, Phoebe,' she appealed wistfully, 'the world of French fashion under one roof. It's my dream!'

'I thought your dream was to make an advantageous love match?!' Phoebe retorted with a laugh.

'Oh it is!' Sophie smiled winningly. 'But my reserve dream, should such a gentleman not be found, is to move to Paris and design fashionable pelisses instead. There's just one tiny drawback...'

'Which is?' Phoebe prompted suspiciously.

'Debutantes aren't allowed to go, on account of there being undergarments on display.'

'I beg your pardon?'

'Well, exactly!' Sophie exclaimed. 'As if I'm likely to be plagued by such a thing when I wear them myself! Plus, they are French,' she added with a shrug. I'd have to be a real ninny-hammer.'

Phoebe closed her eyes with a look of pained denial.

'Sophie, wearing undergarments oneself – French or otherwise – does not make it acceptable to peruse undergarments at a public exhibition,' she uttered in a strangled tone, 'Just imagine what Aunt Higglestone or Harriet would say for a start!'

'Well I hope both would understand that an interest in fashion requires one to have an eye to every detail,' Sophie returned stubbornly. 'Besides, I think it's very silly to pretend to be missish about such female things when I am female too. And I have already thought of a way to safeguard my reputation.'

She eyed Phoebe with a defiant gleam.

'Should I even ask?' her sister replied in a voice of great sufferance.

'But of course!' Sophie smiled winningly. 'The newest darling of the ton, Viscountess Damerel, will escort me!'

Chapter Five

THE ARCHERY PARTY

Another week later

'In fairness, my sister, the Viscountess Damerel, would have been happy to escort me, were it not for the inconvenience of her honeymoon,' Sophie said airily, accepting the bow from Ursula.

'Inconvenience?' Ursula queried with a frown.

'Well, she may not have called it an inconvenience exactly,' Sophie amended, colouring a little, 'or used those precise words, but she did agree the timing could have been better. And I, for one, will never understand the fuss about the exhibition when we all wear undergarments – plus these are French, which is hardly the same at all!'

'Silk stays and drawers?' Aurelia smirked. 'You're right, they're very different to our boring muslin affairs.'

'Silk *thread*,' Sophie corrected knowledgeably, taking her place at the shooting line. 'But cotton in the main and anyway, it's an exhibition of ladies' fashion, not ladies' unmentionables!

In truth, I am much more intrigued by the Duchesse du Barry's new troubadour style than anything else. A square neckline coupled with Renaissance pearls and silk puffs is such an interesting offshoot of Romanticism, don't you think?'

There was a moment's impressed silence while Sophie accepted an arrow from simpering Lord Riley, who offered to place it against the bow for her.

She declined.

'It's only fifty yards to the target. How difficult can it be?' she smiled confidently, stepping up to the shooting line.

'You'd be surprised,' Isabella muttered from the garden table, stirring her tea from six to twelve o clock as she'd been taught.

Which was precisely the moment that both a small and distant visitor appeared on the Hamptons's grand lawn steps, and Sophie let her arrow fly. 'Oh!' Sophie mouthed in sudden realisation, wondering if this would be the first and last archery party to which she'd ever be invited.

'Good Lord!'

'Duck!'

'Not one of *our* guests at least!'

Fortunately, the sudden chorus of alarm alerted the visitor to his impending doom and he dodged the missile with a grace that made Sophie's spirits sink further. Of all the gentlemen in London.

'It was distracting!' she defended hotly, as Lord Riley confiscated the bow without so much as a simpering word.

'Good grief, it's Lord Rotherby,' Isabella muttered faintly. 'My mother would never have forgiven us had we murdered him— Lord Rotherby, Good afternoon!' she exclaimed in the same breath as he made his way towards them. 'I do trust you are quite well?'

'Still alive, Miss Hampton, which is always a bonus!'

Lord Rotherby's moss-green eyes danced as he strode up to the small party.

'And rest assured my business is with Lord Hampton. I have not arrived merely to provide your delightful party with target practice.'

Lord Riley guffawed loudly, as Lord Rotherby swept into a graceful bow.

'Oh, what a pity you aren't staying, Lord Rotherby,' Aurelia said with a sigh. 'Miss Fairfax here was just trying to persuade Miss Hampton of the virtues of the new scandalous ladies' fashion exhibition, and I understand you're *quite* the authority?'

'On exhibitions, or scandalous ladies' fashion in general?' Lord Rotherby replied in an amused tone. 'And I was under the impression that the new exhibition had been deemed unsuitable for debutantes? Either way, my personal view is that ladies' clothing should be as scandalous as possible, of course.'

There was another low guffaw, while Isabella covered her embarrassment with an offering of extra thin ginger stem biscuits. 'I really can't apologise enough for the mishap with the arrow, Lord Rotherby,' she said, turning the shade of their Sèvres teapot. 'I'm sure no one was actually trying to murder you, least of all Miss Fairfax.'

'Oh, I'm not sure that's entirely the case, is it, Miss Fairfax?' Lord Rotherby enquired, making short work of two of the proffered biscuits. 'I wager it might have been quite satisfying for many reasons.'

'Miss Fairfax wished to murder you?' Aurelia smiled coquettishly. 'Now this I need to hear.'

Sophie took a moment to survey Lord Rotherby's languorous figure, wishing with all her heart that Aunt Higglestone hadn't chosen this moment to peruse Lady Hampton's new parlour curtains.

'Lord Rotherby knows full well I didn't intend to murder him,' she returned coldly, 'and I really don't think it's helpful to spread rumour and conjecture either. Perhaps, if my lack of skill has offended him, Lord Rotherby can content himself with the thought that I'm not likely to pick up a bow and arrow again any time soon.'

'What a pity that would be, Miss Fairfax,' Lord Endercott interjected pompously. 'For archery is well known to import both grace and elegance to female deportment, as well as offer a healthy and agreeable pastime.'

'Indeed!' Lord Rotherby drawled, turning a piercing gaze on the foppish young gentleman. 'And are you suggesting Miss Fairfax currently lacks any of those attributes?'

'No, no! Of course not! What I was saying was … that is, I was merely…' Lord Endercott tailed off in confusion.

'Good. Then in future, I suggest you restrict your observations to the weather, and your over-ambitious tailor!' At which point Lord Endercott flushed the very same colour as his overambitious tailor's new line in waistcoats. 'In truth, Miss Fairfax,' Lord Rotherby continued, turning back, 'all you really require is a little knowledge of bow grip – which any one of these young fops might have demonstrated – and you will be a formidable archer. If you will allow me?'

Without waiting for an answer, Lord Rotherby took the bow from the awestruck Lord Riley and positioned himself on the starting line.

'Miss Fairfax?' He indicated the space beside him as though he taught archery to vexed debutantes every Sunday afternoon.

'I have four brothers at home, sir!' Sophie said, glowering.

'All the more curious, then, that not one of them had the foresight to show you how to hold a bow properly. Now, if you don't mind?'

Despite minding very much, Sophie found she could think of no good reason that wouldn't sound churlish the moment it left her lips. So she did the next best thing and joined his lordship with the bristling resentment of a child that was being forced to eat boiled cabbage.

'Hold your bow loosely, like so,' he began, 'then draw your string back… I see your arm is quite rigid. May I?'

Sophie shook her head, determined not to show any reaction. Yet the touch of his fingers was having the most curious effect on her stomach. She blinked, trying not to acknowledge the shiver spreading throughout her tense limbs, whilst simultaneously fogging her thoughts in the most disconcerting way.

'That's it. Make sure the arrow is in the centre. Align your shoulders … aim and … release.'

Then, much to Sophie's irritation, the slim shaft of wood flew straight towards the target board and buried itself within its small black centre.

'Bravo, Miss Fairfax, bravo!' Lord Endercott called out.

'Bravo indeed, Lord Endercott. And, I believe Miss Fairfax may have also demonstrated some 'natural grace and elegance' too?'

'Indeed she did, my lord,' Lord Endercott agreed nervously.

'Excellent. Then we'll part on civil terms – and I believe we'll be adding *archer extraordinaire* to your list of fearless attributes very soon, Miss Fairfax!'

'Oh I doubt that very much, sir,' Sophie returned with a wry smile. She drew a breath, trying to gather the thoughts his proximity seemed to have scattered like more wayward arrows. 'Though my sister, the viscountess, would be most impressed! She'd have much preferred to join our brothers in archery instruction than practise the pianoforte, but my father would never allow it. Like most, he wished us to present as accomplished young ladies who could marry well, when the time arrived.'

'You are fortunate if your father acted with such foresight, Miss Fairfax,' Lord Rotherby replied in a cooler tone. 'Some believe the measure of their offspring lies only in their tally on the hunting field.'

'Yes, I suppose so.' Sophie replied hesitantly.

'Archery aside,' a steady voice interjected, 'I suspect Miss Fairfax has a good many other accomplishments that she would be far too modest to own in company.'

Sophie glanced up in surprise as Lord Rotherby's demeanour shifted again.

'Weston,' he drawled, glancing back at the group of gathered gentlemen. 'How interesting to find you at an archery party when you cannot even abide the sport.' His lip curled faintly. 'And I'm sure no one is in any doubt of Miss Fairfax's accomplishments. Now, if you'll excuse me, ladies and gentlemen, I must take my leave. Miss Fairfax, if you could allow me a sporting head start, I'd be most appreciative! Good afternoon.' He bowed.

'Which brings us right back to French silk drawers,' Aurelia sighed as they all watched Lord Rotherby stride back to the house.

'It's an exhibition of *modern ladies' fashion*!' Sophie glowered, nettled by Lord Rotherby's manner, which had left her feeling wholly unsettled again.

She was no more an archer than she was a murderess, yet he seemed determined to tease her abominably.

'Whatever you say,' Aurelia said with a shrug, 'though I'm sure I only have to be told once that something is unsuitable for me to want to see it – whatever is on display.'

'But you aren't going to see it, are you, Aurelia?' Ursula asked in a hushed tone. 'Particularly if *gentlemen* may be in attendance,' she added, her eyes as round as the porcelain teacup she was holding.

'Oh Ursula, do you really think a flood of gentlemen will be rushing to see pinned French drawers when they can see real ones at the Opera House?' Aurelia exclaimed, rolling her eyes.

'Hush, Aurelia!' Isabella muttered. 'Mama says only wicked girls talk like that!'

'Well I must be quite wicked then,' Aurelia replied with a glint, 'for I believe we are quite safe at an exhibition of ladies' fashion.'

'I am in agreement for once, though I suppose it may attract gentleman of a certain character,' Sophie observed drily.

'True,' Aurelia said, selecting a grape from a dish on the table and popping it into her mouth. 'Though they are usually the most diverting – and, as they say, while a libertine is a scoundrel, there is always a chance of redemption with a rake.'

'Aurelia!' Isabella challenged in an aghast tone, glancing at the nearby gentlemen.

'We aren't supposed to talk of such things. Mama will never let us hold a garden party again.'

'La, is that all you simpletons think about?' Aurelia scoffed, selecting another grape, and starting to peel it in the most fastidious fashion. 'Aren't you in the least bit interested in knowing our potential husbands a little better?'

'You are certainly making us sound quite villainous, Lady Aurelia,' the steady voice interjected again, 'and while I can't vouch for all, some of us happen to be quite civilised.'

They all looked up at Sir Weston's approaching figure, and Sophie couldn't help but smile. His coat wasn't by the most fashionable tailor, his cravat couldn't be tied in a less dashing style and his hair, while smart, lacked the more fashionable waves of his contemporaries. But there was a dependable elegance about his person, and when he spoke, he radiated the kind of quiet authority that made everyone listen.

'Oh, your very proper self excluded of course, Sir Weston,' Aurelia replied. 'I can't imagine you being the least bit scandalous, whatever the occasion!'

Lady Aurelia then proceeded to smile archly across the Hampton's best table linen while Sophie felt an inexplicable rise of annoyance.

'Looks can be deceptive,' Sir Weston returned politely, 'but I for one believe that most ladies would far rather marry a gentleman *with* standards, than a nobleman without.'

At this all the young ladies gushed their heartfelt agreement, while Aurelia rolled her eyes and Sophie took a large gulp of Isabella's terrible tea.

'Dear me,' Aurelia said as Sophie coughed into her pretty lace kerchief, 'anyone would think we were at one of your country bumpkin parties. Don't they teach you anything in the wilds of Devon?' She sighed, delicately covering the smallest of yawns. 'And all this chitter-chatter has made me yearn for something more than archery and tea. How about a turn around your delightful maze, Isabella. I hear there is lovely folly at its centre?'

The bewildered Isabella cast a swift appeal around her select party: Lady Harriet Wakeley, the Farrington twins, Lady Aurelia, Miss Sophie Fairfax, Lord Endercott, simpering Lord Riley, Sir Weston and Ursula.

Her mother had sanctioned an archery party, not a garden jaunt in the maze, but she was also aware it was quite rude to deny her guests anything she could reasonably provide – which left her in rather a quandary.

'Perhaps a short turn then, just to refresh ourselves?' she ventured doubtfully.

'Bravo! What a wonderful idea!' Aurelia exclaimed, already rising. 'Did everyone hear our delightful hostess? Isabella has proposed a new game: a race to the centre of the maze, and the last one to reach the folly must pay the winner's forfeit! We are six ladies though, so you gentlemen had better be on your mettle!' she smirked, snatching up the last ginger thin and starting towards Lord Hampton's pride and joy.

'But Aurelia, wait!' Isabella called in bewilderment, jumping to her feet. 'Ought we not to finish our tea first?'

'Tea?' Lord Riley simpered. 'I'll take a race and forfeits over tea any day.' Then he started after Aurelia, who was already a considerable way down the rolling lawn.

Sophie shot Sir Weston a glance and wondered briefly, if he'd ever played any game in his life. Yet the tea party appeared to be at an end, Phoebe had abandoned her for the continent, Aunt Higglestone was distracted by parlour curtains, and much as she didn't want to take part in any of Aurelia's games, she had even less desire to be left alone.

She lowered her offensive cup of tea.

'Well, I can't murder anyone anyway,' she sighed, wondering if she shouldn't have just taken Matilda to the patisserie instead.

Sophie knew she should have taken Matilda to the patisserie instead.

Not only was she quite lost, but she'd been enduring the whoops of victorious players for some time now, while she'd seen nothing but yards of yew.

'Which only goes to prove that spontaneous games around any maze are rarely as refreshing as they sound,' she scowled, pushing an errant ringlet out of her face.

Briefly, she paused to look up and down the stubborn green corridor, which looked exactly like the one before. She'd already considered scaling the hedge before deciding she'd rather be lost, than risk her frilled sleeves and ivory gloves to an invasion of prickles.

Fortunately, at the same moment she heard the low yet unmistakable tone of a cheerful whistle. She exhaled in relief, certain that of all the gentlemen taking part, only sensible Sir Weston would be composed enough to whistle.

'Do I have the pleasure of addressing the ghost of the maze?' she called brightly, 'and do you come to offer assistance or merely to terrorise those who pass through it?'

'A tricky choice,' came a muffled response, 'though in truth, my terrorising skills are a little rusty, so I trust you will be content with the former?'

Sophie chuckled. 'I promise you, sir, if you can guide me out of this beehive, I shall most likely be content forever,' she replied.

'High stakes indeed, for no female I've known has ever reached such an exalted state,' he countered.

Briefly, Sophie wondered if Sir Weston was prone to philosophical turns of mood, yet she was certain he would know the quickest way out of the dratted maze, and even Aunt Higglestone couldn't object to his anodyne company.

'Then perhaps you are keeping the wrong company, sir,' she replied, her lips twitching, 'Now, how shall I find you?'

'I believe there is a fork at the end of your corridor,' came the muffled response. 'Take the left, follow it round, and with a little luck we should find ourselves in the same corridor. Then I may be certain to guide – or terrorise – you in a much more civilised manner.'

Relieved, Sophie picked up the skirts of her new pink

muslin and ran in what Harriet would have undoubtedly called a hoydenish manner towards the end of the corridor. She was out of all patience with Aurelia's game, and very much looking forward to putting an end to it before anyone could say 'Prinnie wed Mrs Fitzherbert in secret'.

In fact, it was just as she was pondering whether her aunt's favourite piece of court gossip was suitable to share with a gentleman of Sir Weston's very proper character, that she rounded the corner and ran straight into him.

'Oh, I do beg your pardon!' she exclaimed during their momentary tangle, which somehow managed to attach the delicate lace of her frilled bodice to the gilt button of his expensive waistcoat.

'Oh, I am sorry, this French lace is all very well, but it *is* wearisome when—'

Yet the remainder of her sentence evaporated as she stared up into an entirely unexpected face, with cheekbones that had clearly been borrowed from a Michelangelo.

'I defer to your superior knowledge in these matters, Miss Fairfax,' came his amused response. 'I'm just grateful to have progressed from target practice to dress adornment!'

'Oh!' Sophie flushed instantly, taking a swift pace back. 'I beg your pardon, Lord Rotherby. I thought you'd left. I mean, I had no idea you were…'

Sophie tailed off uncomfortably, suddenly and acutely aware of the picture she must present: hot, bothered and making no sense whatsoever, in addition to which, her ringlets were behaving as though she hadn't attempted to recreate this month's cover style of *La Belle Assemblée* at all.

'Ah yes, well that's perfectly understandable,' he replied, unruffled. 'However, since my business with Lord Hampton had concluded, and the afternoon was advancing, I offered my assistance with locating your party. I have navigated this maze once or twice before, you see.' He smiled in a way that left Sophie in no doubt that once or twice was the most conservative of estimates.

'Well, that is reassuring,' she swallowed, to cover her jangle of nerves, 'for I fear these corridors are all quite identical.'

'Nearly,' he replied enigmatically, his eyes gleaming. 'But there is a secret to navigating a maze, as there is with all things, and that is to look up, rather than ahead.'

She nodded, trying to connect this gentleman with the one who'd left so abruptly earlier. She couldn't, and her agitation redoubled. He was the most changeable of gentlemen, and for some reason his proximity seemed to rob her of the ability to think clearly.

'That is most helpful,' she managed, knowing her cheeks were likely the colour of squashed strawberries. 'And I do believe we might be closer to the exit than the centre, so if you would be so kind as to show me the quickest exit?'

'I would be only too happy to oblige, of course, Miss Fairfax,' he replied, 'except my charge is to locate *all* of your group. He paused as a quizzical light crept into his dark eyes. 'Besides which, you have previously led me to believe that a fearless Fairfax will ride bareback through a storm before conceding defeat to anything?'

Sophie bristled. It was true that her family were renowned for their stubborn determination, but she was also aware that spending time alone in Lord Rotherby's company was less than ideal too.

She scowled, spinning one way and then the other, before gazing up at the ancient Hampton oaks in the distance. Begrudgingly, she realised Lord Rotherby's strategy was actually a rather wise one.

'If your intention is to distract competitors by placing them in a spin, I can confirm it is highly effective,' he quipped with a grin.

'*You* are not my competitor. And *you* do not seem to be in any kind of spin,' she retorted, gathering up her skirts and starting in the direction from which he'd come.

'You are vexed with me, Miss Fairfax,' he called, catching up to her in a few easy strides. 'Please accept my apologies. I do not often keep company with debutantes, and my tongue can be a little unguarded. I'm certain we will discover the rest of your party very soon.'

She glanced up to find his dark eyes shaded with sincerity, and his expression altogether gentler. Her confusion and nerves eased a little, perhaps she'd let Phoebe's excessive warnings addle her brain.

'Not vexed, no, it's just I do not wish to lose,' she replied hesitantly. 'You see, the loser must pay the winner's forfeit, and if Aurelia has got there first…' She paused, fearing she had already said more than she should.

'I understand.' He nodded and they set off again. 'A forfeit, like any wager, should never be knowingly underestimated.'

Briefly, she wondered if he was teasing her again, but his eyes were shuttered against the bright sunshine, and he was behaving like a perfectly respectable gentleman. She inhaled deeply. She had to be reasonable; only fools would go their separate ways now because of propriety.

'I believe Lady Aurelia was trying to entertain everyone,' she offered, as they turned a new corner.

It wasn't a complete untruth, she reasoned, though she knew Aurelia was thinking mostly of herself. Lord Rotherby smiled politely, yet she felt the oddest impulse to keep talking and filling the air between them.

Fortunately, at that same moment, the hedge followed around a wide corner and brought them face to face with a gleaming white sculpture, set back in a small alcove.

'Oh, how beautiful!' she exclaimed. 'Does it have a name?'

'It does,' Lord Rotherby confirmed, as they came to a standstill. 'It's Canova's *Cupid's Kiss*, and is supposedly the moment Psyche is awakened from a death-like sleep with a kiss from Cupid, her husband.

'But why was she in the death-like sleep?' Sophie quizzed. 'What happened to her?'

'I believe she lost a forfeit,' he replied, pan-faced. 'Or perhaps it was a wager?'

Sophie noticed his lips twitching and chuckled, despite herself.

'I don't believe she lost anything,' she countered. 'Look at her face. She's sublimely happy!'

'Appearances can be deceptive,' he mused after a beat, 'though I believe Psyche was supposed to have opened some kind of forbidden box. It's the part of the story that has always fascinated me, for how many of us wouldn't do the same?'

Sophie stared at the sculpture, pondering how sorely tempted she would be to lift the lid on any forbidden box. It was hard enough when a letter arrived addressed to one of her sisters.

'Curiosity *is* a part of human nature,' she murmured, mostly to herself.

'Indeed, though society rarely forgives it,' he returned.

She glanced up then, suddenly aware of his subtle cologne. It was entirely unlike her brothers', with soft lavender and citrus notes, and for some reason it prompted a faint warmth to steal across her cheeks. He glanced back, and for just a second his eyes gleamed with something other than amusement.

'Fortunately for us, Apuleius wrote a happy ending,' he continued in a brighter tone, 'and I believe we shall have the same because this corridor leads directly to the folly. Shall we?'

Sophie nodded, suddenly needing to be among more people, even if they did number Aurelia. Lord Rotherby was witty and knowledgeable, but he was also distinctly unnerving, with a talent for making her feel like a hapless ingenue.

Which is what you are, after all, she muttered to herself, as she hurried down the last length of yew, before finally emerging in the centre.

Exhaling in relief, she swept her gaze around the small, enclosed area to spy the rest of her party beneath an old cherry tree that was just beginning to bud with tiny pearls of spring.

'Well, look who decided to grace us with her company,' Aurelia called from the pretty gazebo beneath the tree.

'I do believe you are the *last*, Miss Fairfax, which means you must pay the winner's forfeit as a matter of honour. And since I am the winner…'

She broke off to smile triumphantly, while Sophie cursed all noblemen and their concepts of honour in a very unladylike mutter.

'In fairness,' a low tone interrupted, 'and if you will accept a wild-card entry, I may actually be last?'

Conscious of a blur of gratitude and annoyance, Sophie glanced back to see an unruffled figure emerge from the maze behind her.

'Lord Rotherby!' Aurelia exclaimed, starting forward amid flounces of shimmering lavender.

'Accompanying Miss Fairfax...how exceptionally diverting! Your wild-card entry is most certainly accepted, and as the very last, it looks as though *you* must pay a forfeit instead. Do you wish to know what it is?'

'Wish may be a trifle strong,' he drawled, coming to a standstill, 'but pray do enlighten me all the same.'

'Well,' she paused, her eyes gleaming,' your forfeit is to tell us who broke your heart, for that is the usual reason a bachelor becomes a rake, is it not?'

There was a moment's shocked silence around the space, before everyone turned their gaze to Lord Rotherby, standing alone with a flint smile.

'Oh, it's not that terrible, is it?' she cajoled. 'After all, we ladies need to know if there's any prospect of a vacancy at Rotherby House any time soon.'

There was another low murmur as Aurelia made her way forwards, before drawing to a standstill, just in front of him.

'It is less *terrible*, than barely a forfeit at all,' he shrugged, after a beat. 'But since a gentleman always honours his debts, here is the truth: no one broke my heart, for in order for them to do so I would have had to possess one in the first place.'

There was a poignant silence, while the smile died from Aurelia's face.

'And now, since the game is over, I believe Lady Hampton is waiting.'

Chapter Six

AUNT HIGGLESTONE'S RESPECTABLE, BOURGEOIS LODGINGS

Three days later

Suffice to say, I will not be seeking a career amongst the Royal Company of Archers, and it is not an exaggeration in the slightest when I say you might have been visiting me in Newgate had Lord Rotherby not seen—

Sophie broke off her letter to Phoebe, consumed by conflicting thoughts. That Lord Rotherby nettled her was beyond all doubt, that she was more determined than ever to win the wager was also very clear, but the fact that he intrigued her beyond anyone she'd ever known was much harder to convey.

He was, at times, the most charming and chivalrous of gentlemen and yet, at others, so abrasive and cold too. There were certainly moments when he seemed congenial – kindly almost – but he'd also dismissed the importance of love in a marriage before declaring he had no heart at all.

All of which made him a most confusing gentleman she shouldn't spare a second thought, and yet somehow, despite all her protestations, he'd managed to get under her skin. Absentmindedly, she sketched out a new pelisse design she'd been thinking about on a torn piece of blotting paper. It had Phoebe's fur-lined wedding sleeves, and a diamante clasp she'd glimpsed on a society matron at Almack's, together with a graduated hemline. She paused to admire the glamorous combination awhile, before sighing.

She could hardly understand herself. She'd always been proud and determined, especially when it came to things she cared about, but never at risk to her own plans before. It was how she differed from her sisters: she never allowed herself to be distracted from her course. Mama always maintained she was the one most likely to make a good match because of the way she looked, but Sophie knew better. It was her common sense that made the difference, her determination to use what she'd been given to improve her position in the world – and that began with avoiding risky situations. Yet Lord Rotherby appeared to be risk personified.

She conjured the moment he'd adjusted her grip on the bow, and the way the briefest touch of his fingers had prompted a wave of ... something across her skin. A faint flush reached up her neck and across her cheeks. She could only ever recall one other person making her feel remotely similar, and he'd almost eloped with her sister. She shook her head as she dipped her quill in the inkpot. She really could be quite a fool sometimes.

> *Anyway, you were right to warn me, dearest, for I suspect he has the most duplicitous character, and I do believe Lady Aurelia might yet be labouring under the illusion that he might—*

She broke off again, chewing the end of her quill. Quite what Aurelia believed was a mystery, and her chances of winning a respectable husband this season were slim enough already. Yet she'd made it quite clear she nursed ambitions in the notorious Lord's direction, despite his insistence that he never dallied with debutantes, let alone intended to marry.

She returned to her letter gloomily, wondering if it was the height of selfishness to write of such things while her sister was radiating pure marital bliss.

> *—like her well enough to make an offer. He has been more than clear that he intends no such thing which only seems to encourage her further, and reinforce my present thinking that Lord Rotherby should be avoided at all costs.*

Then she concluded her letter with an account of a recent outing to a travelling circus, omitting the part where Duke Wellington emptied an entire row of paying customers, and focusing on Matilda's ambition to become the first Fairfax fire-breather instead.

It was only when she was sealing the letter with Uncle Higglestone's most sensible brown wax seal that her mind wandered back to the Exhibit of Ladies' Fashion at The British Institution. She did so wish to go, and even more so now Lord Rotherby had taken it upon himself to echo the ton's view.

She bit her lip and scowled.

If only she were married and free to do as she pleased; if only Phoebe hadn't chosen such an inconvenient time for her honeymoon; if only the haute ton didn't impose such unreasonable rules on debutantes.

Then an idea struck that ran counter to every sensible thought she'd ever had. She swallowed, acknowledging the risks, admitting Phoebe would disapprove – though it was the type of thing she might have done herself once – and yet still relishing the prospect of something entirely different to think about, other than Lord Rotherby's infuriating person, for a few precious days.

'I'm sure I only have to be told once that something is unsuitable for me to want to see it – whatever is on display.'

Aurelia's words rang in her head as she drew another sheet of writing paper from her drawer, and dashed off a much shorter letter before she could change her mind.

Lady Aurelia,

I wonder if I might count on the pleasure of your company on a visit to The British Institution in the next few days?

I have been much persuaded by your recent comments regarding the exhibition, and believe an interest in fashion far outweighs any outdated notion of respectability. I am further mindful of the fact that a pair of companionable young ladies attending together, at a discreet hour, will be far less remarkable than one alone.

Do let me know if you are agreeable, so we may arrange a suitable day,

Yours in confidence,
Miss Sophie Fairfax

Sophie exhaled as she signed and sealed the second letter, certain Aurelia would need little encouragement to join her. And while she was aware of some distinct unease, it was swiftly replaced with the intoxicating thought of all Parisian fashion under one roof for her to peruse.

After all, why should she ignore an exhibition of modern ladies' fashion when she'd been sketching it for as long as she could remember?

A small flush of satisfaction crept across her face. Let Lord Rotherby think what he liked. She was a Fairfax, and more than capable of making an advantageous love match *and* attending a fashion exhibition *and* winning a wager, and no one – least of all a heartless rake – was going to stop her.

Then, much pleased with her morning's work, she delivered her letters to Aunt Higglestone's housekeeper, before ensuring she'd removed every last candle from Matilda's bedchamber.

Chapter Seven

THE BRITISH INSTITUTION

Two days later, at a very discreet hour

'Perhaps *La Belle Assemblée* is not quite the oracle of Parisian fashion I thought,' Sophie murmured, wide-eyed as she angled her head to follow the line of the sketch.

'La, you must know the fashion pages are *weeks* out of date by the time they reach us,' Aurelia replied, stifling a yawn with a silk-gloved hand. 'But I suppose you have been living with country bumpkins, and between your suffocating sister and worrisome aunt, I doubt you've worn anything but empire-line muslins before.'

'Actually, I was referring to the puffed sleeves and skirts, rather than the materials,' Sophie replied, trying to suppress a rise of annoyance.

She glanced up and down the gallery again, just to make sure they were still quite alone. She'd experienced such varied feelings since stepping inside The British Institution: excitement, guilt, and more than a little concern that she'd allowed a moment's frustration to prevail over one of her fundamental rules. If they were spotted, there would most certainly be a black mark against them, and she had no desire to be outed to either Phoebe or her doting aunt, who believed her to be shopping for ribbons.

'Take this plain *barège* silk, for example. They've added several rows of the same material – *bouillons* – either in horizontal lines, or in bias. And look, here are flounces in large quiltings, and full wadded bands in bias, I believe… The sheer variety is beyond anything I've ever seen, and so exciting!'

'Oh yes, fascinating!' Aurelia replied, rolling her eyes. 'Now I've seen a few pink-laced chemises I can entertain drawing rooms around London for months. Sophie, I love a new dress like any debutante, but when you start talking about quiltings and bias, you sound like a common modiste.' She paused to shudder. 'In truth, this exhibition is not what I expected at all, and I'm beginning to understand why we're the only ones here.'

Sophie frowned, quietly thankful she'd taken the precaution of leaving her faithful abigail nearby with strict instructions to alert her should anyone arrive who might recognise them.

'To be honest, I was rather surprised to receive your invitation at all,' Aurelia added, her eyes narrowing, 'but then I suppose the sickly sister and the wildling aren't old enough, and the other one is far too busy honeymooning with her stolen husband to chaperone you anywhere.'

'Aurelia, Josephine isn't sickly, Matilda isn't a wildling, and Phoebe is Viscountess Damerel now,' Sophie countered firmly. 'Plus, you know full well that theirs was the love match of last season, so you can't speak of theft either, particularly as you have also been engaged yourself since. Tell me, what *did* happen to the delightfully scented Duke of Cumberland?'

Aurelia opened her mouth to retort, just as the large doors at the entrance to the gallery swung open, admitting a visitor. Sophie spun away, conscious she was tempting fate quite enough already without adding in a public scene.

'I thank you for your company, but I have no desire to listen to untruths,' she forced politely. 'Now, might I suggest we peruse the rest of the exhibition as swiftly as possible, before taking our leave?'

In truth, Sophie had no desire to leave at all. Most of the designs and materials on display were like nothing she'd ever seen before. There were gowns of figured satins with beautiful festoons of roses and their foliage in rich clusters; high-necked pelisses of fine net over white satin, finished with flounces of lace and richly embossed in flowers; and the sleeves were a wonder in themselves, varying from long sheer American styles to daring short ones, with long gloves rucked just beneath the elbow.

But despite all this, and her previous scepticism, it was the vast array of undergarments that had really captured her attention. She'd never seen anything beyond the usual knee-length muslin drawers, yet it seemed Paris considered undergarments an art form in themselves. There were silk pantalettes, held together by a tie at the waist and a multitude of delicate-coloured ribbons in other unmentionable places, as well as pretty satin knickerbockers adorned with broderie anglaise, and a variety of other designs that seemed in every way both scandalous and glorious.

In short, Sophie was quite certain that should her aunt ever discover her attendance at the exhibition, she would not only disapprove but likely confine her to her bedchamber for the rest of the season itself.

'You're still worried we might be seen, aren't you?' Aurelia said slyly. 'Well, much I care for that! My parents are so heartily sick of me this season, they can hardly wait to remove to the country again. Apparently I've exhausted every decent match and I'm to try again next year.' She paused to wrinkle her nose in distaste. 'And if I don't find a husband next season, my parents will marry me off to one of their ancient friends, like the Earl, just to be rid of me. I suppose I don't much mind who it is, but I'd as lief not have a husband as old as my grandfather!'

She paused to laugh, though there was a distinctly brittle edge.

'Surely it won't come to that?' Sophie frowned.

Aurelia shrugged.

'My view of marriage is rather less fictional than the general Fairfax outlook, though I'm not entirely persuaded I might not have a little success this season after all…' She lowered her voice to a whisper. 'Perhaps, if you can keep a secret, I'll tell you who has been setting their cap at me.'

Sophie glanced up sharply. It was the first she'd heard about Aurelia considering a match this season, and surprisingly welcome too. Perhaps it would finally lay Phoebe's marriage to the viscount to rest.

'Well, that is intriguing!' she encouraged. 'Is it anyone we know?' she added, wondering which of this season's eligible bachelors had been threatened into matrimony by the arch-matriarch Marchioness Carlisle.

'Why, you really can be quite obtuse sometimes, Sophie,' Aurelia sighed, fanning herself. 'I thought you must have noticed a certain nobleman's marked attentions lately?'

Sophie stared, aware of the oddest pool of disquiet in her stomach. She'd certainly noticed Aurelia fawning over one gentleman in particular, but she couldn't mean him, could she?

'You mean to say ... that is ... you're saying that ... *Lord Rotherby* has made you an offer?' Sophie asked incredulously. 'Self-confessed notorious rake Lord Rotherby, who claims not to possess a heart?'

She swallowed, trying not to look as shocked as she felt. It wasn't that Aurelia wasn't both attractive and a significant catch. It was just that Lord Rotherby had done nothing but convince her of his permanent bachelordom from the moment they met.

Aurelia surveyed her as though she'd just crawled out from Edward's sleeve.

'La, much I care for that!' she scorned. 'I'm a creature of the real world, and know it is far better to marry with your head than your heart. And no, not an offer *yet* – a girl can only work so fast after all – but he has been paying me considerable attention and I do have a plan!' She smiled smugly, before lowering her voice. 'Lord Rotherby frequently travels to France on account of some extended family living there. I believe they're based in Paris, though there's also a maiden aunt who conducts her life in the oddest fashion, travelling across Europe in the pursuit of artistic endeavours rather than living at Grosvenor Place—'

'I like her already!' Sophie murmured.

'Anyway,' Aurelia continued, glaring, 'the last time we conversed, he said *I'd adore Paris* which was so clearly an invitation that I've made up my mind: I'm going to accompany him on his next trip! It is simple yet brilliant, is it not? Imagine waking up to the scent of freshly baked croissants and le chocolat, safe in the knowledge you're shortly to become Lady Rotherby? Not even my parents will be able to object, and I'll have spared myself a husband in his dotage too. I have to say that this time, I have surpassed even my own expectations!'

Sophie gazed at Aurelia in horror-struck silence, certain all the colour had drained from her face. Aurelia was the most conceited and self-centred debutante of her acquaintance, but even she didn't deserve utter ruin. How she'd convinced herself Lord Rotherby, of all gentlemen, could be relied upon to behave with any kind of honour was beyond all belief.

'But Aurelia!' she whispered hoarsely, 'European shores are not Gretna Green. And what makes you think Lord Rotherby will behave honourably when pressed in this manner? Suggesting you will adore Paris, is not the same as asking you to run away with and marry him! He's a rake and a confirmed bachelor, and much more likely to abandon you in France, without any hope of a match or return to polite society at all,' she finished in a rush. 'Truly, this is a madness, Aurelia, and you will end up ruined and alone.'

Sophie paused to inhale deeply, perplexed by her own reaction. Aurelia's plan sounded beyond foolish, but it didn't explain the rise of agitation she felt at the thought of Lord Rotherby disappearing onto the continent with her either.

'La! What a worryhead you are!' Aurelia retorted with a

dismissive shake of her head. 'Lord Rotherby may well be a rake, but he is also a nobleman, from an old family like mine. We understand one another! I also have an old, beloved friend in Paris who has much influence with him, and if necessary my mother will make such a fuss that he'll have to wed me. Anyway, I'm sure he's already contemplating it, for even a notorious rake is still a man when all is said and done. You're just envious because a darling of the ton wants to show me Paris, while you have yet to secure any interest from anyone!'

She smiled superciliously while Sophie gritted her teeth, wondering why she didn't just consider herself well rid of two of the most obnoxious characters of her acquaintance.

Instead, she adopted a tone Phoebe would have recognised from a Fairfax production of Macbeth three summers before.

'It's your decision, Aurelia,' she replied coldly, 'though in truth, the season has hardly begun. Most debutantes are just getting to know the eligible bachelors and certainly wouldn't be tempted to take such a chance. Indeed, if Phoebe's happiness is anything to set standards by, it is quite possible to hope for a match of the heart, as well as the head.'

'Oh, another love match enthusiast,' Aurelia crowed. 'How exceedingly quaint! Do you plan to steal another's betrothed from under their nose, too?'

Sophie inhaled sharply, as a pale girl in a modest dress and shawl peered around a column a few paces away.

'I said wait outside the library!' Aurelia hissed, making the poor abigail shrink and flee in terror.

'For the last time,' Sophie replied, white-lipped, 'Viscount Damerel broke off your engagement long before he married my sister, as well you know. And now, if you don't mind, the hour is advancing!'

Sophie walked up to the next exhibit, her thoughts whirling. The truth was, no matter how much she believed Aurelia was making the gravest of mistakes, or that Lord Rotherby was highly unlikely to be forced into anything by the threat of dishonour, neither were the type to listen or be told anything. Which left Sophie washing her hands of the pair of them, no matter how oddly her stomach churned at the thought.

She inhaled deeply as she gazed up at a Prussian-blue ribboned corset, wishing for the umpteenth time that she'd been able to bring her own sketchpad.

'Part of your love match plan?' Aurelia nodded at the corset.

Sophie inhaled deeply, wondering if old Phoebe would have landed Aurelia a leveller by now.

'Actually, I've always believed fashion should be a blend of art and functionality,' she replied when she could trust her voice, 'and that there should be room for both. For example, this designer has explored very contemporary lines, with an acknowledgement of the feminine shape which puts our own corsetry to shame. Indeed, most make me wonder if they were designed with females in mind at all.'

'A fascinating insight!' a low and familiar tone interrupted them. 'Even if I am a little surprised to find a young lady expressing it so freely.'

She caught her breath, as all the tiny hairs on the back of her neck began to strain.

'Better a young lady with an opinion, than another one

without one,' a female voice chimed in. 'In my view, the real pity is that such items are hidden beneath the layers of clothing deemed necessary by polite society!'

Then the newcomer tailed off into a throaty laugh that didn't sound polite to Sophie at all.

Sophie closed her eyes in disbelief. It seemed the height of misfortune to run into any of her acquaintance – she'd deliberately selected an early and unfashionable hour, and they'd barely been there above thirty minutes. Yet, when she turned, there was no denying the tall, languid nobleman or the hawk-eyed lady beside him at all. A warm flush crept into Sophie's cheeks as she forced herself to meet his curious gaze. She didn't know his companion, but could read everything into the way she hung off his arm.

'Aren't you going to introduce us, Dominic?' the lady asked coquettishly, tapping his arm with a closed fan. 'We ladies like to know one another.'

'Of course,' Lord Rotherby replied smoothly, though it seemed to Sophie that he was reluctant.

'Miss Fairfax, may I present Mrs Haxby. Mrs Haxby, this is Miss Fairfax of … the fearless Fairfaxes.'

Sophie suppressed a frown.

'Well, how delightful,' Mrs Haxby smiled showing her pearly-white teeth, 'I am honoured, Miss Fairfax.'

She bobbed a swift curtsey that suggested entirely the opposite, while Sophie reciprocated, certain she was being inspected.

'Oh Lord Rotherby, what a surprise,' Aurelia gushed, holding out her hand and ignoring Mrs Haxby entirely.

'Lady Aurelia,' he returned with a barest of nods. 'The

pleasure is all mine, though I'm not sure it's entirely advisable for you and Miss Fairfax to be here,' he quizzed with a faint frown.

Aurelia only laughed coyly, making Mrs Haxby stare.

'Oh, Lord Rotherby, you're always such a rogue,' she admonished. 'As though you would expect me to miss this exhibition, when you have long known my interest in Parisian fashion!'

It was Sophie's turn to stare as Aurelia smiled archly.

'Indeed?' he drawled, pan-faced. 'I admit I had quite forgotten that, though having already benefitted from Miss Fairfax's insights into corsetry design, I wonder if you'd care to share some of yours?'

'Oh, you droll thing!' Aurelia returned with a giggle. 'My only insight is that I believe you would have us ladies traversing around in *only* our corsets given half the chance.'

'Aurelia!' Sophie muttered in a strangled tone.

'I can conceive of nothing more entertaining,' Mrs Haxby purred, her eyes glinting, 'and I daresay I have more to choose from than a debutante, after all.'

Aurelia's doll-like chin lifted instantly.

'I'm sure none of us are in any doubt of that,' Lord Rotherby placated swiftly, 'and now if you'll excuse us, ladies, I'm sure you have many other appointments to keep.'

He nodded abruptly as Sophie flushed, aware he was telling them to leave.

She swallowed, trying to suppress an inexplicable rise of fury. First, he'd all but dismissed her love match ambitions, and now he was offering moral judgement on her decision to attend a modern fashion exhibition with his … *light-o'-love* on his arm? She drew a deep breath just as a grating voice rose above the general background hum.

'But Miss Fairfax! What a surprise! Pray, is your sister, the delightful new viscountess here with you too?'

Sophie looked up to find herself being scrutinised from head to toe by the peacock-styled patroness from Almack's. She was one of the worst matriarchal gossips of the haute ton, and exactly the type of person Phoebe had been determined Sophie should avoid.

She withered briefly, before gathering herself.

'Mrs Hendercott,' she said, forcing with a smile, 'how delightful to see you! Alas, my sister planned to accompany us but had to leave for—'

'Oh, is that Lady Aurelia and Lord Rotherby as well?' Mrs Hendercott cut in, her gaze narrowing dangerously. 'What an unexpected pleasure to see so many familiar faces here.' She turned to Rotherby's companion. 'And you are…?'

Sophie shrank a second time, as Mrs Hendercott's question hung painfully on the air.

'Mrs Haxby, ma'am, pleased to meet you,' she returned in grating tone, bobbing another curtsey.

'Indeed,' Mrs Hendercott returned with one of her piercing gazes. 'One can never be sure who one might bump into on these occasions, and it is *always* a revelation.'

'My sister left for her European honeymoon a full week ago,' Sophie rushed, reading everything into the purse of Mrs Hendercott's lips. 'And my aunt is indisposed today, which is why Lady Aurelia and I brought our abigails instead.' She rattled on, praying Mrs Hendercott was far too interested in Mrs Haxby to notice their distinct absence from the gallery.

'Tell me, how is the General, Mrs Hendercott, and all your talented progeny too? Is Cecily quite recovered from her cold? I daresay her morning hacks are assisting, though my sister said her groom clearly has a challenge in keeping up.'

She smiled innocently, praying her dart had found its target. Phoebe had chanced upon the young Cecily riding through Hyde Park, without her personal groom, on more than one occasion. No one would understand the urge to ride alone better than a Fairfax, but Sophie also knew the pastime was even less acceptable in London than Bath, and particularly as an unmarried debutante.

Mrs Hendercott's thick eyebrows darted together in instant suspicion.

'Cecily is quite recovered now, I thank you, Miss Fairfax,' she returned icily, 'and much too busy for morning hacks with the season underway. And now, as the ladies of the Bridge Club are here in an investigative capacity, we really must take our leave. Lord Rotherby, I must say it is much *less* of a surprise to find you here. Lady Aurelia, Mrs … Haxby,' she concluded waspishly.

Both ladies inclined their heads as Mrs Hendercott took her leave, and Sophie slowly exhaled a breath. She was the victor for the moment, but only because of a fragile snippet of gossip. Yet she was sure she'd blotted her copybook too. Mrs Hendercott would be well aware she'd traded Cecily's minor lapse in good behaviour for a blind eye to her own, but how long would it be before she found a way to penalise her?

'Expertly done,' Lord Rotherby murmured as soon as Mrs Hendercott and her vulturous Bridge Club were out of earshot. 'Though I'm sure you must have been well aware of the risk of attending an exhibition such as this?' He frowned before continuing. 'In truth, while it is admirable to know your passion outweighs societal expectation in all things, I'm surprised your guardian permitted it at all.'

The latter part of his address was uttered softly, but the glint in his eyes was clear. She drew herself up to her full height, unwilling to be admonished by a sanctimonious rake or to be reminded of their wager at this time. His double standards infuriated her, while the narrow escape with Mrs Hendercott had only made her feel foolish.

'I am not interested in your observations, sir,' she replied coldly. 'My interests are not your affair, and now, if you'll excuse us, we've a number of—'

'Oh I do believe we are quite discovered!' Aurelia declared in delight as some boisterous laughter resounded through the space.

Sophie's spirits sank further, as she glanced in the direction of the Institution entrance. A matron of the ton and Lord Rotherby were one matter, a group of young gentlemen seeking frivolous entertainment quite another.

'And what can any young lady do in such circumstances, except throw herself on the mercy of her heroic company?' Aurelia added, smiling at Lord Rotherby, who looked distinctly uninterested in being heroic in any way.

'There's always making an exit with your self-respect intact,' Mrs Haxby murmured.

'In truth there is little need for any heroics,' a sensible tone interjected, 'when there is another exit, just up ahead.'

'Sir Weston,' Sophie exhaled in relief, 'how truly delightful to see you!'

Sir Weston lifted his curly-brimmed beaver hat as Sophie curtsied, unable to help contrasting his steadfast presence with Lord Rotherby's clear disapproval.

Briefly, Josephine's praise echoed through her thoughts.

'Sir Weston has a quiet air of authority that neither seeks attention, nor shies away from it, and his manner always suits the occasion. He neither tries too hard, nor not enough, and always knows just what to say too.'

She smiled faintly, it seemed her younger sister was far more astute than she'd realised, and now she couldn't be more grateful for his appearance.

'Would you be so kind as to escort us home, Sir Weston?' she asked, ignoring Lord Rotherby's silent stare, 'for we find we are quite finished here.'

'I should be honoured, Miss Fairfax,' Sir Weston said, executing a very proper bow which was neither too obsequious, nor too small.

'Thank you, that would be most kind.' Sophie smiled with real gratitude. 'I've not had the chance to thank you for your delightful daffodils either,' she continued. 'They made Damerel Place looked just like Knightswood Park, and my sisters did not stop admiring them for a week.'

'You are most welcome, Miss Fairfax,' Sir Weston replied. 'I believe daffodils possess a true beauty that encapsulates spring – I hoped you might enjoy them.'

'I did,' she replied sincerely. 'They were, by far, my favourite.'

Chapter Eight

ONE HOSTILE RAKE

Three days later

It wasn't exactly an untruth. Daffodils were Sophie's favourite, but even she didn't know why she'd said as much to Sir Weston – except that she'd very much enjoyed the scowl on Lord Rotherby's face when she did so. She wrinkled her nose at the memory. In truth, Lord Rotherby hadn't scowled so much as *glowered*, intently, and even though she had taken the greatest satisfaction from his clear disapproval for dear Sir Weston and his impoverished blooms, it was still a mystery of epic proportions. On reflection, she could only conclude that Sir Weston's sensible coats and genteel manner offended him as much as her determination to make a love match.

Sighing, she gazed out at Hyde Park, wishing for the umpteenth time that Aunt Higglestone had accepted the offer of Phoebe's lilac phaeton while she was away; it was so much finer than a hired carriage, especially for a debutante in her first season.

'Do try and look a little bit interested, Josephine. It'll be your turn soon enough.' Sophie glanced across at her dearest bookworm sister, who was enthralled by a copy of Ann Hatton's *Modern Attachments*.

'I haven't the time,' Josephine murmured, raising an eyebrow.

'I discovered Hatchards Booksellers in Piccadilly yesterday, and it is a perfect treasure trove! I fully intend to return there tomorrow as I found a rather lovely bound copy of *Northanger Abbey* which smelled like old leather and ink and… Anyway, did you know this book was written by Sarah Siddons's sister – the actress who gave Phoebe the theatrical epée she snapped when duelling the high—'

'Yes, yes dear,' Sophie assured swiftly with a pointed look at their abigails, seated opposite them. 'I recall her very well. And I'm sure it's a very fine book, but the whole point of riding out in Hyde Park before dinner is to see and be seen. All anyone can see of you is the tip of your topknot *à la madonna*, and I do believe Lucy positively slaved over it.'

Josephine rolled her eyes before marking her page with her favourite homemade bookmark.

'Aunt Higglestone's maid isn't here,' she pointed out drily, 'and the only reason I'm here is because Phoebe isn't. I know you'd much rather be bowling through Hyde Park, in a fashionable phaeton, with the newest darling of the ton at your side.'

'Not at all,' Sophie frowned, reaching out to squeeze her sister's hand. 'For who else could I rely on to remind me that the season is actually all rather frivolous and silly, if not the most thoughtful and dearest bookworm among us?'

She smiled as Josephine's face lit up, though she was conscious of a dart of concern too. Their mild-mannered middle sister could usually be counted on for her sunny outlook; it was most unlike her to compare herself to anyone.

'I still don't understand why Sir Weston was at the exhibition,' Josephine blurted suddenly. 'I would have thought him the last gentleman to be interested in an exhibition of modern ladies' fashion. He usually seems … above such things.'

'Dearest, Sir Weston was only there as an escort to Mrs Hendercott and her Bridge Club,' Sophie replied, surprised Josephine should fix upon such a point. 'Apparently, he offered to escort them in case there were any exuberant gentlemen present. Though how Sir Weston could offer any more protection than Mrs Hendercott herself, is beyond me!'

Josephine began to chuckle as Sophie glanced across the park at a smart black curricle being driven along the *King's Route* at a vigorous pace.

'She is rather formidable,' Josephine replied, 'like all our governesses and the Marchioness Carlisle rolled into one, only with slightly less peacock!'

At this, they both dissolved into snorts of laughter.

'If anything, I suspect Sir Weston needed protection from Mrs Hendercott!' Josephine added when she could draw breath. 'Though I did think it was gentlemanly of him to escort you home. Did he not ask why you were there?'

'He didn't,' Sophie said. 'He's far too well-mannered for that. Though I did mention having some ideas for my sketch book, so hopefully he realised it was for the sake of fashion... Not that it matters now. The main thing is that we all know just how much of a scoundrel Lord Rotherby can be. Do you know, apart from treating me like an ignorant schoolgirl, he actually had the effrontery to scowl at Sir Weston too – and all with his lady-friend on his arm!'

'A scoundrel indeed,' Josephine replied, eyeing her sister carefully. 'He really is one of Matilda's pigwidgeoned dunderheads!'

'I warrant there are few more cheering sights than an ambush of fearless Fairfaxes choosing their own company over the rest of the ton,' a low voice called with perfect timing. 'Good evening, Miss Fairfax – and Miss Fairfax the younger too, I hazard?'

Sophie started at the familiar tone, before reluctantly turning towards the gleaming sports curricle that had pulled up alongside their own. Instantly she could see it was a fashionable equipage finished, it appeared, with far more care than the driver himself today. She glanced at Lord Rotherby's ruffled hair and swiftly tied cravat, which gave him a dashing, almost heroic appearance in the late afternoon light, and suppressed a frown, for he was neither, she reminded herself. Indeed, he was still the same unpredictable, notorious rake she'd sworn to avoid for the rest of the season.

'Good evening, sir,' Sophie replied, deliberately ignoring his reference to Josephine. 'I trust you are enjoying a pleasurable excursion?'

She waited, as he seemed to consider her question. Unusually, there was a decidedly unsettled air about him, and he appeared entirely devoid of company, save for a scowling tiger seated at the back of his curricle. For a few moments, Sophie wondered if Mrs Haxby had given him his marching orders and felt a peculiar satisfaction at the thought.

'I am enjoying the air,' he replied, 'but in truth, Hyde Park is a little crowded today.' He paused and smiled in a way that didn't quite reach his shadowed eyes. 'Though it is encouraging to see young ladies enjoying all of the distractions London has to offer,' he continued. Indeed, I would be tempted to wager there will be a new darling of the ton very soon, but as I am already in danger of losing my first, I'll offer it as a sincere belief instead. Miss Fairfax, I wish you every success of the season! And Miss Fairfax the Younger, you would do well to study your sister, for I am certain that her unique passion and charms will ensure she takes the ton by storm.'

Then he doffed his hat and drove on.

'Well, what on earth was all that about?' Josephine quizzed, wide-eyed.

'I'm sure I haven't the faintest idea!' Sophie replied.

Chapter Nine

TEACHING A RAKE A LESSON

Two days later

'An ambush of fearless Fairfaxes,' Sophie muttered to herself, re-buttoning her stays and wishing she hadn't had a second helping of baked custard at dinner. 'Well, he was right about the latter part anyway.'

She glanced down at the hastily scrawled letter from Aurelia, and cursed in a way that would make even Phoebe look twice.

My dear Miss Fairfax,

I have heard through a reliable friend that there is movement afoot in a certain noble household, thus providing an opportunity for my plan. I will leave a letter for my parents and ask only that you maintain my confidence until tomorrow evening, when I will send word directly from Paris.

Do think of me at midnight tonight, headed for foreign shores, and the next time we meet you can address me as Lady R!

Until then, mon amie,
Lady Aurelia Carlisle

'Pah! Headed for Rotherby's shores, more like,' Sophie muttered caustically, wriggling into the only muslin she could fasten with a hook.

It was well past ten, her aunt's bourgeois lodgings were quiet, and she'd been deliberating her course of action since receiving the letter at breakfast.

That Lady Aurelia was delusional Sophie was now sure, and that Lord Rotherby was entirely capable of crushing her expectations was also beyond certain. The only question remaining was whether she should thrust her head in the sand, or admit she had the smallest window of opportunity to try and stop Aurelia from making the biggest mistake of her life.

She closed her eyes in frustration. The last thing she wanted was to take any more risks. Her chance meeting with Mrs Hendercott at The British Institution had already resulted in more restless nights than she cared to admit, but there was a chance she'd never forgive herself if she stood by while Aurelia ruined her life – especially for a cad like Rotherby. And so, despite every good reason to climb into bed and ignore the world, she'd begun dressing the moment the housemaid retired.

'Which only goes to show that the possession of a conscience does not always work to one's advantage,' she added darkly.

'You're not running away, are you?' a sleepy voice asked, 'because you know how that worked out for Phoebe…'

'Oh Matty, you scared me to half to death!' Sophie chastised, spying her youngest sister standing just outside her door, holding a candle. 'And why have you got Duke Wellington with you at this time of night? It's long past both your bedtimes.'

'Edward said I could borrow him – and besides, he's half of my new circus act!'

'Your new *fire-breathing* circus act?' Sophie quizzed.

Matilda nodded as Sophie closed her eyes and muttered a short prayer.

'Well, come in and close the door, lest you wake Josephine too,' she urged. 'And of course I'm not running away.'

She paused to consider what phrasing would attract the least suspicion.

'I'm simply … helping a friend.'

Sophie eyed Matilda warily, well aware of her uncanny knack for reading her older sisters like open books.

'I'll be back well before breakfast, I promise,' she added breezily. 'But you could help me by hooking my dress and not saying anything to anyone?'

'I *could* do that,' Matilda replied, setting the toad down between Sophie's cushions from where it proceeded to watch them with disgruntled suspicion.

'But only *if* you do something for me too.'

'And what would that be?' Sophie frowned, pulling on her indigo velvet gloves.

'Find out what's wrong with Josephine!' Matilda complained.

'She's been such a bore since we left Knightswood, always gushing on and on about Sir Weston, and his perfect manners, and his perfect coat, *that is just the right shade of green*,' she mimicked, feigning her most convincing sick face. 'I'm beginning to think her last lung spasm left her addled in the head!'

'Matilda Fairfax!' Sophie eyed her younger sister exasperatedly. 'There's nothing wrong with Josephine. She's just growing up.'

'Well, if growing up means writing for hours in your diary, and being cross for no reason at all, I'm sure I'd actually rather join the circus!' Matilda fired back, throwing herself facedown on Sophie's bed.

Sophie smiled thoughtfully at her wilful younger sister, recalling Josephine's mood in Hyde Park. She hadn't realised the extent of her infatuation, and clearly needed to give it some thought, but it would have to wait for now.

'I promise I'll talk to her,' she said placatingly, turning her attention to the button fastenings on her gloves.

'Now, hook me up, old lady, and we might even visit the real circus soon – but only if you give Duke Wellington the weekend off. He doesn't look entirely comfortable with the idea of being the first fire-breathing toad!'

'The last time we conversed he said I'd adore Paris which was clearly an invitation, so I've made up my mind.'

Sophie hurried from her hackney cab and along the quiet Mayfair street with Aurelia's grand plan ringing in her ears.

She was already beginning to have second thoughts and wondering if she shouldn't have just left her to ruin her life, instead of her own precious new kid boots. And yet, the idea of turning back sent the oddest flare through her veins too, despite it making perfectly good sense.

She scowled as she pulled her cloak tighter and quickened her pace. A midnight rendezvous was certainly not as glamorous as it sounded; there were shadows looming out of every corner, and muddy puddles that seemed impossible to avoid no matter how one tried. She could only hope that Aurelia's delusion would not affect her usual, terrible timekeeping, and that Lord Rotherby would be on his way before she even arrived. She wasn't even certain she would know his residence, despite a sketchy knowledge of Grosvenor Square. She would just have to trust Aurelia's description of Rotherby House as 'one of the grandest in all Mayfair'.

Fortunately, it was accurate enough, and within minutes an impressive façade and marble steps loomed up, together with a gleaming coach emblazoned with his lordship's arms. Sophie exhaled as she slowed, peering through the misted moonlight, praying Aurelia had been misinformed about Lord Rotherby's intended journey. Any fragile hopes were swiftly dashed, however, by the sight of luggage strapped to the top of the chaise, and a tall, unmistakable nobleman loitering beside his groom. She shrank back, cursing her new heeled kid boots as he turned in her direction, and suddenly aware she was quite alone, in Mayfair, at midnight.

'Is that you, my love?' he called in a new tone she'd not heard before.

Sophie froze. She'd planned to wait in the shadows, to

intercept Aurelia if she happened to arrive on time – most definitely not confront him directly.

And now this. She'd heard Lord Rotherby be sardonic, playful and even quizzical before, but never like … a lover. She swallowed a sudden lump in her throat as she realised he *was* actually expecting someone, and a shadow of doubt flew through her mind.

He hadn't seemed that enamoured with Mrs Haxby. Could he be leaving with someone new? *Or perhaps he was expecting Aurelia after all?*

Her blood ran cold for a second, before she recalled his barely concealed animosity at the exhibition, as well as his own self-imposed rules. Lord Rotherby was undoubtedly a rake and a scoundrel, but running off with a debutante just didn't fit.

'You have come. I had begun to wonder,' he said with a chuckle, striding forwards to catch her up and plant a warm kiss on her lips.

For a second, Sophie gasped in complete shock, a multitude of feelings coursing her veins. She'd never been kissed in such a way before, and the sensation was both scandalous and something else she didn't even want to begin to identify. She inhaled raggedly and willed her thumping heart to slow. Of course he would have expectations if he was expecting a lady-companion – the question was how to manage them while convincing him to leave.

Briefly, Harriet's advice about notorious rake reached through her thoughts. She flushed and pulled her cloak hood forwards, more convinced than ever that she was doing Aurelia the biggest favour of her life.

'You wouldn't wish me to appear too eager, my lord,' she said, in her best attempt at a coquettish tone.

He laughed as he slid his arm around her, and began walking towards the chaise, while she tried not to tense every muscle she possessed. His warm proximity was most disconcerting, yet he seemed much too distracted to notice anything at all, which for some reason irritated Sophie intensely.

'Well, not here at any rate,' he replied in a tone that made her itch to box his ears. 'But let us not delay, my love,' he continued in the next breath, 'for I am keen to be away and happy I have provided everything for your comfort, as I promised. Let me show you; it's all waiting inside the coach.'

'Thank you for your effort, my Lord,' she replied, clenching her teeth, 'however, what I actually came to say is that I cannot—'

'Thunder an' turf!' he cursed suddenly, making Sophie's ears redden. 'We appear to have company, so we really must away this instant. There is no time to be lost!'

With a lurch, she followed the direction of his gaze to spy a hazy figure at the bottom of the street, hurrying towards them. Instantly, she knew it to be Aurelia, and her hopeful plan suddenly seemed the most flawed of any she'd ever made. She gritted her teeth, knowing Aurelia's appearance jeopardised everything, and she had just seconds to make a decision. There was no way she could explain everything to Lord Rotherby in so short an amount of time, and a public scene with Aurelia would be disastrous! As far as she could see, she had but one option left.

Swiftly, she turned and climbed into the chaise, telling

herself she would share her identity and ask to be set down as soon as they were clear of Mayfair. Lord Rotherby was many things, but a kidnapper he certainly was not.

'We will talk, my love,' he promised in a rush, 'just not here. I look forward to joining you properly in Dover, when our real adventure will begin!'

Then he slammed the door shut and strode towards the front of the chaise.

For a second, Sophie could only stare at the dark leather interior of the door. How could she divulge her identity, and demand to be set down, if he wasn't travelling inside the chaise with her? Her answer was a muffled shout, before the whole equipage lurched forwards into the night.

Instantly her numb limbs flushed with life and, seizing the door handle, she forced it open, only to find the street flying past at such a rattle-pace she could barely close it again. Then she turned and started banging on the solid wood frame, shouting for the chaise to stop. But whether it was the luxurious interior muffling the sound, or the noise of the racing wheels over the cobblestones, her appeal went unheeded.

Finally, she sank down against the seat, cold fear swirling, as the enormity of her situation began to materialise. So much for avoiding scandal! She'd done nothing but court it since coming to London, and for what good reason?

To show a rake she was more worldly than she actually was?

To show a debutante she was right about a scoundrel?

What had she actually achieved, except to prove herself to

be the most naïve debutante who'd ever entered the marriage mart at all?

'I look forward to joining you properly when we reach Dover.'

Sophie swallowed, trying to order her thoughts, as his parting words struck a cold toll through her. Aurelia had said he was intended for France, but his mention of Dover made everything very real. It was also some seven hours from London, which meant it was imperative she got out as soon as possible. Rapidly, she tried to recall her knowledge of coaching inn stops along the London road, certain Thomas and Fred had mentioned a few. But quite how far along they were – or how far Lord Rotherby would drive before stopping – was a mystery.

She clenched her fists in the folds of her muslin skirt, reminding herself he would have to stop for her comfort, if not his own. The thought was her only consolation. Travelling as far as Dover would not only take her some significant distance from Aunt Higglestone and the rest of her siblings, it would also mean being in Lord Rotherby's company for an entire night, *unaccompanied*. No one would believe her virtue to be intact after such a duration, especially given Lord Rotherby's reputation. She would be as good as ruined! Her aunt would have an apoplexy; Thomas would try to force Rotherby into marriage; Phoebe would think she'd taken leave of her senses; Josephine would suffer another lung spasm; Matilda would likely run away and join an actual circus, while Aurelia…

For a full minute, Sophie's mind turned cartwheels, imagining all the ways Aurelia would wreak her revenge, if she did not find a way out of her current situation.

She stared out at the shadowy night. The main roads with

which she was familiar had disappeared and she could see only the occasional cluster of buildings and long stretches of countryside. Clearly Lord Rotherby had chosen a lesser-known route from London, and briefly she recalled his unsettled air at Hyde Park.

She exhaled shakily.

Had his dark eyes been contemplating this midnight escape back then? What had occurred to prompt such a flight?

Warily, she eyed the expensive-looking boxes on the opposite seat.

'I am keen to be away and happy I have provided everything for your comfort, as I promised.'

With a burst of fresh purpose, she reached across the swaying coach to the first dress box and pulled it onto her knees. If her only option was to catch the stage or mail coach back to London, she'd likely benefit from a few extra layers. Resolutely, she pulled off the box lid and stared briefly at the folded material within, before realisation dawned. She reached out to touch the expensive silk in wonder. She'd never seen such fine material before and briefly she imagined Lord Rotherby selecting the flimsy undergarments, together with the thoughts that might have run through his mind.

Had he pictured his companion wearing them? Removing them perhaps?

She flushed scarlet, confused by the myriad emotions coursing through her veins. She had nothing but contempt for Lord Rotherby, so why did the thought of him picking out such items fascinate her so? Swiftly, she reached for the next box, and then the next until she'd opened every box and discovered nothing but stays, stockings, petticoats and the type of scandalous nightwear that only endorsed Lord Rotherby's view on ladies' clothing.

Finally, she paused to stare at the most expensive and impractical pile of clothing she'd ever seen. No wonder Lord Rotherby had attended the exhibition; he was quite the fashion connoisseur already! A wave of fiery determination engulfed her. She would not let such a cad ruin everything. She had to make a plan. Furiously, she cast her eye around the inside of the chaise for anything that could serve as a makeshift weapon. She might not be Phoebe, but she was still a Fairfax!

Seconds later, her eyes alighted upon two sleek leather pockets stitched to the inside of the padded doors. They looked suspiciously like Thomas's pistol holders, and with a lurch across the seat, Sophie thrust her hand into the first. Triumphantly, she withdrew a small silver pistol which, on closer inspection, turned out to be a deadly Webster flintlock, and pulled back the muzzle. Yet to her intense disappointment, the pistol was completely empty, and the pocket likewise.

Scowling, she pushed the pistol back into its holder and slid over to the second pocket before inserting her hand again. This time, she withdrew a small silver crossbow, inset with a row of gleaming mother of pearl. It was a very pretty little weapon, fashioned with considerable skill.

'But do you actually work?' she whispered, noticing the small quiver of darts attached to its slim shaft.

Carefully, she eased a sharp dart from its holding place and turned it over between her fingers, her mind flooding with the times she'd confiscated similar contraptions from her brothers. She might not be willing to jump into a duel with a highwayman, but she could certainly wield such a weapon if needed.

Anxiously, she sat back and pulled a fur throw over her knees, unable to help admiring its quality – Lord Rotherby might be all manner of rogues, but he certainly didn't compromise on style or comfort. Then her thoughts wandered to Aurelia, and to whether she'd returned home by now, furious her big plan had gone awry. She felt a pang of guilt, despite everything.

'Yet I'm certain you'll never thank me,' she muttered to herself, resting her head back against the seat.

It had to be near one in the morning, which meant she had less than two hours to board a public coach back, if she was to have any chance of returning to her bedchamber before breakfast. It was tight, but he would have to stop at some point, and if there was any difficulty in parting ways, she would simply threaten him with the crossbow.

Convinced she had a plan that would work, Sophie allowed herself to relax a little. His lordship really did drive at breakneck speed, but there was something about the pace that was oddly lulling and, under any other circumstances, she could allow herself to get very comfortable indeed. She yawned and pulled the throw further up, even though there were no draughts at all in his well-sprung chaise and she already felt quite cosy. No matter how well-intentioned, she'd acted impulsively – she could see that now – and thoroughly deserved the scolding she had no doubt was coming when she relayed the whole affair to Phoebe.

But she was also just as capable as her sister of taking care of herself, and she *would* make it back that same night, if it was the very last thing she did.

Chapter Ten

THE ARROW AND DASHER

Several hours later

The first sound she heard was the faint cry of a paddle steamer, echoing the gulls.

Sophie woke with a violent start, conscious the comforting blanket of darkness had been swapped for cold, clingy tendrils of morning, and a complete desertion of the courage she'd felt at midnight.

Tentatively, she blinked – once, twice – denying the changes around her before fresh fear began seeping through her veins. It had to be impossible, and yet stark reality said otherwise. Somehow, she'd swapped the luxurious interior of Lord Rotherby's chaise for an even more luxurious bedchamber, that also appeared to be moving!

Furiously, Sophie patted her person and clothing, all of which appeared to be intact, before scrambling off the comfortable bed and lurching to a small, oddly circular window. For a second, she stared in numb denial at the busy harbour walkway, and then a nauseous twist reached up from the pit of her stomach. Somehow, she'd not only fallen asleep, she'd slept right through a transfer to a tethered yacht too! A vague dream of whinnying horses, banging doors and muffled shouts began to seep into her thoughts. Back at Knightswood, she was famous for sleeping through everything, including thunderstorms, but even she couldn't have slept though her only chance of saving her own neck, could she? *And how had they not discovered her identity?*

She swallowed, staring at the early harbour workers through the grey mist, and trying to force her dazed brain to work. She'd assumed Lord Rotherby would be travelling by either *The Arrow* or *The Dasher*, the new cross-Channel wooden paddle steamers Phoebe and the viscount used to start their honeymoon, but of course he would have the comfort of his own yacht. He'd never travel in anything, but the lap of luxury.

Panic-stricken, she spun from the window and rushed to the cabin door, determined to get off while she still could. She had no idea how to catch the public stage all the way from Dover, or if she could arrive at her aunt's lodgings with anything like a plausible story, and yet the alternative was too awful to contemplate. If the truth became known in the polite world, she would've as good as absconded with Lord Rotherby, thus tarnishing her reputation forever. She would be no better than Aurelia, if not a whole sight worse.

Yet, even as she reached for the door handle, there were footsteps outside and a brusque knock at the door. Horrified, she shrank back and pulled her cloak hood as far forward as possible, before fumbling for her pocket. By some miracle, the miniature crossbow still appeared to be secreted within her skirts and she felt a moment's reassurance. Whatever his reaction, she still stood a chance of getting away before the rest of Dover witnessed her shame.

'Guv'nor sends his best compliments,' came a gruff, unknown voice, 'and asks if you have any special requests for refreshment?'

Sophie blinked as her disbelief evaporated. Lord Rotherby had dared carry her aboard his boat, and now he didn't even have the decency to face her?

'He has already requested coffee and a selection of—'

But whatever his lordship had requested was lost entirely as Sophie yanked the door open to find his tiger standing there, looking much more like a recalcitrant child than a respectful groom.

Momentarily she glowered, wondering whether to scream or try to run, but then she noted his querulous face and felt a flicker of hope. He didn't seem at all concerned by the absence of Mrs Haxby, and looked every inch a cross wildling, entirely different to the pan-faced grooms she was used to seeing around town. Perhaps he could be persuaded to help.

She pulled her cloak tighter, suddenly conscious of how much she needed to use a water closet.

'Thank you,' she said, nodding abruptly.

'Who placed me in this cabin please … sorry, I don't know your name?'

'Me, and it's Horace, Miss' he replied tersely. 'Guvnor needed to brief the crew and didn't want no one else doing it. I was very careful,' he added swiftly. 'Just left you sleeping, like the guvnor said.'

'I see,' Sophie replied slowly, realising that if Horace had carried her aboard, it meant her identity could actually still be a secret.

'Horace, I find I need a few moments alone before I meet his lordship. A few ... *lady* moments, that is. Could you escort me, discreetly, to the inn, do you think? I promise it won't take much of your time.'

She forced a beguiling smile then, the one she reserved for family and people she actually liked, and for a second the redoubtable Horace stared before he scowled again.

'The guvnor asked me to check for any special requests and that's all,' he growled, making Sophie sorely regret her initial impression. 'Not that you don't seem a nice enough filly,' he continued in a kinder tone, 'but I don't get to make orders, jus' follow 'em. And I daresay you can still 'ave them lady moments as this yacht has more luxuries than I've 'ad 'ot dinners,' he added with a shrug. 'You jus' need to ask the guvnor w'en he gets 'ere.'

'I'm not asking your guvnor anything!' Sophie replied fiercely. 'Please stand aside so I may—'

'We leave as soon as the tide is with us,' came his lordship's faint tone, framed by the sound of brisk boots across a wooden deck.

Sophie shrank back again, suddenly feeling more exposed than ever in her life.

'Thank gawd,' Horace said with relief. 'I ain't got the patter for fillies an' no mistake,' he added, before walking away.

Furiously, she gripped the crossbow in her pocket and stiffened at some faint laughter, starkly aware some of the deckhands must have witnessed her undignified embarkation on board. She stepped back in a rush, suddenly fearful of everything; and then he was in the doorway, his tall figure silhouetted in the brightening morning, a roguish light in his eyes.

'Good morning, Mrs Letitia Haxby,' he began silkily, starting towards her. 'I trust you have rested well my love? I have taken the liberty of ordering breakfast for you, but just say if you'd like anything in particular. I apologise for the swift journey, the tide waits for no man, but now we are *finally* alone we can begin to—'

'Stop right where you are, Rotherby!' Sophie growled, pulling out the small crossbow and aiming it directly at his lordship's chest.

There was a sharp curse as he pulled up short and scrutinised her in utter astonishment.

'Miss Fairfax?' he exclaimed in genuine shock. 'What in the name of every blackguard known to England are *you* doing here?'

Chapter Eleven

STILL TEACHING A RAKE A LESSON

A few seconds later

'I would consider staying and breaking my fast with you, Lord Rotherby,' Sophie enunciated icily, keeping the crossbow trained on his person, 'but I have a stagecoach to catch if I'm to make it back to London before this day is done. Suffice to say, I will never speak of this night, and neither will you!'

'Stagecoaches be damned, I asked a question! What in the blazes are *you* doing here?' Lord Rotherby thundered, his eyes narrowed to shards.

Sophie suppressed a shiver. She'd never witnessed a gentleman in such a fury. Her father had a quiet nature, and Thomas always vented his anger on the local rabbit population. But this was different; she could feel Lord Rotherby's fury as keenly as though it were her own, while the gleam in his eye was distinctly unnerving.

She drew a steadying breath and reminded herself she was

the one holding a crossbow, and that no one, not even Lord Rotherby, was impervious to silver darts.

'Lady Aurelia interpreted your comment about her *adoring Paris* as an invitation to accompany you on your next trip,' she replied with forced calm. 'She had no idea you planned to take Mrs Haxby, and was convinced you would offer marriage in the morning. My intention was to intercept and dissuade her from coming with you, but when you mistook me for Mrs Haxby everything changed. I … panicked, and let you think I was she until Aurelia approached Rotherby House, when I realised I was risking a public scene. I thought it better to reveal my identity in your coach, and ask safe passage home. But *you*, sir, decided to drive all night, making it impossible for me to do so.'

'Lady Aurelia? Adore Paris?' his lordship expostulated, his eyes flashing with anger. 'I never said any such thing, and if she had some fairytale ending in mind she would have been sorely disappointed!'

'Aurelia does not believe in fairytales,' Sophie replied stonily, 'and her plan was hardly honourable, particularly if what you say is true. But that does not excuse the fact that your rakish behaviour, sir, is an insult to all females!'

She paused as a dark scowl spread across his face.

'My rakish behaviour? All females? I pride myself on my strict rules about companions, and I most certainly have *not* in any way encouraged Lady Aurelia,' he expostulated furiously. 'Any interest she may have perceived was entirely on her side or, as I am more tempted to believe, wholly exaggerated to justify her own ambition,' he continued scathingly. 'In truth, I believe the only person who has been duped, my dear, is you.'

Sophie felt a dull flush rise across her face as she realised the full extent of her folly, but held her weapon steady. Even if Lord Rotherby had never mentioned Paris to Aurelia, he was still culpable, by virtue of his very nature.

'In some ways I am not surprised by Lady Aurelia, for she has been forever making cow's eyes at me,' he continued, his lip curling contemptuously. 'But you…' He scowled intently, making Sophie feel suddenly and inexplicably vulnerable. 'I would have expected so much better of you. Why a young lady of your breeding and understanding of the world has got embroiled in this mess – for the sake of *Lady Aurelia*, of all people – is beyond my comprehension. Do you realise what you have done? What any member of the ton will think?' He took a step forward, raking his hand through his perfectly unruly Byronesque locks. 'They will assume you've spent the night with me, Sophie,' he ground out intensely. 'Do you know what that even means?'

Sophie blanched at his use of her first name. Somehow it felt even more intimate than it should in his luxurious cabin, aboard his personal yacht.

'It means you're as good as ruined,' he added bluntly. 'You do understand that, don't you? I've never pursued debutantes, but my reputation is such that everyone will assume I've—' He closed his eyes and inhaled deeply. 'They will assume I've had your virtue, and by God, I've—' He pulled himself up swiftly, before a fresh scowl spread across his features. 'You cannot blame my choosing to drive *my chaise* through the night,' he continued scathingly, 'when *you* took it upon yourself to rescue a friend who did not need any kind of help. I would have known exactly what Lady

Aurelia was scheming and sent her on her way, but instead…'

He paused to groan and run his fingers through his dishevelled hair again, while Sophie didn't know where to look.

'And yet, it doesn't matter who I thought you were, only that you're here now and you've shattered your own reputation to achieve it. Why would you do such a thing? Your dream of making an advantageous love match lies in tatters, while Aurelia sleeps soundly in her bed. No self-respecting gentleman will make you an offer if they think I've had first dibs,' he added roughly.

'How dare you!' Sophie gasped in outrage. 'I only intended to try and save Aurelia from making a huge mistake, and no lady, not even Mrs Haxby, should be addressed in such a manner.'

'It's the hard truth, you little fool!' Lord Rotherby blazed.

Sophie eyeballed the hostile rake for a few moments with vehement dislike, before trusting herself to speak.

'I've been gone for less than a day,' she said, ignoring the wave of fear the words generated in the pit of her stomach. 'If I'm back by dinner, I can say I've been with a sick relative. My aunt will—'

'You left London, in my chaise, at midnight!' he growled. 'By now, most of your household will be breakfasting and you will be distinctly absent! And if I know the female mind at all, you will have told *someone* you were slipping out to help a friend – or some other such incriminating thing.'

Sophie flushed instantly, recalling the brief conversation she'd had with Matilda along very similar lines.

'Precisely,' Lord Rotherby said, nodding with dangerous calm. 'Which means whoever you have told will have announced your intentions at breakfast this morning, prompting your fond relatives to make your absence known to all their friends in Mayfair by now. It will take a matter of seconds for Lady Aurelia to work out what has happened and turn it to her advantage. Do you really not know the character of your friend? She would never protect you, especially if there is a scandal to be created from it!'

Sophie suppressed a shiver as she pointed the small crossbow in the weak morning light, her chest pounding.

'So much for winning the wager, Miss Fairfax,' he added, taking a step forwards. 'You've won nothing except a lifetime of regret.'

Briefly, she stared at Lord Rotherby's hard eyes and noble lips curling in contempt, wondering how she ever allowed herself to be distracted in Almack's. He was the rudest, most obnoxious man of her acquaintance – which only made his correct assessment of her situation all the more galling. By now, Matilda would have told Aunt Higglestone, who, never known for her restraint, would have alerted half of breakfasting London. There would be no easy return without a fictional account of epic proportions, and no guarantee Aurelia hadn't hijacked her chances already.

Yet she couldn't accept any alternative either. She clenched her fingers, and wracked her brain for an answer. Perhaps she could return to Knightswood with her sisters for a while, or at least until the scandal subsided.

'Come, come,' Lord Rotherby muttered testily after a beat. 'It's not quite as terrible as you might think. If I were the heinous rake you believe me to be, I'd undoubtedly leave you here in Dover to make your own way back and face the music, but I am a Rotherby and, as all this is one huge, calamitous mistake, I am honour-bound to offer you my protection. Your actions this night might leave you few options, but your reputation will not be tarnished at my hand.'

'Your protection?' Sophie blazed furiously. 'I would rather employ the protection of your dubious tiger who, I hasten to add, also has the manners of a jungle cat.'

'A jungle cat?' Lord Rotherby repeated with a harsh bark of laughter. 'Poor Horace will be heartbroken, for he was quite taken with you!' Sophie tensed as he loosened his cravat and took another step forward, closing the distance between them. 'You must understand you have inflicted this situation upon both of us with your ramshackle and foolish intentions,' he challenged furiously. 'Which means you may not wish for my company, and the Lord knows I won't force it upon you, but our lots have fallen together and we—'

'Take one more step and I swear I'll fire!' she growled, training the crossbow on his waistcoat's topmost gleaming button.

His lordship pulled up in surprise.

'Well, it wouldn't be the first time, would it?' he returned scathingly. 'You know, I really am quite regretful that I won't see the outcome of our wager, for I do believe you are that rare combination of spirit, accomplishment and beauty one so seldom sees among today's debutantes. In truth, I also believed you might achieve that love match of yours, and that it would be well deserved, but now you will have to make do with me instead. Alas, it is truly a poor exchange.'

'I am not interested in your regret, or your fake laments,' Sophie ground out, keeping her aim steady, 'any more than I am interested in being aboard your ridiculous yacht one second longer—'

'Be that as it may, you *are* here,' he interrupted, exhaling frustratedly.

'And you must have known the risk you were taking the moment you let me kiss you,' he added, his eyes darkening suddenly.

'I did not *let you*!' Sophie rattled, trying to catch her breath. 'And if you didn't drive like the devil, I wouldn't be standing here now.'

'I have a reputation to uphold!' he threw. 'And I was keen to reach Dover.'

Sophie shivered despite herself, the sudden heat of his kiss flooding her mind. She flushed as a sardonic smile flickered across his face, and she was sure he was recalling exactly the same moment.

'Besides which, that silver crossbow is ornamental, you little fool,' he added a little less roughly. 'An expensive trinket, but no more. You may keep it if you wish, but it is no more a weapon than your sister's infamous epée!'

Sophie caught her breath as Lord Rotherby's eyes gleamed with cold humour. Yet all she could think was that he'd ridiculed her beloved sister – and that was her right alone.

'My sister, sir, is a viscountess!' she hissed, inadvertently squeezing the crossbow in her fury.

It was already too late when she heard the tiny click, releasing a small, determined arrow that flew directly at Lord Rotherby's upper arm. And when it sank, they both stared at the silver shaft protruding through his shirt in momentary silence, before Sophie let out the loudest shriek of all her eighteen years.

'Surely it is I who should be yelling?' Lord Rotherby said testily. 'You don't have an absurd toy protruding from your arm!'

'It's not an absurd toy,' Sophie wailed, with a look of stricken grief. 'I shot you! I shot you with a crossbow!' she sobbed. 'And now look at your ruffled French silk shirt…'

'You do seem to be rather predisposed to shooting me,' Lord Rotherby scowled in pain, 'and I would suggest my ruffled French silk shirt is the least of our troubles. I'm more concerned about the important tissues you will have undoubtedly severed, leaving me with no option but to have my arm sawn off by a local butcher!'

'Dear God, no!' Sophie shrieked again, more wildly this time. 'There must be something we can do? I'd rather cut up Phoebe's primrose muslin for my brothers' grubby knees than be responsible for such a fate,' she sobbed.

At this, Lord Rotherby's shoulders began to shake violently, while he inclined his face as though in prayer.

At first Sophie thought he was having spasms of such terrible pain he couldn't even look at her, but on closer inspection she found he was actually having convulsions of uncontrollable laughter.

'Well, I don't see what's so funny,' she wailed. 'I am ruined, you have been shot with a crossbow, and all you can do is laugh? Matilda always said you were addled in the head!'

Yet if Sophie intended her derision to bring his lordship to his senses, she was very much mistaken, for all he did was laugh even harder.

'And I do believe the fever has set in already,' she moaned. 'To think I thought you so worldly, and now all you can do is stand there and laugh at your own downfall. Well we must send for a doctor this instant for that dart needs extracting and — Oh!' Sophie gasped as Lord Rotherby suddenly reached up and pulled out the protruding shaft in one swift movement. He winced before smiling apologetically as the bleeding intensified. 'That's it. Sit down this instant and give me your cravat,' she demanded.

Lord Rotherby sat down much more meekly than Sophie expected, while she snatched up the offending dart.

'You're not going to shoot me a second time, are you?' he enquired in a mollified tone.

'Hush now, or I'll let you bleed to death,' she admonished, deftly scoring the fine silk of his shirt sleeve.

Then she took hold of the sodden material and ripped until she had a clear view of the puncture wound. Swiftly, she pressed his cravat to the wound while making a tourniquet with the torn sleeve. Seconds later, his lordship was sporting a makeshift bandage and sling, and looking unusually impressed.

'Am I to add nursing skills to your string of highly commendable attributes, Miss Fairfax,' he asked.

'Am I Miss Fairfax again because I've bound your arm?' she countered, raising her eyebrows. 'I have four brothers,' she added. 'And through them I've dressed more injuries than I care to remember. This bandage is only temporary though; we still need to fetch a doctor.'

'We do, do we?' Lord Rotherby replied with a gleam. 'And since when did we start making decisions together?'

Sophie eyed Lord Rotherby with fresh loathing before treading swiftly towards the door. She yanked it open to find Horace leaning against the corridor wall outside, eyeing her with the oddest mix of curiosity and suspicion.

'Exactly how long— Oh, never mind!' Sophie shook her head, exasperatedly. 'His lordship needs a doctor, and quickly! He has already lost quite a bit of blood,' she added in a more urgent tone.

'Too late,' Horace replied with a shrug. 'We weighed anchor about ten minutes ago, miss. His lordship gave strict instructions to set sail as soon as the tide turned.'

For a moment Sophie said nothing, though she had the feeling every drop of blood may have drained to her feet. Then she was conscious of a million ungracious thoughts before they morphed into something else entirely.

Outrage.

How dare Lord Rotherby make such a decision when she'd made it abundantly clear she would rather face public shame than continue to Calais with him! How dare he assume control, simply because he could!

'Well, you can turn this miserable little bathtub around and sail right back then, can't you!' she snapped, before spinning on her heel and storming back into the cabin.

'No doctors immediately available?' his lordship quipped, though Sophie could see the set of his lips was harder, as though he was suppressing pain.

She surveyed his person in cold fury. He'd moved to a comfortable armchair and attempted to pull on a gentleman's brocade dressing gown that looked as expensive as the undergarments she'd discovered in the coach. From this vantage, she could also glimpse a dark stain of blood that had managed to seep through his makeshift bandage, but she felt no guilt, only an unbridled sense of satisfaction. His lordship could force his presence on her all he liked, but she'd shot him in defence of all females everywhere.

A faint smile threatened, despite everything.

'None offering their services beyond the harbour!' she growled instead. 'Please be good enough to instruct your men to turn around, sir. I have no desire to travel to Calais and wish to save myself a cold swim if at all possible.'

Lord Rotherby gave a bark of laughter then, before wincing.

'Turn around be damned!' he cursed. 'We are away now and will be in Calais by suppertime. From there we'll travel to Paris, the Alps and then on by boat to Italy. You should see Rome and Venice of course, but we could also include the excavations at Herculaneum and Pompeii,' he pondered thoughtfully. 'Then we could move on to Spain and Portugal. You might like to get your portrait painted, but of course Rome is always best for that…' He trailed off as he looked back at her. 'What do you think, Miss Fairfax? Do you have any decided preference?'

Sophie stared at the injured nobleman in disbelief. He'd not only ignored her express wishes, he was now describing a European tour as though he hadn't just abducted her at all. He had clearly gone stark-raving mad.

'What I think is that you have taken leave of your senses entirely!' she hissed. 'You may have grown used to behaving however you like, whenever you like, but may I remind you, sir, that I have a guardian – my eldest brother, Sir Thomas Fairfax – who will demand satisfaction when he hears how you have insulted his sister. Let alone the Viscount Damerel, of course, who is at this very moment traversing through Europe with my sister, the Viscountess Dam—'

'Oh Lord, spare me the entire family tree, I beg of you,' Lord Rotherby groaned. 'I am well aware of the extent of your delightful relations, and I am scared of none. I would also remind you, if you recall correctly, that *you* decided to join me. I didn't bundle you into a coach at midnight! Besides which, I am persuaded that even if Tom Fairfax can drag himself away from Newmarket long enough, the news that his younger sister has become Lady Rotherby will hardly have him reaching for his pistols – unless you wish him to meet an early demise of course?'

Sophie eyeballed the pithy lord, knowing he was speaking the truth. Thomas most certainly wouldn't object to having another Fairfax off his hands, even if it was under scandalous circumstances.

'Now you wish to marry me?' she repeated, feeling as though she would very much like to shoot him again, given half the chance.

'Now I'm honour-bound to marry you,' his lordship corrected, 'despite a lifetime avoiding the thing,' he muttered darkly.

'You are insufferable!' Sophie expostulated. 'And if you don't tell your men to make all haste this instant, I shall have no choice but to swim to shore!'

'But certainly,' Lord Rotherby replied, smirking. 'You need only ask… Horace?'

The door opened instantly, confirming Sophie's suspicions that he was indeed listening to every word being spoken.

'Miss Fairfax has bid me to instruct you to make all haste to Calais!' Lord Rotherby ordered abruptly. 'Please ensure her request is treated as though it were my own, for she is shortly to be my wife. Oh, and she has also recommended the attendance of a doctor when we dock, which is probably a good idea, if only for the sake of my shirts.' Lord Rotherby looked down at his discarded torn shirt and sighed. 'It's *Italian* silk by the way,' he amended, as though the words offered all the explanation in the world.

'Oh!' Sophie exclaimed, enraged. 'Horace, please ignore his lordship's order,' she countered, before the long-suffering groom managed to close the door. 'I do believe his wound has become infected already for he certainly seems to be delirious.' She paused to steady her voice. 'I am in no way betrothed to Lord Rotherby, nor expecting to be, and if you can't turn around, I require only to be set down at Calais, from where I shall join my sister, the Viscountess Damerel.'

Horace waited stoically as though accidental abductions, crossbow shootings and brief betrothals were all commonplace features in his life.

'You'll do no such thing,' Lord Rotherby interjected in his quiet, glittering voice. Horace eyeballed his employer darkly. 'No not you, Horace,' he added in the next breath. 'You may withdraw and do as I request, while Miss Fairfax and I continue our … discussion.'

The blinking Horace eyed them both disparagingly, before backing out as swiftly as he could.

'And now we've upset Horace,' Rotherby said with a sigh. 'Be so kind as to pour me a glass of bourbon, my dear. I'm finding this crossbow wound a little *de trop*…'

'I will not!' Sophie replied witheringly. 'If you wish to develop the fever and die when we reach land, please do so with my compliments. Until then, however, you are my responsibility and I will not assist you to an untimely demise!'

At this, his lordship's eyes widened. He sat forward, his dressing gown falling open to reveal a glimpse of his golden throat.

'You know, you are the most intriguing female I've ever met,' he murmured, before wincing. 'No one, not even my indefatigable tiger, has ever denied me anything to my face. Yet here you are, within my world, behaving as though I were the one in my short-tails.' He stood up and made his way towards her, his eyes oddly bright. 'You really are refreshingly singular, Miss Fairfax, and I find, quite disconcertingly, that I care more for your reputation than for my own at present. It is both irregular and mystifying, but no one has ever shot me and then taken the greatest care to ensure I didn't die before.' He smiled in a strained fashion. 'So we will just have to make the best of it instead.'

Sophie stared, feeling as though she'd fallen into a nightmare, from which there was no waking.

'But—'

'I will seek out an English pastor as soon as we land in Calais, though of course it may take a few days. In the meantime, I have a friend in Paris, and a most sensible aunt travelling through Europe who, if discoverable, would make the perfect companion until we can be wed. With a little luck, it won't take long to find a pastor, for I have no desire to duel with every member of the Fairfax family before the sennight is done.'

Rotherby paused in front of Sophie then and, taking her hand, slowly raised it to his lips. He was standing so closely that his subtle cologne made her senses swim, and she had the most irrational urge to reach out and touch his warm, golden throat, to see if it felt as good as it looked. Instead, she clenched her teeth, determined not to show how he distracted her.

'I know this is a damnable business, Sophie, and not at all what you expected, but I will make it right in the eyes of the world – I give you my word,' he murmured, touching her shoulder briefly.

Startled, her eyes flew to his, to find his expression gentler than she'd come to expect, yet she knew he was well-versed in the female mind too.

'And uncomfortable though it must seem, I believe it would be prudent for you to practise addressing me by my first name, Dominic,' he added with a frown.

'We have a part to play when we reach European society,' he continued, 'and while I intend to place you under the protection of my friend or my maiden aunt as soon as possible, the French haute ton will expect a certain familiarity between us…' He smiled faintly. 'Are we agreed?'

Sophie caught her breath as a bewildering mix of feelings coursed through her body, echoed by the question in his eyes.

'No, we are not agreed!' she replied heatedly. 'I have not given you leave to call me by my first name, and I refuse to confuse things further by using yours. I have no intention of marrying, and once we reach Calais, I will do everything possible to distance myself from you. If you have any sense of self-protection, you will do the same!' She paused to draw a steadying breath then and watched a shadow flit across his face. 'I've no idea what prompted you to flee the country in such a rapid fashion,' she continued, 'but I assure you that, despite my predicament, I have no desire for my name to be further besmirched. So, if you are quite finished trying to decide the rest of my life, I will happily remove myself to the other end of this boat, and remain there until land is reached.'

'On the contrary, Miss Fairfax,' his lordship replied, all trace of his previous charm eradicated. 'You will remain here in the master cabin while I take the second, and I will brook no dissent. We may disagree on many things, but on this I remain firm.'

He strode to the door then, his dressing gown falling open and prompting a ready blush in her cheeks, as he turned to address her for a final time.

'I prefer not to discuss the circumstances under which I left London, but suffice to say they are temporary, and less detrimental to my name than your current situation is to yours. In the meantime, perhaps the solution I have proposed will be more acceptable if I clarify it will be for the avoidance of scandal only. It will be a *mariage de convenance*, if you wish it.'

Sophie watched a muscle flex in his jaw as he spoke.

'What I wish is of no relevance to you,' she replied icily,

'and I assure you that *any* marriage with a Rotherby would be considered a *mesalliance* by a Fairfax!'

There was a silence then when his eyes darkened, before he nodded and walked away, leaving Sophie with the most curious sense of regret.

Chapter Twelve

PRESSED DUCK AND CALAIS

Several choppy hours later

It was just as Sophie was considering whether she shouldn't have just jumped yacht and swum to shore after all, that a knock came at the door.

'The guvnor trusts yer enjoying a quiet crossin' and sends 'is regrets that he won't be able to join you for supper,' Horace announced in a voice of deep sufferance. 'He also wants you to know that we will reach Calais in less than an 'our, and r'spectfully requests you stay in your cabin 'til such time that he's arranged accommodation.'

There was a poignant pause while Sophie inched open her door to find Horace bearing a supper tray and deeply suspicious expression.

'The guvnor asked me to ask—' he started again.

'Oh Horace!' Sophie exclaimed in exasperation, before he turned any more purple with the pressure of recalling his instructions. 'Wouldn't it be easier if I speak to Lord Rotherby directly? He's in the cabin opposite, isn't he?' She scowled. 'And what, in the name of King George, is that?' she asked, nodding at the brown heap on the supper tray.

'Pressed duck, miss,' Horace replied defensively. 'The guvnor's chef doesn't like to compr'mise when'e travels. Though the kitch'n is a bit small,' he conceded in a mollified tone.

'That may be,' Sophie replied, gathering her skirts and walking briskly towards the cabin door. 'But I do generally like to be able to identify what I am eating. Now, if you will just take me to his lordship…?'

'I can't, miss. He's restin' and specific'lly asked—'

Sophie pushed her chin into the air in the manner of one well past caring, before rapping on the opposite cabin door twice.

'Thunder an' turf, don't just stand there dawdling!' came Lord Rotherby's exasperated response. 'Get in here, man!'

Then she threw a glance back at Horace, who appeared to be quite frozen in horror, before opening the door.

'Much as I appreciate the efforts of your chef,' she began, unprepared for the sight of Lord Rotherby reclining in a deep armchair, and without a stitch on his toned upper half, 'I hardly think *pressed duck* the right food for a fever.'

She swallowed, never more aware that he was the most carelessly handsome man she'd ever set eyes upon, as well as one of the most intractable. She waited as he stared back, his hair ruffled wildly, before an intense scowl settled upon his face.

'I don't give a tinker's damn about the fever!' he threw back irritably. 'Bag of moonshine! And who made you my nursemaid? Send in Horace and a bottle of Burgundy this instant, or I'll have you thrown overboard for being a meddlesome tabby!'

Sophie took a hard look at his lordship's flushed face and the tiny beads of sweat that had settled along his hairline, before pursing her lips in a way her sisters would have recognised as a distinct warning sign.

'Neither I nor Horace will do any such thing!' she replied firmly. 'It's as plain as a pikestaff you have the fever, and little wonder too. You should have had the wound sterilised and bound hours ago! Horace, I've changed my mind. You *can* bring me that bottle, but not for his lordship to drink – and fresh bandages or cravats too, I mind neither – as well as a bowl of tepid water.'

Horace gaped at his new mistress with barely concealed awe. Clearly no one had ever overridden his lordship before.

'Now please, Horace!' Sophie demanded.

'Of course, miss. Right away, miss,' Horace replied, scurrying away despite his guvnor's thunderous expression.

'I suppose you intend to relieve the skipper of his role too, and sail us straight into Calais!' Rotherby expelled with a short, pained laugh.

'Not unless I have to,' Sophie replied, rolling up her muslin sleeves. 'And I'm not playing nursemaid either. As I said before, I am simply not letting you die on my watch. The moment we reach Calais and a doctor has been fetched, I'll consider myself free of my duty but until then, my lord, I'm your best hope of avoiding a pernicious pyrexia of the blood.'

At this, Rotherby gave another bark of laughter that ended in a painful wince.

'I'd also thank you to sit still while I make this a little easier,' she instructed, calmly unwinding her previous handiwork, 'for jumping around like a jack-in-the-box won't aid either of us.'

It took several heated exchanges, many colourful curses and countless dark mutterings about interfering debutantes before Lord Rotherby finally eased himself back into his chair, looking a lot more comfortable.

Sophie had taken the precaution of dousing and washing the angry wound with his lordship's finest bourbon wine, much to his vociferous disgust, before binding it carefully, but he was still running a fever. She pressed a clean, damp cravat to his forehead and watched as his eyelids lowered in relief.

'Don't go getting too comfortable just because I'm laid up,' he muttered with a ghost of a smile. 'I know every route out of Paris, and even if you got that far, I would find you. I'll not let you ruin yourself, even if you think it preferable to being tied to me. I told you I won't bother you … but you'll have the protection of my name if it's the last thing I do.'

Sophie withdrew the cloth and stared into his pained eyes, which at this close vantage appeared to be the colour of a dusky spring evening at Knightswood. She closed her own eyes and silently berated herself. Lord Rotherby was a cad and a rogue – albeit one with the oddest sense of chivalry – but a cad and a rogue all the same. The sooner they docked and she was free of his company, the better it would be for both of them.

'I have thought about my situation carefully,' she replied, avoiding his searching gaze. 'And while I am sensible of the offer you make, of its generosity, I am not willing to partake in a liaison that has come about so scandalously and which will undoubtedly bring us both great unhappiness in the end.' She paused, and refreshed the cravat for want of something to do. 'I have a plan, and I intend to put it into action once we reach Calais.'

'A plan?' Rotherby scoffed. 'Write to your sister and demand Damerel put a bullet in me, I've no doubt.'

'Actually no,' Sophie countered, lifting her eyes and forcing herself to meet his distracting gaze. 'I will put my family's minds at rest of course, but given the fact I cannot return to London for some time, I intend to make my own way,' she said, with much more confidence than she was feeling.

Inwardly, she shrank. Phoebe may have relished the idea of joining a band of travelling players, or riding bareback across clifftops at midnight, but she had never wanted anything more than her sketchpad and a love match. And now that her marital ambitions were all but shattered, she had no choice but to plough her energies into the former. She had no idea how hard it was to find work with a Parisian modiste, particularly as she had no references or designs with her, but it was all she could think to do. And, if she could make it work, she would be an independent working person; even Phoebe would have to respect her for that.

She lifted her chin.

'Oh, well, that's settled then,' Rotherby threw scornfully. 'I'll just abandon a young debutante to the mercy of every miscreant and guttersnipe in Paris without a backward glance! I give you two days before you find yourself penniless and alone in the Rue Saint-Denis!'

'Where?' Sophie said, frowning.

'Never mind,' he muttered. 'Come on then, Miss Fairfax, out with it. What is this famous plan that is so vastly better than shackling yourself to me?'

'Why, I don't see that it is any concern of yours,' she returned haughtily, 'but if you must know, I am a reasonable artist with some talent for…' She tailed off, thinking about her scrapbooks of fashion designs back at Knightswood, and how useful they would be now. 'For designing pelisses,' she finished, colouring faintly.

'Ah yes, the infamous fashion exhibition,' he drawled, but his eyes sharpened. *'I've always believed fashion should be a blend of art and functionality…that there should be room for both,'* he paraphrased. 'Have I got it right?'

Sophie flushed, recalling how he'd discovered her at the exhibition with Aurelia.

'It *is* my belief,' she replied, bristling, 'and I would thank you not to ridicule it. It is also my intention to offer my services to a French modiste. It'll be respectable work, and once some time has passed, I might be able to return to Knightswood – if Thomas agrees.'

'You mean, if he isn't six feet under by then for trying to put a bullet in me?' Rotherby muttered brusquely.

Sophie stared at his feverish face and wild eyes, and had the oddest desire to push back the damp hair that had fallen forward onto his forehead. He was opinionated, spoilt, and very stubborn, but there was something about him that was oddly endearing too.

She swallowed.

'A letter will exonerate you, my lord,' she replied quietly.

'There is no gain to be had by adding a scandalous duel, so I will simply inform Thomas that I left of my own free will—'

Sophie was stilled by a sudden, firm grasp of his fingers around her wrist, stealing the remainder of her thoughts.

'Is the thought of a life with me so very repulsive that you'd prefer eking out your *livres* by the light of a guttering candle?' Lord Rotherby asked intensely. 'I would take care of you, you know, and you could try to … improve me? As well as sew as many damned pelisses as you want.'

Sophie smiled faintly, withdrawing her hand.

'Do you recall our wager, my lord?' she asked, steadfastly. 'My desire has not changed, though my course is diverted for now. I will make a love match in the end – or none at all. And I find I am quite content with the prospect.'

'Hell and damnation! Why can't you see that what I am offering is safety? You are in the most precarious position, there is no guarantee your plan will work, and I never shirk my responsibilities!'

Sophie regarded Lord Rotherby's flashing eyes. She'd seen him witty, provoking, stubborn and furious, but never concerned before. It seemed an odd emotion for a rake to possess, despite his regard for his reputation.

'But why should you be forced to marry when, by your own admission, you have never sought it?' she replied carefully.

There was a moment's silence, during which Sophie was aware only of the drum of blood in her ears. Then she stood up and walked to the cabin door, feeling as though the waves were still rough beneath her feet.

'I thank you for your consideration, my lord,' she repeated, avoiding his intense scowl. 'But the moment we reach Calais, and you are under the care of a doctor, I will consider myself free to go my own way.'

Then she closed the door behind her and returned to the safety of her own cabin, where she sank onto the bed, and tried not to give in to the whirl of fear inside. It was only when she was steadier, that she shook back her shoulders, blew her nose, and forced her mind to her plan. She might not be the most courageous Fairfax, but she had always been the most cunning.

An hour later she stared down at two letters, one addressed to Phoebe at her last address in Athens, and the other to her brother, Thomas. Each was crafted to reassure, without providing any specific details – Rotherby wasn't entirely unrealistic about Thomas challenging him – and she had no desire to add murdered family members to her growing list of scandalous wrongdoings.

She was quietly confident her plan wasn't so terrible either. She *was* talented, and had always dreamed of working as a real fashion modiste. It was just the thought of not finding respectable employment that sent her thoughts into a spiral. Would she end up on rue *wherever-Rotherby-had-said*? She'd heard rumours about opera girls offering more than musical entertainment but had never fully understood exactly what – only that it sent her aunt into a fluster if she enquired.

It was with all these thoughts competing that Sophie finally made ready to leave the yacht. She wasn't fool enough to believe Rotherby would wave her off with a smile, but this wasn't Dover at dawn, and even he wasn't brazen enough to throw a screeching female over his shoulder in the middle of a busy dock. Then, once alone, she would make her way to the nearest jeweller, where she intended to sell the miniature crossbow to pay for modest lodgings until she found work. She stared down at the pretty pearl-inlaid piece and felt a brief pang of guilt before reminding herself she wouldn't need to sell it at all, if his lordship hadn't acted like one of Matilda's pigwidgeoned dunderheads. And even though he'd acted fairly honourably since discovering her identity, she was sure it was only because he feared further damage to his own name.

She scowled. Most people would think her very foolhardy indeed to refuse an offer from one of the most eligible bachelors of the ton with so much at stake. But despite every good reason to accept Lord Rotherby, she found herself unable to entertain the notion. He had teased her from the moment they met, and she had risked everything in return. How could she consider marriage to a man who brought out the very worst in her? Their match, no matter how sensible, would end in heartache and disaster.

She sighed heavily, just as the faint shouts of the deckhands filtered through from above.

'Calais,' she whispered, and after one final glance at her cloaked countenance, made her way up on deck.

Despite the promise of dry land, it was the chaos on board that stole Sophie's attention at first. Not only did Lord Rotherby keep a far bigger crew than she'd first realised, they also seemed to know their way around the complex sails and rigging blindfolded. It was a comforting thought as they navigated their way into the busy port, which seemed to be spilling over with every kind of trader, vying to dock and unload their wares.

She waited tentatively, trying not to think of the coldness that had crept into her bones, and focusing instead on her plan. Yet as the first faint French words began to reach across the churning water, she became conscious of a shadow behind her.

'Please don't try to dissuade me,' she murmured quietly, 'for my mind is quite made up.'

'That may be as you say, miss,' came Horace's perturbed response. 'But it's the guvnor, miss. He's tak'n a turn for the worse.'

One look at Horace's wide-eyed fear was enough to convince Sophie that this was not a ruse cooked up by Lord Rotherby to stall her plan.

'Take me to him,' she replied without hesitation. 'And send for a doctor as soon as we dock.'

Moments later, Sophie was anxious to see that the wound had indeed become inflamed, and his lordship delirious with it. Instantly, she set about implementing all she'd learned from nursing Josephine's lung spasms and feverish deliriums, but with minimal effect.

'I am loathe to move him,' she whispered to Horace, when she had settled him as best she could. 'Yet I do believe we stand little chance of breaking his pernicious fever while he's stuck in this stuffy cabin. We must remove him to a more comfortable lodging, just as soon as it can be procured.'

'Right you are, miss,' the fiery tiger acquiesced, his swift agreement only serving to make Sophie even more anxious. 'I'll send enquiries immediately.'

Sophie nodded before returning to Rotherby's side in a much graver mood. Awaiting ruination as a debutante was one matter, facing the gallows as a murderess quite another.

Chapter Thirteen

MISCREANTS AND GUTTERSNIPES

Several fretful hours later

It was one bumpy coach journey, two harried conversations – during which Sophie couldn't recall the French for *niece* for love nor money – and several fretful hours later when the doctor finally arrived.

Horace had secured lodgings on a quiet Calais street and while they weren't the finest, Sophie was satisfied the sheets were clean and the surroundings respectable. The landlord also seemed happy to put things on account, especially when Sophie bestowed her most beguiling smile, restoring her faith that on most people, and on most occasions, it worked.

'About time too!' Horace scowled while watching the doctor's ponderous approach out of the bedchamber window. 'For 'ow long the guvnor has been talkin' to hisself, no one knows.'

Sophie nodded, frowning. She too had heard Rotherby's

feverish mutterings, that had suggested something was playing on his mind.

'He's mentioned the word *mark* a few times,' Sophie whispered. 'Might it have something to do with why he left London?'

She'd wracked her brains but could think of little that may have prompted a midnight flight by an established member of the ton. To her surprise, however, a shadow of genuine concern passed across Horace's face.

'That's not for me to say, miss,' he said, his lips set loyally. 'Tis a serious matter, to be sure, but the guvnor weren't r'sponsible of course. He was jus' coming to Paris for time to sort 't out.'

Not for the first time, Sophie wondered at a world in which a notorious rake of the ton earned the undying loyalty of a dockland tiger. And yet, with this cryptic utterance Sophie had to be content, for *le médecin* had finally arrived at the bedchamber door.

The doctor turned out to be a portly gentleman of advancing years who smelled of tobacco and bourbon. He pronounced Lord Rotherby's wound to be *très enflamé*, and recommended a thin oxtail gruel and a course of leeches.

'Leeching always seems a barbarous practice to me,' Sophie whispered upon spying the bottle of creatures in the doctor's open bag.

'May look it, miss,' Horace growled knowledgeably, 'but works better than bloodlettin' and cuppin'.'

As Horace predicted, the prescribed course turned out to be surprisingly calming, and once the doctor had left, Sophie returned to his Lordship's side.

'I'll have you know I am a Rotherby!' he muttered, turning his brow into her hand unseeingly.

'Well, it's encouraging you've not forgotten your name, at least,' Sophie replied, her tone belying her anxiety.

There was no escaping the seriousness of his infection, and yet the longer she stayed in his company, the higher the risk to herself.

'...Roseby and O'Sullivan are JPs ... Sir Giles and Weston too strait-laced ... it's a damnable matter ... marked during the game ... it has to be one of us...' he murmured, before settling again.

Sophie frowned, more convinced than ever that Lord Rotherby's feverish mutterings related to his scandalous midnight flight in some way.

'I prefer not to discuss the circumstances under which I left London, but suffice to say they are temporary, and less detrimental to my name than your situation is to yours.'

'What did you do?' she whispered, mostly to herself.

'It was you who shot me, remember?' Rotherby murmured weakly.

Sophie's eyes flew to his, which were still closed.

'Well, yes, but you were such a pigwidgeoned dunderhead I had no choice but to do it,' she said with a faint smile.

Rotherby gave a dry chuckle.

'If that is what you truly believe,' he replied softly, 'then why are you still here?'

There was a short silence during which Sophie acknowledged the question she'd been avoiding since the doctor left.

'You know I've no wish to add *murderess* to my list of

misdemeanours,' she replied carefully. Thankfully, the doctor believes we will avoid it, if you follow his instructions.'

It was the truth. Lord Rotherby was ill, but he was also young and strong, and the doctor was only too delighted to add him to his expensive daily list of patients to visit.

'I have sent my letters,' she added, mostly for her own benefit. 'And I expect to leave just as soon as your fever has broken.'

'I expect you do,' Rotherby murmured, drifting away. 'And I wager I'd find you before nightfall.'

Sophie smoothed the forget-me-nots on her cotton quilted bedspread, knowing she didn't feel quite as she ought.

It was three days since Lord Rotherby's fever had abated and, despite his vociferous objection to almost every plain and healthy dish she'd ordered, he was making swift progress. And in between threatening to throw his every meal to the gulls, she'd formulated her plan, sent her letters and waited until she was convinced he was out of danger. Yet now the day had arrived, the thought of leaving was unexpectedly hard.

Briefly, she closed her eyes and let her mind conjure the moment he kissed her outside Rotherby House, and then the moment in his cabin just before she shot him. His eyes had darkened with a visceral heat she barely recognised, and yet, it had prompted such an intense coiling of *something* in her core she'd been almost tempted to throw caution to the wind. To do what exactly?

She flushed, recalling all the hints, whispers and

innuendoes about marital liaisons that she could. What was it Phoebe had said?

'I do believe you will much prefer to discover the mysteries of marital relations with your husband...'

Would the discovery with Lord Rotherby be worth the fall from grace?

Sophie flushed even harder as she realised she was contemplating complete ruination just to understand what Lord Rotherby had in mind – which was only further proof that she needed to get as far away from his influence as possible before she threw all her scruples to the wind and actually turned into Aurelia.

Briskly, she pulled on her cloak, picked up her gloves, and slipped out of her bedchamber. Then, pausing only to pull her hood forward, she slipped down the back stairwell and into the quiet backstreet outside.

The first thing she noticed was the faint aroma of sweet pastries, combined with more tobacco and something far less inviting too. She wrinkled her nose in distaste, before making her way down the quaint, cobbled street, nodding at two ladies who greeted her in such a friendly fashion that Sophie couldn't help but feel a little heartened. Then when she reached the end, the street divided into two more bustling directions. Sophie hesitated only briefly before choosing the sunnier of the two, which turned a corner and meandered quietly until the reason for the less inviting aroma became clear.

For a few moments, Sophie gazed around at Calais' quiet dockside. The afternoon water was murky and still, while the loading area was now entirely empty, save for piles of discarded fish entrails and the occasional marauding gull.

Suddenly, it seemed so far from Knightswood and everything she knew, that a pang of homesickness reached through her. She drew deep breath, and forced herself to look around, wondering which direction might lead her to some shops and a jeweller.

'*Es-tu perdu, chérie?*'

Sophie glanced up as the two friendly ladies approached her with wide smiles.

'Oh ... *non* ... *merci*,' Sophie replied, unable to help wondering at the design of their plunging corsets. '*Mais ... c'est... Je cherche un* ... jeweller's ... *s'il vous plaît...*?' she added in what she hoped was a passable French accent.

'Ahh, *un joaillier* for the English lady!' the second lady cried in such excitement that Sophie immediately forgave her the rouge wedged between her yellow front teeth.

Not everyone had the benefit of a vanity mirror about their person after all.

'*C'est proche.* Near... *Suivez* ... follow, follow!' the first lady insisted, beckoning so vigorously, while the other stood by and grinned, that Sophie began to feel a little unsure.

And yet, jolly female company had to be far less risky than traversing the streets of Calais alone, particularly when they did seem to know their way around.

Smiling politely, Sophie fell in beside the chattering ladies, who seemed only too delighted to lead the way to the local traders. And for the first few minutes she was quite content to have the local sights pointed out via a mix of stilted French and happy gesticulations. Indeed, it was only when they swapped the open dockside for squalid, shady streets with grime-streaked urchins and leering faces, that she began to wonder if she might have been a little hasty. She wasn't too sure a jeweller's in such a district would be very interested in a pearl-inlaid crossbow, particularly when half of the inhabitants looked as though they could barely afford food.

Anxiously, she slipped her hand into her cloak pocket, wondering how to excuse herself, only to discover her pocket was completely empty. Swiftly, Sophie fumbled for her left pocket, telling herself she couldn't have been so naive as to lose her only means of paying her way within a half hour of leaving Lord Rotherby. But much to her mounting horror, her left pocket was empty too.

For the briefest of moments, Sophie's eyes prickled uncomfortably, and she had the feeling she might actually bawl like Edward the day his grandfather newt died. Then she recalled that no amount of tears had prevented the newt's Viking funeral across Knightsmoor lake in a rain that had extinguished three of cook's best candles. And crying certainly wouldn't change the stark and unwelcome conclusion that her newfound friends weren't really friends at all.

Rapidly, Sophie considered her options before alighting on the only item she had remaining that might help her cause: a hairpin. With just a moment's sorrow for her curls à *la Sévigné*, she reached up and dragged the pin out, leaving the rest of her curls to fall around her face in what she hoped was more of a renaissance tumble than a hedgerow-bird's-nest. Then she gripped it tightly, and waited until they turned onto a busier street, with market traders hawking a number of wares that looked as though they deserved burial, more than someone's plate.

'Oh, how pretty!' Sophie exclaimed, feigning interest in a

small arrangement of dead flowers she wouldn't even give to Aurelia.

Her companions leered momentarily, giving Sophie the opportunity to thrust her arm into her pocket with a dramatic flourish.

'I think I would like to buy— Oh!' she gasped, channelling a Fairfax production of *Oliver Twist*. 'I've been robbed! But who would rob an innocent lady in broad daylight, I ask you?'

Then she clamped her hands together, with a most appealing expression.

'*Non, non!*' her first companion shushed, taking her arm tightly.

'*Venez avec nous* ... come with us ... *et nous le chercherons.*'

'*Arrêt! Quittez la jeune femme!*' the woman selling the dubious flowers called out.

'Yes, let go of the young lady,' Sophie repeated loudly, before lifting her boot and driving it down onto her captor's toe.

Her captor obliged instantly, her painted face twisting up in a toothy grimace that gave Sophie the most delightful sense of satisfaction before her companion closed in with a coarse laugh.

'*Bravo, ma petite, bravo!* Vous êtes *une naturelle!*' she said loudly, gripping Sophie's other arm and extending her other as though they were on stage.

'*Et maintenant* ... we go ... *au théâtre!*'

It was clear no one was convinced, and briefly Sophie wondered how even she could have been so easily duped. Yet, they'd stolen her only means of paying for food and lodgings, and there really was no time for regret.

'Really?' Sophie threw fiercely, 'but we already have an audience right here!'

Then she jabbed her hairpin directly at her captor's hand, who yelled, as Sophie tried for what her brothers would call a stranglehold – to find herself counter-thrusted, unceremoniously, onto the cold, wet cobbles instead. Furiously, she used all her strength to pull her captor down with her; resulting in the most undignified roll through a muddy puddle which did not improve her complexion at all.

'How dare you!' Sophie gasped, gripping her opponent's hair, only to find it lifting away in her hands entirely.

A shocked gasp rippled through the watching crowd as Sophie gazed at the mangled item in disbelief, before offering it back. There were some things even she couldn't fix.

'*Non, non, non!*' the furious woman moaned, grabbing the wig and attempting to replace it, just as a black barouche rounded the end of the street.

Sophie glanced up, too distracted by the offence on her captor's head to be much disturbed by a hire barouche. Yet when it careered to an abrupt halt beside them, and a familiar tiger jumped down with a deprecatory look that confirmed he did not understand the gravity of her situation one bit, reality began to dawn.

'Not quite la Rue Saint-Denis,' drawled a familiar voice, 'though damnably close and a little swifter than I predicted too. Regrettably, the show is over, my dear, and it is time for you to say farewell.'

Slowly Sophie swung her gaze, fully aware of the comical figure she must present, to find Lord Rotherby regarding her back with a highly amused expression. Inhaling deeply, she drew herself up and hobbled towards the barouche, as though one approaching her own funeral.

'Well, you needn't look so pleased with yourself,' she hissed, climbing in opposite the shadowed lord, who'd given in to a silent mirth that only enraged Sophie further.

Yet he only wiped his eyes and tipped his hat, before swinging his attention back to the watching crowd.

'I must extend my thanks!' he called out in perfect French, to the gawping females who'd held Sophie captive. 'There are two gendarmes behind me who were most interested to know you'd taken my young friend under your wing. Pray tell them the crossbow is a pretty toy I took from a highwayman back in Somerset, with the compliments of Lord Rotherby!'

There was a short silence before a ripple of understanding filled the air, peppered by muffled gasps and suspicious glances. And then, two things happened at once.

The first was that the pretty fake was lobbed through the air like a tiny glinting arrow, directly at the barouche; and the second was that the gawping, muddied females took off down the street at impressive speed. Lord Rotherby watched with a smile of satisfaction as he leaned out to catch the weapon, before calling to Horace to drive on.

'You shouldn't be here,' Sophie said, noticing his grimace of pain as he settled back in the seat opposite her.

'Neither should you,' he retorted.

She stared at his furrowed eyes and damp brow, and realised how much the excursion had cost him physically.

'How did you find me?' she added in a softer tone.

A mischievous smile flitted across his face.

'It wasn't that hard,' he replied in amused exasperation. 'I simply asked Horace to find out if anyone had seen a young lady in the company of known rogues. You know, you really are the most stubborn and wilful female I've ever met,' he added through half-closed eyes.

For a moment, Sophie just wanted to laugh.

'Surely it would be easier for you just to close your eyes and let me go?' she asked instead. 'You could say you provided me with safe passage, and I went on to stay with friends in France. You could carry on doing whatever it is you do, and in the end, they would all forget.'

'Whatever it is I do?' he repeated, his eyebrows arching. 'I exist in a space where no one gets hurt Miss Fairfax – what's so wrong with that? Far too many are ignorant of the impact of their actions, and I swore a long time ago never to join them.'

There was another silence while Sophie observed him.

It wasn't the first time he'd said something curiously honourable, and it was unexpected for a nobleman she'd written off as the worst kind of rake.

'And anyway, the ton never forgets. You know that.'

She glanced down, acknowledging the truth of his statement, despite her wishing it a thousand times otherwise.

'But in answer to your question,' he added softly, 'I also believe it would be quite sad for a flame to burn so brightly, only to be snuffed out by a mistake. I would hate to be responsible for that fate, Miss Fairfax.'

'As for your terrible judge of character, I claim no responsibility for that at all.'

Sophie chuckled, suddenly grateful for the darkness inside the small barouche.

'Perhaps I have a penchant for rogues,' she muttered.

He smiled wryly.

'Perhaps,' he concurred. 'Though you certainly seemed to have the upper hand when I arrived and, while unusual, there is a certain charm to your … current raiment.'

Sophie flushed as she cast an eye down her muddied and torn gown, never more aware of the bedraggled figure she must present.

'Does it hold some sentimental value?' she tried to distract, with a nod towards the crossbow. Lord Rotherby's eyes gleamed with mischief.

'A little,' he acquiesced, 'but I'm quite partial to diamonds and mother-of-pearl too.'

Sophie bit her lip to stop herself laughing.

'I must say I'm impressed,' she replied when she could, 'to know the full extent of your duplicity. But then why, if the crossbow is so precious, did you give it to me?'

'I knew you would try to take off as soon as you could,' he replied. 'It was the most I could do to ensure you were not penniless when you did so.'

'But … you owe me nothing,' Sophie murmured.

'I exist in a space where no one gets hurt, Miss Fairfax,' he replied quietly, 'and I am quite determined to stay there.'

Chapter Fourteen

L'AUBERGE NOTRE-DAME, PARIS

Three days later

Sophie leaned her forehead against the cool glass window, watching the fine mist of rain wash away specks of dirt. There weren't many. This was a much more respectable establishment than their lodgings in Calais, which Lord Rotherby had pronounced 'a dubious backwater Horace should have known far better than to patronise while he was indisposed'. And while Horace had muttered extensively about headstrong young ladies who led them all a merry dance, he was too relieved about the recovery of his guvnor to complain.

Sophie had been far more vocal, pointing out the many advantages of such a dubious backwater until such time that they agreed their story, but Rotherby remained unimpressed.

'I may not be gentlemanly in the way you would wish, but I draw the line at grubby sheets,' he muttered, when they made the journey to L'Auberge Notre-Dame in Paris, which boasted a sparkling view of the Seine and the historic cathedral.

Yet even the superior view couldn't allay Sophie's cold fear that she'd made a very big mess of things indeed. She'd planned to be employed by some quiet, respectable modiste by now, not still in Lord Rotherby's company, and getting more anxious with every passing minute. Gloomily, she thought of Phoebe and how much better she would have fared, especially when it came to a muddy back-alley brawl with two of the worst rogues in Calais.

And now she had no plan, no crossbow, no personal possessions whatsoever – at least not until hers had been washed and mended. She glanced down at the lace-trimmed jade muslin Lord Rotherby had provided while her own dress was with the seamstress. She was well aware it became her burnished curls and sea-blue eyes better than anything she'd ever owned – that Lord Rotherby appeared to have a considerable knack for picking out expensive Parisian fabrics and colours to suit – but even this acknowledgement failed to cheer her for long, as it was clearly down to much practice on his part.

Exhaling, she recalled the blur of the past few days. Lord Rotherby had insisted on making the journey from Calais to Paris, despite his wound re-opening and needing further care. Sophie had had little choice but to oblige until they reached Paris, and Horace had been her constant shadow ever since. She was certain his vigilance had far more to do with her care of his precious guvnor than any regard for her skin, but it had limited opportunities all the same.

Then, finally, Lord Rotherby had proposed a new

arrangement: he would arrange for her to remove to the home of a friend outside Paris, if she postponed any new escapes.

Sophie had to admit that the prospect of some time to make a new plan, rather than traipsing through Paris in search of a modiste prepared to take a chance on an ingenue without a sketch to her name, was very tempting. And, once they'd established his friend was a respectable childhood connection and not one of his past light-o'-loves, she'd readily agreed. This unexpected reprieve had also helped her weather numerous curious glances from L'Auberge Notre-Dame chamber maids, who clearly hadn't believed the story about a sick abigail in Calais.

It was with the promise of this removal uppermost, that Sophie made her way down L'Auberge Notre-Dame's wide guest staircase. Horace was running errands while Lord Rotherby was resting, leaving her to enquire about progress with her dress. The hotel staff had been polite so far, but she was sick with fear they would change their minds the longer the party stayed without an appearance from the redeeming abigail. Indeed, it was just as she was wondering if whether she could persuade one of the curious maids to fill the breach, that she heard a voice that filled her with the oddest mix of hope and chagrin.

'I require only a modest bedchamber, nothing special, and a light supper please,' a most sensible voice requested.

'*Mais, monsieur,*' the landlord protested in his horrified tone. 'L'Auberge Notre-Dame does not have zis ... modest *chambre*. Only ... grande!' he boomed, gesticulating wildly.

'Then the smallest of your grand rooms, *s'il vous plaît,*' the calm tone persisted. 'I am passing through Paris and will be checking out in the morning.'

At this the landlord shook his head emphatically, vastly unimpressed by any gentleman who refused to see how superior the L'Auberge Notre-Dame was in comparison to other Parisian establishments.

'*A small* grand chambre? *Mais non! C'est une tragédie!*'

'I assure you it is not a tragedy. I simply wish to book…'

'Sir Weston?' Sophie inquired, her heart hammering.

Sir Weston's calm and unruffled figure turned to peer up the shadowy stairwell.

'Miss Fairfax?' he asked incredulously, 'Is that really you?'

Sophie smiled wanly, feeling as though a thousand years had passed since he came to her assistance at The British Institution.

A shadow flitted across his face as he regarded her.

'I'll take any room that's free – *grande*, *petite* or anything in the middle,' he threw at the landlord, who was muttering darkly about the 'eccentric English and their ways'.

'Are you well? What are you doing here?' he added in an urgent undertone, striding across to meet her. 'I heard you'd left for Paris rather suddenly, but didn't dare hope I'd run into you…'

Sophie nodded, barely trusting her own voice, and suddenly aware of a few heads turning their way.

'Please excuse any indelicate questioning on my part,' he added, lowering his voice. 'I am just so surprised to see you here… Would you care to join me in the parlour? Partake in some refreshment?'

Sophie nodded without hesitating, the prospect of being in

Sir Weston's calm and reassuring company for a short time eclipsing all her concerns. Gratefully, she followed him into the parlour, where he proceeded to order glasses of the landlord's recommended Bordeaux – a request that appeared to redeem him a little – and find a private booth beside the parlour fire. Then, haltingly, Sophie repeated the fictional story about the sick abigail, though Sir Weston's earnest face made the task almost impossible.

'Though of course you are free to draw your own conclusions, and who could blame you after all,' she finished, hanging her head.

'Do excuse me, Miss Fairfax,' Sir Weston replied gently, 'but it seems to me you are not quite yourself at all. You are under no obligation to tell me anything of course, but as Lord Rotherby and I are related, you are free to confide in me with all confidence.'

Sophie glanced up sharply.

How did she not know Lord Rotherby and Sir Weston were related? And how could two such dissimilar gentlemen be related at all?

And yet, as she looked at him, the truth of his words was undeniable. They were different gentlemen in every way, but now he'd said it, she could see little else. Sir Weston was fairer, but otherwise they had the same jaw, the same high brow and, when they chose it, the same glint in their eye too. It was inconceivable, yet so obvious too – like two sides of one coin.

'You should also know, I am quite aware of Lord Rotherby's ... character, and can assure you of my utmost discretion, were your situation to be *slightly* different to that which you have described?'

'Oh,' Sophie replied, trying to resist the temptation to tell kind Sir Weston everything, and failing instantly. 'I was only trying to dissuade Aurelia,' she confided falteringly, 'and then Lord Rotherby thought I was Mrs Haxby … and so he didn't actually know I was in his coach until Dover when I shot him with the crossbow … which was when the whole marriage thing came up,' she exhaled heavily.

'Mrs Haxby … marriage thing … you *shot him*?' Sir Weston repeated in a bewildered tone, making Sophie wonder if he'd caught a chill, or had the headache perhaps. 'And he's staying right here in L'Auberge Notre Dame?' he added through gritted teeth. 'I will put a stop to this right now, Miss Fairfax. I will call him out for there can be no marriage without a bridegroom, after all!'

Sophie frowned. It was a tricky situation by anyone's reckoning but she couldn't imagine anyone less likely to get the better of Lord Rotherby in a duel than kind, sensible Sir Weston.

'We're both here, in separate bedchambers,' she confirmed hastily. 'He tells everyone I am a distant relation he is delivering to my parents, though I fear that tale has not been as persuasive as we might wish. Still, his Lordship *is* recovering from a wound at the moment, and since he has behaved quite properly since the whole street brawl—'

Sir Weston eyed her with such horror then that she considered sending for a jug of water.

The whole situation was undoubtedly a mess, but she'd never imagined Sir Weston being quite so enraged on her behalf.

'I cannot fathom why you were forced to defend yourself

with a crossbow,' he said heatedly, 'any more than I can bear the thought of you being mixed up in a street brawl! I will not abandon you to your predicament, Miss Fairfax.'

He stood up then to kick a log into the dancing flames before turning to face her with an expression she barely recognised.

'I understand more than you know,' he continued in a low, gritty tone, 'and this is not the first time I've known Lord Dominic Rotherby to act dishonourably. Do you trust me, Miss Fairfax?'

Sophie had the distinct feeling that she was wandering further into hot water, but was unable to fathom an escape.

'Well, yes … of course,' she said faintly.

'Then you will trust me to arrange things to your advantage?'

She hesitated again, before he stepped closer and took her hand.

'Lord Rotherby is a known libertine of the ton, and I may not be as rich, but I warrant I am *twice* as honourable!' he declared intently. 'You'd need never shoot me, I promise.'

Sophie stared, as though in a trance, as Sir Weston lifted her hand and planted a small, chaste kiss on her fingers. It was so different to Lord Rotherby's kiss that it was almost disappointing, and yet the intent behind his words mattered more.

Was he actually offering what she thought he was offering?

'How very affecting,' a voice drawled from the parlour entrance, 'and yet a display of affection that is entirely excessive, for Miss Fairfax is shortly to become Lady Rotherby. Pray unhand her, Weston. I'm not in favour of any lady befriending buffle-headed buffoons, least of all my future wife.'

There was a moment's silence, then a dark flush rose up Sir Weston's neck, as he turned and locked eyes with Lord Rotherby. Transfixed, Sophie watched as each one regarded the other in some kind of murderous stand-off, until the full ridiculousness of the situation dawned on her.

'When you are quite finished with your theatricals,' she said coldly, gathering her skirts, 'I shall be in my bedchamber, actually planning a way out of this mess.'

'Don't over-tax yourself,' Lord Rotherby replied, his eyes softening briefly. 'For I have news of my own. But firstly, I will see Sir Weston to the door, as I do believe L'Auberge Notre-Dame cannot accommodate any more guests. Is that not the case, Gérard?'

Lord Rotherby raised his voice so loudly that the long-suffering landlord had little choice but to approach the small party.

'Weren't you telling me this morning how full L'Auberge Notre-Dame is, Gérard?' Lord Rotherby continued smoothly. 'After I rented the remainder of the rooms on my floor.'

'*Mais ... c'est vrai*, my lord, unfortunately...' the landlord replied, when he managed to control his gaping mouth.

'Unfortunately indeed. So, you see, Sir Weston, I do believe you must find a room in some other establishment, for Gérard's rooms are already being used by esteemed guests of L'Auberge Notre-Dame.'

Lord Rotherby smiled then, though it wasn't a smile of condolence, but one of vehement dislike.

In disbelief, Sophie watched as the bemused landlord

looked from Lord Rotherby to Sir Weston and back again, before looking to the ceiling and muttering something very rude under his breath. Then he bowed stiffly and began explaining to Sir Weston in a stream of apologetic French how Lord Rotherby had booked out the last of *les chambres* earlier that day.

Knowing he was beaten, Sir Weston picked up his hat, bowed to Sophie and strode towards the door.

'You will meet me for this, sir!' he hissed as he passed between Lord Rotherby and the round-eyed landlord.

'Another challenge, Weston?' Lord Rotherby drawled. 'I'll expect a withdrawal within the hour then.'

Sir Weston stopped abruptly and turned towards Rotherby, and from this vantage point there was no denying that they shared a bloodline. Their stature and scowls were nearly identical, though one was controlled, while the other was wild enough to make the landlord throw up his hands in horror.

'I do not accept your insults, and Miss Fairfax certainly does not deserve to endure your company,' Sir Weston said through tight white lips. 'You will hear more on both but unlike you, there is a limit to what I will say and do in front of a lady. And you can keep your view,' he threw at the landlord, 'because I never liked those damned gargoyles anyway!'

At this, Gérard turned a very deep and resentful purple, but had the good sense not to pass comment.

'I depart your faithful servant, Miss Fairfax,' Sir Weston concluded, turning back to Sophie. 'But trust I *will* be in touch!'

Then he strode from the room, while Lord Rotherby and the landlord looked on with a mix of disdain and puffed-cheek forbearance.

'Shouldn't you be resting?' Sophie demanded.

'Probably,' Lord Rotherby replied, his eyes glittering, 'except my betrothed seems determined to attract the attention of every gutter-dweller in France. Including those who wish to shoot at me with alarming regularity – not that Sir George Weston poses a serious threat of course.'

Sophie scowled as the landlord walked away muttering some very rude, very French things.

'How could you behave so to a gentleman who was only seeking to assist a friend? she threw furiously. 'You consider yourself a nobleman, but what is noble about insulting another before denying him a roof over his head? And a kinsman too, I am led to believe. It is the act of a villain, and I for one could never imagine Sir Weston engaging in such behaviour, no matter his reason.

She paused to watch Lord Rotherby's lips tighten and felt a dart of satisfaction. Somehow, she'd got under his skin.

'Why did you have to leave London so quickly?' she added. 'Why can you not return? And why do you pretend you are invincible, when it is so very clear you are not?!'

She glared at Rotherby's injury, which was clearly causing him considerable discomfort, and waited for the usual derisory retort, but instead he only regarded her through half-shuttered eyes.

'Above all things, I consider myself honourable,' he replied grittily. 'I do not lead or make false promises to ladies, any more than I accuse a gentleman unjustly, yet I cannot explain it, so you will just have to trust me when I say Weston is not all he appears to be. I left London because I was falsely accused of villainous behaviour – that

I *will* disprove. You must accept my word that this is truth.'

He paused to smile darkly, and Sophie wished she didn't find him so convincing.

'As for Weston, better for him he's out of my sight. You know my reputation. I never miss – it's a Rotherby thing.'

There was a brief silence while Sophie scrutinised him intently.

'I accept that there are some things gentlemen prefer not to discuss,' she replied quietly, 'in the same way ladies do not divulge all their secrets. But I cannot accept Sir Weston's nature is as you describe. He has only ever treated me with the utmost respect and gentlemanly regard so I think Lord Rotherby, given all the circumstances, I will make my own mind up about who I do and don't trust – it's a Fairfax thing!'

Then she gathered her skirts and swept from the room, wishing with all her heart that her sisters were there to agree.

It was one hour, and nearly two foiled plans later, when a scratch at her door revealed a rather sheepish-looking Horace.

'Guvnor says you're to come with me, miss,' he muttered, not quite meeting her eyes.

'Does he?' Sophie returned in an arctic tone. 'Well, please tell your *guvnor* that I've no wish to go anywhere with him, or anyone remotely connected with him, now or in the future, thank you, Horace.'

Sophie made to close the door, only to find Horace's boot in the way.

'Guvnor said you'd say that an'…' He paused to scratch his head. 'Well, he said to say it's in your best interests, miss. He's managed to arrange the stay with 'is relation, miss, a *Madame Dupres*, while he conducts some bus'ness. He says it's not 'propriate for you to stay 'ere anymore, an' she's from one of the best fam'lies an—'

Sophie yanked open the door with the force of a small tornado.

'You can tell his lordship,' she hissed, 'that I've changed my mind and I'm not being foisted off on some poor, unsuspecting female relation while he jaunts off in search of someone to marry us! I have my own plan, and I'm—'

'Beggin' yer pardon, miss,' Horace persisted, 'he said I was to give yer back this, miss?'

Sophie frowned as the awkward tiger pressed a familiar miniature crossbow into her hands.

'Guvnor says yer have a right to be angry, miss, and if he doesn't arrange things to your sat'sfaction, miss, well, you can shoot 'im, or anyone else you choose, with 'is blessing, miss.'

For a moment, Sophie said nothing. Then she took the crossbow and drew in a deep breath.

'I will come then, but only so I may arrange my future to my satisfaction, and to that purpose, female company will be infinitely more useful.' She tucked the crossbow into the pocket of her jade muslin.

'Right y'are, miss,' Horace said, regarding her with new respect.

'And Horace?'

'Yes, miss?'

'It was entirely his lordship's own fault that I shot him.'
'Yes, miss.'

Chapter Fifteen

MADAME MARIE-LOUISA DUPRES

The following day

Madame Marie-Louisa Dupres was so very captivating that Sophie was a little suspicious at first. However, her suspicions were swiftly allayed by her very respectable Parisian *maison*, in a respectable Parisian *arrondissement*, and after a while even she had to accept that Rotherby seemed capable of conducting respectable female relationships.

'Oh, la! My Dominic said you were too good for him, and I thought to myself, this cannot be true. No lady is too good for my Dominic. But now I see he did not lie at all, *ma chérie*. No wonder it has sent him careering all over France in, what is it you English call it? A spin?'

Sophie could think of several other choice words to describe Lord Rotherby's behaviour but instead she only smiled at the alluring girl with thick ebony hair, lustrous skin and a vivacious laugh to match. To Sophie, she looked a beguiling, lost princess from one of Josephine's heroic novels.

'Now, we will be very best friends, *n'est-ce pas*? And you can tell me about *all* your adventures, for I warrant there have been a few with my Dominic ...'

A few more enquiries swiftly elicited the fact that Madame Marie-Louisa Dupres – or Lu Lu, as she preferred – was about as distant a relation to her precious Dominic as she could be without making a complete nonsense of the claim. She'd grown up on the outskirts of Paris, the only offspring of a distant second cousin, and been wed for six months before the dreaded smallpox had claimed her sickly, older husband.

'However, it is not at all sad,' she reassured Sophie, with a dazzling smile. 'For now I am at liberty to attend as many parties and soirees as I please, without any provoking debutante rules.'

Sophie smiled politely, wondering if Lu Lu was drawing quite the right conclusion from her very short marriage, but had to applaud the spirit all the same.

More surprisingly however, it seemed as though Lu Lu was the closest thing Lord Rotherby had to a confidante, and knew their whole sorry tale already.

'The problem is,' Sophie confided, pirouetting in a rather fetching taffeta gown Lu Lu had persuaded her to try, 'I know he has gone to look for that dreadful pastor but I cannot marry his lordship under any circumstances. I need help finding work as a modiste, or a seamstress? Lord knows, I'd probably settle for a governess just now!'

Sophie bit her lip, recalling her poor progress with mathematics, while Lu Lu regarded her incredulously.

'Is it possible you do *not* wish to marry my dear Dominic?'

she whispered, her eyes as round as Aunt Higglestone's precious china teacups.

Sophie swallowed. She'd avoided a direct question so far, yet there seemed to be little other way to convince his adoring relation.

'I appreciate his lordship's effort to *rectify* the situation,' she replied carefully. 'But I cannot imagine anything worse than for someone like his lordship to be tied to someone like me, because of one mistake. I have always been determined to make a love match, while his lordship intends never to marry at all. We are, quite simply, a recipe for disaster, and I believe tying our lives together will only exacerbate a situation that is already beyond retrieval.'

Her tone was hollow and her expression set, but she'd said it, and when she lifted her gaze Madame Dupres was smiling.

'Ahh, but you must not worry, *ma chérie*!' she gushed, squeezing Sophie's hands. 'We will fix this, and you know, *l'amour* can spring from the most curious and unexpected of places. Why, only yesterday I had a visit from an old English acquaintance who turned out to be quite the surprise! He was so very delightful and proper, he made all the French gentlemen of my acquaintance seem most uncivilised.'

Lu Lu paused to blush prettily and Sophie wondered if she could possibly be speaking of Sir Weston. He was, after all, the most properly mannered English gentleman of her acquaintance, and it would be no surprise if they knew of each other through Lord Rotherby.

'And dear Dominic is *so* wild and wilful, but he can also be kind and good – as well as *very* determined once his mind is made up,' she said, waggling a jewel-clad finger. 'But, if you remain set against this marriage I will help you, after this week's *cercles* at Le Palais des Tuileries, where all Paris will be in attendance! And please, no more talk of being a *modiste* or *governess* when this is Paris? *Quelle horreur!* I think we can set our sights a little higher than that! Indeed, you may not wish to marry my dear Dominic, but unless Paris learns of your situation you are quite safe with me – and that means there is no reason why we cannot find you another husband. Come, at the very least we will have a little fun, *n'est ce pas?*'

It appeared that on the question of fun, Madame Marie-Louisa Dupres would brook no dissent, and by the time the evening at the Royal Tuileries Palace arrived, and Sophie was bathed, corseted and dressed afresh in one of Lu Lu's most fetching blush-pink satin gowns, she'd begun to think it might be just the tonic for lifting her spirits.

'For I am still Miss Sophie Fairfax when all's said and done,' she reminded herself, as she pulled a ringlet free from her elaborate Psyche knot, and turned to inspect the effect.

For a moment she wondered what her sisters would think if they could see her now. She'd always been the one considered least likely to take any risks. Yet it seemed the universe had rather different ideas.

Sophie pulled a face in the looking-glass, resolving that she would not feel sorry for herself, come what may.

'For this is a situation of your own making, after all,' she admonished.

Briefly, she recalled her last conversation with Matilda, so certain she would be able to return before dawn. How could she have been so naive? Lord Rotherby had a reputation for being one of the worst rakes in all Georgian London. Why she had taken it upon herself to try and intercept Aurelia with so little consideration for her own reputation seemed a foolishness of gargantuan proportions. And now that same rake, with more secrets than anyone she'd ever known, demanded blind trust.

She closed her eyes and conjured his scowling noble face, eyelids sunk low and lips curling.

'Above all things, I consider myself honourable, I do not lead or make false promises to ladies, any more than I accuse a gentleman unjustly … I exist in a space where no one gets hurt… You must accept my word that this is truth.'

Sophie exhaled. He'd left London society abruptly, had ignored her entreaties to let her take her chances, and treated Sir Weston abominably – so why did she feel so confused?

'Ah, ma chérie, you know l'amour can spring from the most curious and unexpected of places.'

Lu Lu's voice reached through her thoughts as she gazed into her own anxious eyes. It was true that he was likeable, in a careless, roguish kind of way, and also that he frustrated her beyond all things reasonable. But could there be anything else? Could she have hidden a partiality for Lord Dominic Rotherby, even from herself?

She caught her breath. The notion was almost ridiculous, and yet, *hadn't she indulged him from the start?*

Carefully, she recalled their meeting at Almack's, her rash wager, her behaviour in the maze and her reaction at the exhibition when Aurelia shared her plan. Then there was the moment he kissed her outside Rotherby House in the moonlight. She flushed to think of it, even now, but the warmth of his lips had somehow reached right through her, creating a feeling of such intense longing it had haunted her dreams ever since.

And finally, there was her decision to stay and nurse him when she should have abandoned him to his fate. She had told herself she was doing the right thing, the noble thing even, but was that the real reason? Or had there been something else at play?

Sophie swallowed, her heart beating a note of betrayal.

'I do believe you've liked him more than you've admitted, right from the start,' she accused her pale countenance. 'Which is all the more reason he must never find out,' she added, watching her lower lip wobble. For a heartless rake, who never intended to marry, could never return the same regard.'

And now there was Sir Weston.

'This is not the first time I've known Lord Dominic Rotherby to act dishonourably. Do you trust me, Miss Fairfax?'

Sophie inhaled deeply. Why every gentleman of her small acquaintance seemed intent on asking her the same felt a little pointed, to say the least. She finished her toilette, and drew on the fur-trimmed pelisse and soft kid gloves Lu Lu had loaned her to finish her outfit. Their quality was far in excess of anything she possessed at home and she paused briefly to admire their velvet lining before collecting her thoughts.

In truth, it wasn't so much that she *trusted* Sir Weston, as that she'd *deceived* herself about Lord Rotherby, and despite Lu Lu's optimism, she had zero expectation of making a love match during her short stay. This left her with one real option, and it was with this thought uppermost in her mind that Sophie left for the Palais des Tuileries, determined to fulfil her plan, no matter what Lu Lu might think of it.

'Look, *ma chérie, c'est magnifique,* is it not?' Lu Lu whispered as her carriage drew up at the Royal and Imperial Palace on the right bank of the River Seine.

'And I do believe King Louis XVIII is in residence at the moment – though everyone says he has much to do since Napoleon's *you know what*,' she added in a hushed tone.

Sophie nodded, recalling Matilda's painstaking reenactment of the defeat and exile of *little Boney* over the library atlas, using the bulging-eyed Duke Wellington as the advancing British army.

'It's very beautiful,' Sophie replied thoughtfully, gazing out of the window.

It was no lie. Despite the revolution and subsequent 'Terror', the palace and its gardens were amongst the finest she'd ever seen. Not only did the imposing building appear to stretch on endlessly into the night, the formal Italian gardens, illuminated by a hundred flickering lanterns, were a truly mesmerising sight.

'*Oui*, springtime at *Les Tuileries* is very special,' Lu Lu said, sighing happily. 'It is, how you English say … *merveilleux, oui*? Perfect for a little dalliance perhaps?'

She raised her eyebrows mischievously as Sophie suppressed a smile, wondering exactly how she could expect to have a dalliance when most of her old life hung by a thread.

'Are you sure no one I know will be there?' she asked again, a little anxiously.

'Ah, ma *chérie*,' Lu Lu replied with a wry smile, '*cercles* at Le

Palais des Tuileries are purely for the Parisian haute ton to outshine one another. And this fortunate fact means you and I will be of absolutely no interest at all.'

A few minutes at the Tuileries Palace was more than enough to convince Sophie that Lu Lu's assurances were well founded, for not only was there a sea of Parisian ton, they seemed much more interested in seeking acquaintances and approval from within their own circle, than in meeting anyone outside it.

Sophie stared in wonder as she gazed around at the grand formal ballroom, flickering softly with more candelabras and gilt-edged mirrors then she could count. It was an enchanting and mesmerising sight that she would have cherished in any other circumstance. Yet Parisian society also had an edge that made London seem almost staid by comparison.

'They call it the Bonaparte effect,' Lu Lu whispered, beside her. 'No one is quite comfortable knowing he lived here, and yet this palace holds so many good memories too.'

Sophie watched as Lu Lu nodded her feathered head at a circle of exquisitely dressed ladies across the room.

'If you would you just excuse me for two minutes, *ma chérie*? I find I need to powder my nose.'

Before she had time to respond, Lu Lu had swept away in her rustling lavender silk, leaving Sophie to feel the absence of her sisters more acutely than ever.

She took a deep breath and made her way to a nearby table where a surly footman misunderstood her request for lemonade, and presented her with a tall glass of champagne.

Far too polite to refuse, Sophie thanked the haughty steward before making her way to the back of the room. It was just as she was enjoying her first tentative sips of the sparkling wine, and considering that perhaps the Parisian ton weren't quite so terrifying after all, that a faint English tone reached her ears.

'Why I keep underestimating bourgeois bumpkins, I'll never know.'

The sudden acerbic tone caused Sophie to pause mid-sip, while all the hairs on the back of her neck slowly strained to attention.

It couldn't be, could it?

'And this may be Paris, but any one of tonight's patrons would be difficult if they knew the truth.'

A dull flush began to reach across Sophie's cheeks as she listened, praying she was mistaken.

'Of course, it only takes one reliable soul to share the news, and the whole pack of cards comes tumbling down.'

There was a brief titter then which only confirmed all of Sophie's worst fears, as she shrank back into the shadows looking for something, or someone, to hide behind. But it was already too late as two elegant ladies came to a standstill in front of her, one of whom was instantly dismissed. Slowly, Sophie lifted her eyes to meet Aurelia's penetrating gaze, never more conscious of the moment outside Rotherby House, when she'd glimpsed her figure hurrying through the cold midnight mist.

'But how very fortuitous,' Aurelia greeted in a glittering tone. 'I do believe it is the infamous Miss Sophie Fairfax herself. I say, Miss Fairfax, how *are* you? Do tell all, for you are quite the talk of London. Are you being treated well? There must be some reward, for Dominic is very generous, or so his reputation goes…'

She paused to titter again as Sophie cast a frantic gaze around the room, feeling caught in the slew of a nightmare.

'Certainly, that gown is much finer than anything you wore in London, and your earrings too… Though you should take care you don't catch a chill. I hear springtime in Paris can be quite *short-lived*!'

There was a painful silence while Sophie stared into Lady Aurelia's glacial blue eyes, wondering how to begin.

'Sophie?' Aurelia persisted icily. 'Whatever is the matter? Did you think no one else could cross the Channel? The Carlisles have plenty of old friends in Paris, and it wasn't hard to persuade my mother to take a trip – once I realised your departure coincided with Lord Rotherby's.' She paused to let her eyes sweep over Sophie's becoming Psyche knot hairstyle with its pale pink ostrich feather Lu Lu had insisted she add, just before they left.

'You know, you look well, my dear, but I worry for your future. You must ask Dominic to help you when he grows a little … fatigued? These bachelors can be *so* unreliable, but I'm sure he has plenty of gentlemen friends who would take you on – in Austria or Italy perhaps. Anyway, I'd love to stay and talk longer, only Mother is here too, and very keen I don't associate with … well, I'm sure you understand?'

'Aurelia, you must know I am not what you suggest!' Sophie countered finally, unable to believe she'd ever compromised herself for a girl who didn't even understand the concept of friendship. 'I did not intend to run away with Lord Rotherby, and I most certainly have not become his *mistress*!'

She paused to glance around. 'You insult me to suggest such a thing!'

'*I* insult you?' Aurelia returned, her eyes flashing with fury. 'I took you into my confidence, and you stole my plan and husband for yourself! Not the first time for a Fairfax either. What is it, some kind of family sport?'

'He was not your husband! And he had no intention of offering marriage under any circumstances,' Sophie continued in a low yet furious voice, aware of the curious faces starting to turn their way. 'I was actually trying to help you, and unless you wish the whole of Paris to know about your *big plan*, I suggest we continue this conversation outside.'

'Fine!' Aurelia snapped.

The lantern-lit gardens of *Les Tuileries* looked even more magical now, wrapped in the long reach of the inky night sky. Yet all Sophie could think about was the burning injustice of it all. She knew assumptions would be made amongst the English ton, that there was a chance the whispers might follow her to Paris, but to hear such allegations directly, and from the person she'd sought to help, was beyond everything.

'Let me be clear,' she ground out, as soon as they were alone. 'I was not seeking to take anything that was yours, but rather to try and dissuade you from your plan. I certainly never intended to accompany Lord Rotherby who, I hasten to add, always planned to take *Mrs Haxby* anyway, and I am only here because he thought I was she!' She paused to draw breath, while Aurelia scowled even harder. 'And he may be a nobleman,' Sophie continued heatedly, 'but that is all he is – he is most certainly not *any* sort of gentleman!'

She gritted her teeth as the oddest feeling of remorse

seeped through her. He was a heartless rake who'd teased her from the outset and rubbished all her attempts to fix her situation – including throwing the kind Sir Weston out onto the street at L'Auberge Notre-Dame – but he'd also tried to shelter her from total ruin too.

She swallowed as his shadowed face reached through her tangled thoughts, trying to explain why he hadn't simply let her go. *How could anyone exist in a space where no one got hurt?*

Aurelia's eyes flashed as they forged further into the gardens, their twinkling surroundings a stark contrast to their heated exchange.

'I hear your excuses,' Aurelia scorned, 'but I also watched your face every time you were in Rotherby's company. You were besotted with him, and I have only your word he intended to take Mrs Haxby! I said my mother would have made sure I became Lady Rotherby if he failed to act honourably, so there was no good reason for you to interfere. Well, I'm sure I wish you well in your new … endeavours, while I satisfy myself with assuring your relatives, and all the ton, that you are enjoying life as a courtesan very well indeed!'

At this point, Aurelia picked up her puce silk skirts and swept away, while Sophie could only look on in despair. Her continued stay with Lu Lu was entirely dependent on her story remaining in London – and even then she'd told herself there could be a thousand respectable reasons for a debutante to disappear for a while – but Aurelia's determination to destroy her reputation would ensure she could never return to England.

And it was all her own fault.

Suddenly, the faint yet joyful waltz of the violins was

more than her jangled nerves could bear and, picking up her gown, she hurried through an arbour of orange blossom, before plunging along a garden trail. Then she ran until the only sound was the hum of a lone bee among some tulips, when she finally allowed herself to sink down on a stone bench. Breathing unsteadily, she reached up to fix her loosened curls, while trying not to give in to the swirl of panic inside.

She'd told herself she could find a way, that she could be heroic like Phoebe, but the harsh reality was that she'd created a scandal that Aurelia would never let the ton forget. Her life, as she knew it, was over and worst of all, she'd brought deep shame on the Fairfax name. Sophie dropped her head into her hands, and for the first time since leaving Dover, felt truly and horribly alone.

'I am always surprised by the Tuileries,' a low voice murmured quietly. 'It is a veritable treasure trove of hidden delights, though I must admit, you are my first debutante. I do hope you're not seeking more rogues, Miss Fairfax, for I thought we'd exhausted them as a source of new friends?'

Sophie caught her breath somewhere between a laugh and a sob, quite aware that if Lord Rotherby learned of her current despair, he might use it to accelerate his own plan.

'And in truth,' he continued, 'when Lu Lu suggested an evening at Les Tuileries, I thought a little music and dancing might be of interest to a newly betrothed young lady – entertain her even? Either way, I certainly didn't expect to find her quite alone in these beautiful gardens, which leads me to wonder whether it is Lu Lu's company, or your intrepid curiosity, which is to blame?'

Sophie drew a steadying breath, never more grateful for the cover of darkness for her blotched face.

'Madame Dupres is not responsible for my current situation, my lord,' she replied with a catch in her voice, 'and we both know I am not your betrothed!'

Exhaling softly, Lord Rotherby closed the gap and sank down on the stone seat beside her. Sophie stiffened, aware of a thousand competing feelings, but mostly of the strange air about his person tonight. He seemed thoughtful in a way she'd not seen before, and it softened all his movements.

'Are you avoiding company?' he asked.

Briefly, she glanced at his midnight blue coat, a colour which contrasted vibrantly with his mossy eyes and dark locks swept back à *la Brutus*, while his spotless pantaloons and gleaming Hessians only accentuated his long limbs. Yet it was his distracted face, silhouetted in the half-light, that really stole her attention, taking her back to the night he kissed her. Sophie swallowed. He really was the most carelessly beautiful man she'd ever known.

'Tell me,' he pondered aloud, 'what sends a fearless Fairfax out into these lonely gardens, when I would have thought she might benefit from being seen tonight, especially looking as radiant as she does?' Sophie glanced up swiftly, but there was only sincerity in his expression. 'Lu Lu shared with me her plan to find you an alternative husband as I 'wasn't to your taste',' he added with a faint smile, 'but I'm not entirely certain you'll find one in the rhododendron bushes. Furthermore, I'm not sure my presence will add the right note of ... brotherly guardianship.'

Sophie smiled wanly. He couldn't be any less someone's brotherly guardian.

'You know, the whole world will be a kinder place again if you would but take my name.'

The words were uttered so gently that the garden seemed to still momentarily. Sophie clenched her fingers, steeling herself not to soften towards the melodic persuasion in his voice, to recall that he was a skilled rake, and that someone without a heart could never be trusted with hers.

And yet there was such a curious ache in her chest that she could hardly meet his gaze.

'I know this is not what you planned,' he added, laying a hand over hers and sending a jolt through her cold limbs. 'It isn't what I planned either, but I believe we can make sense of this mess, and it will be vastly better than an existence eked out in some quiet backwater of Paris.'

'But why?' Sophie replied. 'Why, when you have made it your life's work to avoid this precise situation? You may feel a degree of responsibility, but I made the decision to intervene the night you left London. You owe me nothing.'

He paused as a shadow flitted across his face, and his eyes fixed on the mid-distance.

'When I was a small boy,' he replied after a beat, 'my father would force me to watch while he slit the throats of the animals he'd hunted. Then he would hang them and go inside and beat my mother.'

Sophie stilled as he spoke entirely without emotion, as though describing the colour of his boots.

'She was everything good and kind,' he continued. 'At night she would read stories until I fell asleep, just so I wouldn't lie awake, thinking about him. And she never complained, but he was, in every way, a father and a husband to be despised. He drank, he gambled, he whored and he beat. There was nothing redeemable about him whatsoever. Yet all this I overlooked, for the sake of our blood tie, until the night he killed my mother and unborn sister.'

Sophie stared in shock, knowing she had gone as pale as the blossom at her feet.

'He … killed them?' she whispered so faintly even she could hardly hear her own words.

'He beat my mother repeatedly when she was with child, so she barely had strength enough for herself, let alone an unborn baby,' he went on, his profile unflinching. 'Which meant when she came to her labour, she was far too weak … so yes, he killed them.'

He broke off then and exhaled roughly, while Sophie felt as though she'd been allowed a glimpse through a dark veil.

'I swore that night never to marry, or to allow a Rotherby to harm anyone else. I would exist in a space where no one got hurt, and that is precisely what I've done. Except this situation will hurt you, if I *don't* act.'

He looked at her then, his velvet eyes sending the oddest flare through her veins. He was only a breath away, his scent stirring an impulse that started behind his eyes, and reached right through to the tip of her toes, an impulse to do something extremely foolhardy. She inhaled shakily as a nightjar churred nearby, yet was conscious of such sudden longing that she didn't stop his fingers tracing a gentle path to her face. And when his thumb brushed gently over her lips, she only gazed back with absolute certainty that whatever he wanted, she wanted it too, so that when he leaned closer, and let his lips graze over hers, she was conscious only of yearning regret when he paused.

She exhaled raggedly, locked in his gaze, their lips a fraction apart. Then his arm slid around her, pulling her tight against him so his lips could return with a burning heat, and she kissed him back until her head spun. It was a kiss so unlike his last – hungry and intimate – the kind of kiss that existed only in dreams, and for one intoxicating moment she let herself envisage a whole life with this impossible man, until the memories began to reach through.

'Even the strongest of attachments rarely last a lifetime… no one broke my heart, I would have to possess one in the first place… It will be a mariage de convenance only…'

With a huge, forcible effort she thrust him away, and tried to assemble her scattered wits.

'Aurelia may delight in telling the ton I'm your courtesan,' she forced out, 'but I am still a Fairfax – and a debutante too!' Lord Rotherby drew back as she stood up. 'This situation has stolen so much from me: my reputation, my self-worth, my family,' she continued, avoiding his gaze. 'If I marry you now, it will take the only thing I have left: the freedom to bestow my heart where I choose! I am not some debt to honour, Lord Rotherby. And I have yet to learn of one reason why I should marry someone who is running from scandal himself.'

There was a tense silence, before Lord Rotherby stood up too.

'I've told you all I can,' he replied tersely. 'I left London to clear my name, but that has nothing to do with this situation. And I would far rather you accepted my offer freely, but if you are set on pursuing a path of self-destruction, I will have no choice but to insist! In truth, if Lady Aurelia is here, as you suggest, then the matter is even more urgent than I thought. You should not be seen in my company again until we have made our vows. Fortunately, my time away was fruitful, and I have made some progress in locating an English pastor. I intend to ask him to marry us before the week's end, and would thank you to accept this, Miss Fairfax, as a *fait accompli*. Now, I suggest we return to the Grand Salon before we are missed.'

He proffered his arm then as though escorting debutantes through the moonlit Tuileries gardens was the most normal thing in the world, all traces of their recent entanglement as distant as the music from the Salon.

Sophie stared, trying not to give in to the violent feelings coursing through her veins.

She took a deep breath.

'Lady Aurelia is indeed here, and would be more than happy to oblige you in your pursuit of a marriage, if you are so inclined,' she returned coldly. 'But I believe I have made myself quite clear: we are not suited and my path will be chosen freely. I intend to be gone before the week's end, and I would thank *you* to accept this, Lord Rotherby, as a *fait accompli*!'

Then she picked up her skirts and made her way back to the palace quite alone.

Chapter Sixteen

A PATH OF SELF-DESTRUCTION

The following day

It was exactly one day and three whisked raw eggs later that the letters came. All were marked urgent, and all were scrawled in great haste by hands she knew.

Sophie stared at them, her head still woolly from the night before, her spirits as low as they'd ever sunk. She'd spent the remainder of the evening glued to Lu Lu's side, drowning her path of self-destruction with the amply flowing champagne, while her fond companion regaled her with stories of cotillions, quadrilles and waltzes, including two with her very delightful and proper English acquaintance. A few more enquiries confirmed that the neat-stepper in question *was*, in fact, her distant relation, Sir George Weston; and if it seemed a coincidence that in all Paris, Sir Weston had chosen to attend the very same soiree as herself, Sophie contented herself with the fact that at least Aurelia's outburst seemed to have gone largely unnoticed.

In truth, if it wasn't for the persistent ache around her toes, and intense thumping in her head – the former the result of Lu Lu's tightly fitting ball slippers, the latter the result of Lu Lu's generous hand – she might have considered she'd handled herself with considerable Fairfax style and aplomb. Yet this made little sense of her anxious heart every time she recalled Lord Rotherby's exit from the Tuileries later that night, without so much as a glance in her direction.

Frowning, Sophie made haste to break the seals and spread the sheets before her.

Knightswood Manor, Devon
12th March 1821

Dearest sister,

I trust this letter finds you well and adjusting to your new life as Lady Rotherby.

I must own to being taken by surprise by the news of your sudden flight, but as Lord Rotherby has since written to explain the swiftness of your mutual attachment, I have attributed any confusion on my part to the mysteries of the heart, and only wish you both well.

As a happy aside, since you have saved me the expense of numerous public announcements, a tedious engagement party, and another interminable family wedding, I have been able to offer Lord Rotherby a not inconsiderable dowry, which I hope will be to his satisfaction.

Perhaps you will write to your sisters and brothers soon, as I am sure they are keen to hear news of your happy nuptials, directly from your hand.

Your brother,
Thomas
Sir Thomas Fairfax

A dark scowl passed across Sophie's face as she screwed Thomas's letter into a tight ball. It was so predictable of her eldest brother to ignore her letter and treat Lord Rotherby's account as truth, so long as it accorded with his Monstrous Marriage Masterplan. Phoebe maintained that he was vastly improved, but Sophie suspected it was only the change in her sister's marital state that had prompted his improvement. As far as she could see, he was only concerned with notching up another husband for another sister. So much for riding to defend her honour – he couldn't wait to shake Lord Rotherby by the hand!

Seething, she threw Thomas's letter into her bedchamber fire and drew the second letter forwards. She turned it over and observed the Damerel seal with mixed feelings. Phoebe might be traversing the continent on her honeymoon, but as the eldest Fairfax girl, she was also fiercely protective of her siblings. Of all people, Phoebe would be the one to understand – and judge – her the most. She broke open the seal with trepidation.

Florence
12th March 1821

Dearest Sophie,

> *Alexander and I were most concerned to receive your letter*

detailing your current situation and plan to be in Paris within the sennight.

In the meantime, I urge you to remain where you are in as quiet a fashion as possible, for the viscount intends to call on Lord Rotherby, without delay.

Your loving sister,
Phoebe
Viscountess Damerel

Sophie eyed the second letter with misgiving, her mind in a new whirl. It was short but to the point, with several large blots conveying her sister's anxiety better than all the words in the world. And while she'd half expected Thomas's indifference so long as the Fairfax name was not sullied, she knew Viscount Damerel would not suffer from the same shortcomings. He took his position as new brother to the Fairfax brood very seriously, meaning there was every chance he would call Rotherby out for his behaviour.

Sophie pictured her sister's husband measuring his paces before facing Lord Rotherby's deadly pistols, and closed her eyes briefly. It would be a more even match than Thomas or Fred – if Fred ever challenged anyone to a duel – but hadn't Lord Rotherby said he never missed?

And if Rotherby *did* lose, what then? The viscount would be forced into exile for killing a gentleman, and Phoebe would never talk to her as long as she lived. Sophie swallowed as she drew the last letter forwards, conscious this was no longer about protecting her honour as much as protecting her family from ripples of her scandal.

Inhaling deeply, she broke open the last letter and laid the single page on the table in front of her.

Paris
16th March 1821

Dear Miss Fairfax,

Please forgive the direct nature of this letter. I am only emboldened to write by what I perceive to be the nature of your current predicament. If I have misunderstood in any way, please burn this missive and think not on it again.

As I understand it, the engagement between yourself and Lord Rotherby does not have your consent, and you are therefore labouring under the heaviest obligation. I would not usually presume to involve myself in such private matters, but I am convinced I know the true nature of the gentleman to whom you find yourself committed, and it is with no small amount of imperative that I say I empathise wholly with your caution.

I share neither Lord Rotherby's income nor his luxurious style, but I can offer you protection from his unwanted attentions if you agree to be my wife. Once wed, I would propose travelling on to Venice for a suitable time, before a quiet return to England when the opportunity arises.

Should this proposition be of interest and comfort to you, please let me know without delay, and I will make the necessary arrangements.

Your most faithful servant,
George.
Sir George Weston

Sophie stared in silent shock at Sir Weston's neatly penned letter, each word as carefully turned out as his person. It was the most correct offer of marriage she'd ever received, and one that undoubtedly sprang from the greatest consideration too, so why did it make her feel so very wretched?

She closed her eyes wearily and pictured the perfect Sir Weston, in his perfect morning suit, eating his perfect breakfast, before penning his perfect letter. It was a picture she'd daydreamed about before Josephine started to wax lyrical about him, but now it was accompanied by such discomfort.

She frowned, barely understanding herself.

'Weston is not all he appears to be. You must accept my word that this is truth.'

And yet Sir Weston seemed equally as determined to convince her of Rotherby's villainy too.

Why did two gentlemen, who shared a blood tie, detest each other so vehemently? Could their relationship have anything to do with it?

Sophie stared at Sir Weston's offer, imagining Lord Rotherby's reaction, and a strange heaviness crept into the pit of her stomach. He seemed to dislike him so much, and yet he was complex and unpredictable too.

She paused to recall the moment Rotherby had described his father's treatment of his mother and unborn sister, and swallowed. His childhood had been so unlike her own, that she was no longer surprised he considered himself heartless. How could anyone wish to have one after such an ordeal? And yet… She flushed, recalling his kiss in the Tuileries gardens. It was the kind of kiss that belonged to a real flesh and blood hero, not a heartless rake with a dark past.

'I left London because I was falsely accused of villainous behaviour that I will disprove. You must accept my word that this is truth.'

Her thoughts hardened.

Lord Rotherby may have had a terrible father, but he still hadn't divulged the real reason he left London, and no matter how much he protested his honour, his reputation suggested very differently.

She drew in a deep breath and forced all traitorous thoughts to the back of her mind. She had no more desire to marry a respectable gentleman for escape, than she did a rake for the appearance of respectability – and both would mean Lord Rotherby had won his wager. Furthermore, she had even less desire to be the cause of a duel that resulted in her new brother-in-law's untimely demise.

Which left her squarely with her own plan.

Sophie eyed herself severely in the looking-glass. Now was not the time to be addle-pated.

'Mais non, *ma chérie*!' Madame Marie Louisa Dupres squeaked when Sophie explained, in halting sentences, why she could no longer presume upon her goodwill. 'This is a madness, certainly! You have no family, no connections, no wardrobe to call your own... I will not allow it! And besides, my Dominic would never forgive me.' She paused as a frown passed across her pretty face. 'If I let you go jaunting across Paris looking for ... how is it you say ... a position ... without so much as a backward glance, he won't just be angry, he'll be furious. *Enormously* furious,' she emphasised in a stricken tone. 'He—'

'Believes a little music and dancing should be sufficient to distract a newly betrothed debutante?' Sophie quizzed in Lord Rotherby's own words from the Tuileries.

'Mais, ma cherie, it was just to distract you from your situation,' Madame Dupres flushed.

'But that's just it!' Sophie urged.

'I don't want to be distracted from my situation, I need to do what I can to salvage it! And even if my reputation is in tatters, I don't accept that a *mariage de convenance* is my only option. I wagered I'd not settle for anything less than a love match, and I'd rather have none at all than compromise.'

Lu Lu regarded her as though she'd finally taken leave of her senses.

'*Mon dieu!* So is it you wish to design *les pelisses* or teach *les mathématiques*?' she asked, fanning herself as she sank down on her favourite peach damask chaise.

'Pelisses,' Sophie assured, suppressing a smile. 'Truly, I would pity anyone who had to learn *les mathématiques* at my hand.'

'But is it really true you do not hold any *tendre* for my Dominic at all, *ma chérie*?' Lu Lu coaxed again in disbelief.

'Can you not see yourself married, even one little bit? I must confess to having been tempted by the prospect again of late, and while Dominic can be headstrong, he is certainly a very fine catch, *n'est ce pas*?'

Sophie gazed into her friend's large opal eyes, wondering if her new temptation was responsible for their sparkle. Briefly, she recalled Phoebe's doing the same, despite all her protests about the viscount, before Lord Rotherby's dark and unsettled gaze crept back into her thoughts. She frowned and was momentarily tempted to tell Lu Lu everything; to confess she could barely hold a thought around him, that he was the most frustrating, stubborn and tantalising person she'd ever known; that she longed to be free of him and yet could think of nothing worse too.

But none of those words came out. Instead, there was only a heavy silence, before Sophie cleared her throat.

'You know Lord Rotherby is running from a scandal himself, don't you?' she asked quietly, Horace's words reaching through her thoughts:

'Tis a serious matter, but suffice to say the guvnor weren't responsible of course. He was jus' coming to Paris for time to sort 't out.'

'*Mais oui*, though Dominic does not tell me quite everything,' Lu Lu replied with a frown. 'But whatever this scandal is, he is not guilty! My Dominic is a gentleman – a wild one, to be sure, but honourable and very kind too.'

Sophie stared at the troubled Lu Lu, wondering how well she truly knew her Dominic. She pictured him teasing her in Almack's, his fury on board his yacht, his treatment of Sir Weston at L'Auberge de Notre Dame and the way her refused to tell her anything about his own scandal. And then finally, the moment in the Tuileries Garden which had very nearly weakened her…

Sophie's thoughts whirled. The truth was, she had no idea who he was, except perhaps a master of disguise.

'*Ma chérie?*' Lu Lu entreated, reaching through Sophie's

thoughts. 'At least stay until Le Grand Bal Masqué de Versailles? It will be *the* ball of the Parisian season. All the best families will be there. And who knows, perhaps even a surprise for a young lady looking for a *mariage d'amour*?' she coaxed.

'Versailles?' Sophie frowned, 'I thought the King resided at the Palais des Tuileries?'

'Oh, he does!' Lu Lu nodded enthusiastically. 'It is just that the south wing of *Le Cour Royale* has recently been finished, and there hasn't been a ball since *you know who* was banished, so it will be quite the spectacle! It could be just the thing to help you salvage your situation, *ma chérie*,' she pleaded winningly, 'and besides, do you not wish to see Versailles?'

Sophie could think of few royal palaces she yearned to see more. Unlike *les mathématiques*, she'd always enjoyed history, and had spent considerable time studying the Palace of Versailles as a centre of art and culture, as well as royal power. However, the revolution had changed so much, and despite the restoration of the King, she was well aware that Versailles had fallen from favour.

'It is also a masked ball,' Lu Lu added with a mischievous smile, 'so you need not be known, unless you wish it, and there will be music and fountains and fireworks. It really will be *la soirée de l'année*!'

Sophie smiled faintly, wondering if Lu Lu's excitement was driven purely by the promise of entertainment. She'd mentioned her temptation a few times in passing, and wondered if she intended to try and persuade the neat-stepping Sir Weston to attend the ball. A faint wave of guilt reached through her as she recalled his letter; she had no desire to shatter any illusion her whimsical friend might have, particularly when she'd been nothing but kind. Yet in truth, it was also just the sort of prestigious ball Sophie would have moved mountains to attend in her old life – and could well be her last before she disappeared.

She closed her eyes briefly at the thought. How she, the most sensible of the Fairfaxes, had arrived at such a place was almost comical; and yet here she was all the same, with her life in tatters but her dreams still intact – and no one was more surprised than she by how fiercely she would protect them.

Sophie nodded as she picked up her teacup.

'On one condition,' she said, eyeing Lu Lu intently over the rim of her chocolate.

'*Mais oui, ma chérie*,' Lu Lu beamed with a flourish, 'please, just name it.'

'Let there be no more mention of *les mathématiques*!'

Chapter Seventeen

REVOLUTIONARIES AND RUMOURS

The following day

If Madame Marie-Louisa Dupres was suspicious about the slim parcel Sophie clutched to her chest the following day, she was far too distracted to mention it. And once they reached the shop of Madame Montmartre, *modiste to Parisian gentility*, she was much too enraptured by the dove-grey cloak with ermine trim in the window to loan it any special attention.

Indeed, it was only when Sophie continued to carry it with her into the tiny shop that Lu Lu looked at her slightly askance, though it soon became clear that Lu Lu hadn't been *entirely* honest about the Versailles ball either.

'I have heard it called many things already,' the petite modiste chattered, gathering and pinning a fine cream satin in swathes around Sophie's waist. 'A ball, a *soirée*, an *assemblée* … it is not easy, you know, for many families will be absent…'

She paused and eyed them from beneath her long, perfectly pared eyelashes, giving Sophie a sudden image of the tiny

Frenchwoman at the head of a baying crowd, a torch in one hand and a tape measure in the other.

'Yes, indeed,' Lu Lu agreed carefully. 'It has not been that long and I understand the King has called it a *commémoration*, which seems a sympathetic approach, *n'est ce pas*? Though I believe Versailles will always be a museum now.'

'*Mais oui*,' the modiste said with a brief nod. 'In truth, it is hard to envisage otherwise. Despite the restoration of the House of Bourbon, there are too many ghosts at Versailles.'

The modiste's eyes gleamed again as Sophie listened, unable to help comparing this visit to her last in Bath. All she'd had to think about then was an impromptu parasol fight, not a ghost palace scarred by revolution, bloodshed and turmoil. She turned to observe herself in the gilt-edged glass, suddenly homesick for her sisters and afternoons by the parlour fire.

And yet she could not deny the skill of the petite modiste either.

She turned to the right, and then the left, admiring the new satin gown Lu Lu was insisting upon. It was cut in the new Romantic fashion, with her waist cinched in, her skirt a wide bell, and with gigot sleeves cut so wide that she looked more a heroine from one of Sir Walter Scott's novels than Miss Sophie Fairfax of Knightswood Manor, recently disgraced. It was everything she tried to capture in her own designs, and so much more flattering than her old Empire-line gowns.

'I can just imagine a pelisse to go over this,' she suggested quietly, when Lu Lu disappeared to take a closer look at the dove-grey cloak.

'*Mais oui? Quelle couleur?* And how high the waistband?'

the modiste asked through a mouthful of pins, stabbing a mannequin with considerable violence.

Sophie reached for her package of pelisse designs.

'Well perhaps ... like these?' she replied, spreading them out on the modiste's small threads table.

For a few seconds the modiste said nothing, and merely gazed at Sophie's careful designs, reworked over several evenings, in the back of one of Lu Lu's old sketch books.

'These are good, non?' She frowned, pinning a wrapped satin rose on Sophie's bodice before adding another lace frill to one of her sleeves. 'I have a cousin in Rouen who designs for several English ladies,' she added, with a curious glance, 'though she has never mentioned clients presenting their *own* designs before.'

'Well, they aren't for me, exactly,' Sophie replied, feeling a faint flush start to creep up her neck, 'but I was just wondering if you might be interested…'

'*Mais oui, oui*, don't worry, I understand!' the modiste replied urgently, sweeping up all Sophie's designs as footsteps approached. 'I have to say, your artistry'—she paused to tap Sophie's designs—'is very impressive.' Then she winked again, quite deliberately. 'I will study these as a matter of urgency and let you know. *Et maintenant*, how did you find the cloak, Madame Dupres? Is she not a beauty?'

She spun to face Lu Lu as Sophie stared, certain her first attempt at finding employment had not gone as intended at all.

'Ah, you look *très belle, Sophie!*' Lu Lu exclaimed, still wearing the cloak.

'It is too expensive,' Sophie mumbled, wondering what the

etiquette was for reclaiming personal sketches from a volatile revolutionary.

'La! We do not count cost for Versailles,' Lu Lu reprimanded. 'You are my guest, and besides, the gown is entirely suited to the occasion. Now for the domino, if you please, Madame Montmartre? I will draw the curtain so we may see the two together.'

Sophie watched as the modiste swiftly wrapped a voluminous black silk cloak around her shoulders, before fitting a theatrical mask to the upper half of her face. The effect was quite magical, despite everything, and she suppressed a small thrill as she stared at her reflection.

'Exquisite,' a low tone offered suddenly.

Startled, Sophie spun to peer around the numerous mannequins and piles of fabric to the threshold of the small shop. She hadn't heard anyone come in, but the space was cluttered with every kind of tool for dressmaking, and the rain outside was heavy.

'Dominic, you wicked creature! Sneaking up on us like that!' Lu Lu exclaimed, clapping her hands together. 'But doesn't she look like a young Parisian noblewoman? Now, *ma chérie*, you will need to watch your step for she will truly be the belle of the ball!'

'I have no doubt about that,' Lord Rotherby replied, doffing his hat with a faint smile.

Sophie gazed at his dampened hair, recalling his abrupt exit from the Tuileries Palace, before realising the shop had fallen silent.

'What brings you here, Lord Rotherby?' she asked coolly.

She felt the modiste glance from her to his lordship with a

suspicious frown. Sophie inhaled quickly, feeling the visit get more complex by the second.

'Business,' he returned abruptly. 'Please do excuse my intrusion, ladies. Madame Dupres's butler was kind enough to furnish me with your location, and I come only to confirm news which I hope may have already been shared.'

At this, Lu Lu looked horror-stricken, while Sophie's hopes sank fully into her new silk slippers.

'Oh, *ma chérie*, please forgive me. I was so thrilled about Versailles, and then Madame Montmartre, and the divine cloak… And now you and Dominic will both be *so* cross, and it's all my fault…'

Lu Lu's hand flew to her mouth, while her eyes were so wide and guilty that Sophie forgave her instantly.

'*Alors*,' she rallied valiantly. 'I will tell him what *we* agreed, *ma chérie*. Dominic,' Lu Lu said sternly, 'Miss Sophie is not to be told what to do. She must be allowed to salvage herself, no matter if her reputation is in tatters!'

Sophie closed her eyes, while the modiste looked on with suspicion.

'Miss Fairfax is in tatters?' the modiste asked, frowning, her hands on her hips.

'Oh hush, madame,' Lu Lu chastised, 'I have it on good authority you still take orders south of the Seine, so I'll have no Cheltenham tragedies or Canterbury tales from you!'

At this, the modiste pressed her lips together defiantly, while Sophie drew a breath.

'What news?' she asked Lu Lu quietly.

'Why, *ma chérie*, only that dear Dominic has located an English pastor he wishes you to meet in Chartres,' she replied with a nervous smile. 'But really, we have many other things to think about just now because it is Le Grand Bal Masqué de Versailles very soon, *oui*?'

Sophie lifted her gaze slowly, while the modiste muttered something about heroic ladies and wicked m'lords beneath her breath.

'The truth is, my dear Miss Fairfax,' Lord Rotherby replied seriously, 'that while a mask will serve you for now, the moment anyone removes it, you are defenceless, which is why we must proceed with my plan, with all speed, as soon as possible.'

Sophie felt herself pale as she took in Lord Rotherby's unflinching expression.

'I exist in a space where no one gets hurt.'

And yet she would now, no matter what happened.

'I will go with you to Versailles, Lu Lu,' Sophie replied steadily, 'but I shall not presume on you any longer than the week's end, and I will certainly *not* be travelling on to Chartres with Lord Rotherby.'

It was Madame Dupres's turn to pale, as Lord Rotherby's frown deepened.

'As you wish, *ma chérie*. You see, Dominic, she likes *les mathématiques* far too much to be with you.'

'No, it is not for *les mathématiques*, Lu Lu,' Sophie corrected in a low voice, 'or for any reason other than I cannot envisage a life beside his Lordship.'

She closed her eyes briefly then, partly to stop his shadowed greens whispering words that sent a hollow ache through her core, but mostly because she'd lied. She *could* envisage a life with Lord Dominic Rotherby so easily, and yet how could she bestow her heart when he could give her none?

She drew a breath, and forced a tone she was far from feeling.

'And my mind is quite made up.'

17th March 1821
Paris
Dear Sir Weston,

Sophie paused to chew the end of her quill, wondering again how a visit to a modiste could have changed so much. Yet the location of the pastor meant she'd run out of time, and she wouldn't put it past Lord Rotherby not to bundle her off en route from Versailles.

Silently, she let her eyes drift to Sir Weston's previous letter:

> *I share neither Lord Rotherby's income nor luxurious style, but I can offer you protection from his unwanted attentions if you agree to be my wife.*

She swallowed, and continued writing.

> *I thank you for your recent correspondence, which was such a comfort to receive. In truth, while it goes against every natural feeling to presume upon your kindness, I find myself in such a fix that…*

She paused again, recalling Josephine's brief infatuation.

'He seems to be exactly what a real gentleman should be…'

She'd said as much herself, and Lu Lu clearly thought him a gentleman of great character and kindness, all of which made a nonsense of her finer sensibilities now. She swallowed and forced herself on. Sir Weston had offered her the hand of friendship, and right now she needed it if she was to make it away safely. Her recent attempt at finding work had also made her realise that her best chance most likely lay in a quiet town, outside the city. Briefly, she recalled Madame Montmartre's reference to a dressmaker cousin in Rouen and was conscious of a quiet spark of hope. Perhaps there, at last, she might find a place in which she could live and work for a while.

If you are intending to attend Le Grand Bal Masqué de Versailles,

She wrote, hoping Lu Lu had been successful in persuading him to attend.

I could meet you there – it will be busy, and most everyone distracted…

Sophie exhaled, hoping Lu Lu would forgive her for borrowing her delightful English gentleman friend for a short while; she wanted so much to tell her everything, but her relationships with Rotherby and Sir Weston made it too much of a risk. She also wished, with every bone in her body, that she could wait for Phoebe. But if the viscount and Rotherby were to duel, it could be disastrous for them all, whereas a sister who'd quietly disappeared would swiftly be forgotten by the ton.

Wanly, she imagined Lord Rotherby's face when he learned of her flight. He would be incandescent, not least because he would presume she was leaving to marry Sir Weston – one of the very good reasons why she never could, he wouldn't survive the week. Yet a female travelling alone in the small hours of the morning wouldn't do either.

Your offer is the greatest kindness shown by one friend to another, but our hearts are not engaged, and I always said I would marry for love alone…

Sophie didn't allow herself to read the letter back. Her path was set now and while she'd never regained her sketches from Lu Lu's excitable modiste, she was certain she could come up with new ones – she was still a Fairfax after all, even when a million miles from the rest.

Briefly, she closed her eyes and pictured Matilda encouraging Duke Wellington across the library floor with shouts of 'Banish Boney!', in her most convincing general's voice. Her eyes misted as she swallowed, and then she addressed the letter before she could change her mind.

As far as she could see, Le Grand Bal Masqué de Versailles was her very last chance.

Chapter Eighteen

MIRRORS, MASKS AND MAYHEM

Three days later

The morning of Le Grand Bal Masqué de Versailles arrived very swiftly, bringing two distinctly unexpected things.

The first was a further letter from Phoebe, announcing her imminent arrival in Paris along with the Viscount Damerel, who, she wrote, intended to call on Lord Rotherby without delay. Sophie eyed her sister's hurried scrawl with deep foreboding. She already feared a meeting between the viscount and Lord Rotherby, but she could barely bring herself to imagine a meeting with Phoebe. Her sister had left her on the brink of social success, and now she was almost destitute, with the scandal of the season brewing over her name.

The second was an expensive, scented box, containing folds of cream satin wrapped around the most delicate gold filigree mask she'd ever seen. It was breathtaking, and for a few moments Sophie did little but gaze at the swirling design and gleaming rhinestones, inset to reflect the flicker of candlelight. It was entirely different to the carnival mask Madame Montmartre had provided with the domino, and she was perplexed, until she spied a short, handwritten note also hidden within the silk:

Wear this, so I shall I know you.

'Oh, mademoiselle, it must be from an admirer,' Veronique, Lu Lu's dresser gushed as she dressed Sophie's natural ringlets à la Chinoise. 'You will spend the whole evening guessing, until he reveals himself!'

Sophie felt quite certain she knew the identity of the sender already and suppressed a brief sense of disappointment. Of course it made perfect sense for Sir Weston to send something by which he could identify her. How else was he to know her amidst the crowd?

She placed the mask back into its box and forced a smile. It was just the sort of gift she'd have adored in her old life, and yet it was far too close to her new one now – a life of masks and whispers, where nothing was quite as it seemed. She closed her eyes and wished she could leave this very second; starting again in Rouen felt like her only chance of escaping the scandal and living honestly.

Or escaping Lord Rotherby, and living dishonestly?

A sudden ache fanned out from her core. There was no doubt she was escaping Lord Rotherby, but how could a marriage of unrequited love be more honest than making her own way and trying to forget him? She forced her thoughts to the very short, very properly worded letter of confirmation she'd received from Sir Weston:

Your wish is my command, Miss Fairfax. I will make the necessary arrangements and look for you at Versailles.

She frowned as she glanced down at her new cream satin gown, with a delicate fabric rose sewn into the layers at her waist. She'd never worn such a fine dress, even in London, and yet all she could think was that the only link between her old life and her new, was a gentleman who talked like an etiquette book.

'C'est magnifique, mademoiselle,' Veronique said, clapping her hands. '*Et maintenant*, with the domino, like so, and your new mask…' She stepped back to admire her handiwork, a smile of satisfaction spreading across her face. '*Vous êtes très, très belle,*' she whispered, her eyes dancing as she guided Sophie to the looking glass. '*Regardez!*'

Sophie stared, and had to agree that Veronique had completely outdone herself, for the lady looking back was no longer Miss Sophie Fairfax, but Madame Marie-Louisa Dupres's mysterious and elegant friend, passing through Paris for just a few days.

She pulled her domino drape over the expensive satin and adjusted the delicate filigree mask beneath her hood. She was part debutante, part deception, part something she didn't even know yet. She had a plan and was a hair's breadth from making her escape, so why then did she feel so hollow?

'*Bon chance,*' she whispered to herself, though the words echoed coldly.

The journey to Versailles turned out to be unlike any Sophie had undertaken before. Not only did the distance necessitate several liveried outriders, but Horace also managed to take charge of the whole ensemble.

'For the guvnor said I should drive you meself,' the disgruntled tiger said with a scowl, squeezed into a comical affair of mustard and green velvet.

One glance at Lu Lu's penitent smile only confirmed Sophie's suspicion that she'd had little choice but to accept the tiger's assistance. Yet when they joined the cavalcade of coaches, phaetons and barouches making their way out of Paris, she was relieved he held the reins.

'*Mais oui*. He has overtaken the dreadful Comtesse d'Avignon with her enormous hair!' Lu Lu giggled as their coach lurched and swung around another.

Sophie gazed at her charismatic friend, her black domino contrasting starkly with her voluminous gown of primrose silk, and wished she could capture the moment. In truth she was a vision, with her sparkling ebony hair draped luxuriously against her creamy skin, and her cherry lips smiling mischievously beneath her mask.

She exhaled beneath her own intricate gold filigree affair. Lu Lu had offered friendship when she'd needed it most, yet tonight she would have to deceive her. It was a sombre thought as the coach lurched forwards again, speeding them towards her very last ball, for while she could hope to live quietly in the provinces, there was no doubt the ton would never accept Miss Sophie Fairfax again.

It was nearly two hours later, when their coach finally pulled into the grandest courtyard she'd ever seen in her life. Sophie peered out of the coach window at the dusk-bathed palace, and was briefly lost for words.

'Ah, the first time you see Versailles... It is special, is it not, *ma chérie*?' Lu Lu smiled from the seat opposite.

Sophie nodded wistfully, wishing her sisters were there to witness the shimmering horseshoe-shaped palace, alight with more flickering lanterns than she could count. It was truly a palace of dreams, set in an immense and extravagant park, featuring fountains, follies and pale, gleaming statues.

'It is indeed very grand, just as the Sun King intended,' Lu Lu added as a liveried footman handed them from their coach. 'But wait until you see the Hall of Mirrors, *ma chérie. C'est magnifique!*'

Sophie nodded again, suddenly grateful for her domino as she glanced back at the long line of coaches behind them. She was not expecting to know anyone other than Sir Weston and Lu Lu, but there was always a chance some of the London ton might be in attendance at an event as grand as this. Then she turned to gaze at the formal wings and entrances to the palace and gardens, that were untouched by the ravages of revolution. The whole park still echoed with the voices of the rich and powerful, and briefly, she recalled Madame Montmartre's reservations. She frowned fleetingly. It was true there was a strange excitement lacing the air, almost as though the palace was not yet ready to forget its recent history.

'Well then, Versailles, we are a pair, for we have both fallen from grace,' Sophie whispered, collecting her skirts. 'But maybe tonight we can begin again.'

Then she swept into the torch-lit Cour d'Honneur, with her head held as high as any fallen ghost.

Sophie had never seen anything as elaborate and ostentatious as the Palace of Versailles, despite Napoleon's recent occupation. Each successive apartment was filled with more flickering chandeliers, rich gold-thread wall hangings and marble busts depicting Roman deities and emperors that Josephine would have known in a heartbeat. Yet, despite the new King's will for the palace to shine like the crown jewel it once had, the scars of the revolution were still there, in the damaged walls and gilded moulding that seemed too fragile to have survived.

'*Regarde, ma chérie!*' Lu Lu exclaimed, seemingly oblivious to the history around her, 'a champagne fountain!'

'*Bienvenue, mesdames*,' a footman in a black mask said, handing them both a glass.

Lu Lu beamed in delight, while Sophie accepted warily, conscious her friend had not exactly proven herself to be a responsible escort at the last gathering. Yet even she could not deny the atmosphere was intoxicating, as though the palace herself recalled grand balls of the past and was permeating the air with their echo. She took a delicate sip, and was alarmed to find herself surrounded by masked guests almost immediately, vying for their attention.

'La! *Monsieur*, I have told you already I don't dance with peacocks,' Lu Lu said, rapping one gentleman with a jade cloak and excessively sculpted hair.

'Let me guess,' another murmured behind Sophie. 'Helen of Troy, perchance?'

He circled in front of her while Lu Lu gurgled with laughter.

'Not even if you're Achilles himself,' Sophie said flatly, side-eyeing Lu Lu who'd been distracted by another Casanova with a dish of sweet cherries.

'Ah but you would certainly be my Achilles's heel!' He grinned, lifting her fingers to his lips.

'Appealing!' Sophie replied with a good-natured smile. 'Though I aspire to slightly more than being the back end of a foot, demi-god or not! Lu Lu,' she hissed in the next breath, grasping her friend's arm and dragging her away before she committed every faux pas known to polite society.

'*Non, non, ma chérie!*' Lu Lu protested, giggling, 'I was just starting to have some fun!'

She paused to throw a last cherry at her willing accomplice, before Sophie pushed her up some wide, stone steps.

'Achilles's heel indeed,' she muttered, before catching Lu Lu's eye and starting to chuckle.

'It is a compliment, ma cherie,' Lu Lu replied, her eyes dancing, 'and just the beginning I warrant!'

It was a good while later, after they'd toured many more impressive apartments brimming with drunken revellers, amorous couples and the occasional lost soul, that Sophie felt her spirits begin to fall. How she would find Sir Weston in a palace containing two thousand rooms and half of Paris – most of whom seemed intent on behaving as though they belonged within the pages of a forbidden novel – was a real concern.

Briefly, she found herself wondering what Lord Rotherby would make of it, before collecting her thoughts.

'He would enjoy it immensely of course,' she said to herself, ignoring the ache within.

'Pardon?' Lu lu enquired, fluttering her silk fan at a new admirer.

'Nothing.' Sophie shook her head, determined not to get maudlin.

'*Oh ma chérie*,' Lu Lu exclaimed excitedly, 'we should go to the Galerie des Glaces! It is supposed to be a wonder, especially at night, and we can see the fireworks from there too.'

Sophie smiled briefly at her excitable friend.

'It sounds wonderful,' she replied, retrieving Lu Lu's fan from another passing admirer. 'Let us go at once.'

Unfortunately, while the Hall of Mirrors felt like a very good place to look for Sir Weston, it seemed half of Versailles was on their way there too. Indeed, once they'd shaken off the attentions of an overly familiar musketeer, they only had to join the steady thrum of people moving through the palace to find themselves, finally, in the infamous Galerie des Glaces itself.

For a moment, Sophie stood amidst the blur of noise, letting her gaze run up and down the long walls of grand candle-lit mirrors, before travelling upwards to the impressive Sun King himself. The effect was truly magnificent, and she caught her breath, wishing Josephine was there to share the moment.

'*Il est incroyable, n'est ce pas?*' Lu Lu murmured, before making her way towards a new table laden with glasses and champagne.

Sophie nodded, trying to memorise every detail so she could capture its likeness one day. Unlike Phoebe, who'd always yearned for heroic adventure, Sophie had only ever dreamed of touring the galleries and museums of European cities. But if she lived out her life in Rouen, it was unlikely she would ever visit such places.

'It is breathtaking, isn't it?' a languid tone offered, making Sophie start and spill her champagne. 'Though I am caught by its meaning every time. What do you see, *mademoiselle*? Is it *incroyable* as Madame Dupres says, or do paintings offer some truth too?'

In a heartbeat, Sophie was back in The British Institution, only this time there was a dart burrowing straight into her chest. She caught her breath; she hadn't expected to see him, and now all she could think was that it was the last time. She fought to collect her scattered thoughts, knowing Lord Rotherby's discovery of her amidst the crush could put her entire plan in jeopardy, that it would be doubly hard to slip away with Sir Weston now.

'I believe there is little truth here,' she returned, ignoring the pounding in her ears. 'It is impressive, but to me, the greater part is about … position and control.'

Clenching her fingers, she kept her gaze fixed on the painting, trying not to think about his faint cologne, or golden skin that somehow seemed to exude a warmth that wrapped itself around her whenever he was near. She had only words to persuade him to take his attentions elsewhere, and quickly, despite the confusion flooding her veins.

He moved then to face her and, although he was masked, she perceived the shadow in his eyes at once. The dart twisted, and instantly she wanted to tell him she didn't mean it, that she knew he'd tried as much as any heartless rake was able. But instead she was silent, while everyone else receded, until they were quite alone in the vast and shimmering hall.

'An excellent observation, Miss Fairfax,' he said, his jaw tight. 'Though I, for one, believe *position* and *control* can sometimes mask—'

He broke off, letting a poignant silence envelop them, as Sophie mapped every tiny muscle in his lower face, trying to commit them to memory.

'My father would force me to watch while he slit the throats of animals he'd hunted. He drank, he gambled, he whored and he beat. Yet all this I overlooked, for the sake of our blood tie, until the night he killed my mother and unborn sister.'

He smiled as the roar of the room returned.

'I do not intend to interrupt your evening,' he said with a nod. 'I only wanted to inform you I had a letter from your esteemed brother-in-law the Viscount Damerel today.'

Sophie felt a sudden coldness reach through her. She hadn't anticipated her brother-in-law contacting Rotherby before he reached town.

'He would like an urgent meeting, which is understandable, and I will attend of course.' He broke off to stare at her. 'In truth, how you manage to look quite so downcast wearing a mask of gold filigree is impressive,' he added in a softer tone, 'though I flatter myself it is the perfect match with your gown tonight. You really are quite breathtaking, Sophie.'

There was a moment's silence.

'Did you…? Was it you who…? Thank you,' she faltered, her mind in a new whirl.

She looked into his unsettled eyes, feeling her world contract. All this time, she'd believed Sir Weston had sent the mask so he would know her, and they could slip away before anyone noticed. But if Lord Rotherby had sent the mask, not only had she created entirely the wrong impression, she had little means of being identifiable to Weston amongst hundreds of guests.

She closed her eyes and tried to steady her thumping heart, aware that even Lu Lu seemed to have disappeared.

'You're welcome,' Lord Rotherby replied, eyeing her intently. 'I was hoping that by wearing it … that perhaps … it might indicate a change of—'

'Rotherby? I'd know that jaw anywhere.' The tone was jovial and came out of nowhere. 'What the deuce ails you, sir? Heard you had to skip London because of some damned faro nonsense. Refused to believe any of it, of course, yet no one knew where you were, and then you turn up here like the devil himself. Well, sir, I'm delighted to see you and no mistake!'

To Sophie's utter astonishment, Rotherby paled beneath his mask before turning to greet the newcomer, a large hook-nosed gentleman with dancing eyes and a kindly face.

'O'Reilly!' Rotherby exclaimed, though Sophie could sense his instant guard. 'Thank you, old friend. It's good to see you too. Tis a pity a few others aren't so ready with their belief, but I'm confident I'll clear the air soon. Anyway, what of Mrs O'Reilly?' His tone warmed a little. 'I trust you are both enjoying the continent? Versailles is quite the spectacle, is it not?'

Suddenly, and as if on cue, the windows overlooking the gardens lit up as though a thousand stars had fallen, while an orchestra far below burst into life. Sophie watched as the waterfall of light reached across Lord Rotherby's face, accentuating its contours, and in that moment he'd never looked less assured. His lips were pressed and white, his dark eyes wary, while a tiny muscle in his jaw pulsed with strain. Her gaze narrowed as fresh rivulets of doubt invaded her thoughts.

Then another burst of fireworks followed the first, once again lighting the crowd, but this time he was smiling again, as though he had not a care in the world.

'Aye, that it is, though give me Burgundy over champagne any day of the week!' O'Reilly bellowed, earning a reproving look from one of the footmen. 'I'm glad to hear you're making progress though,' he added in a lower tone. 'Never did like that other fellow, a shade too smooth for me! Do me a favour and give him a trouncing when you've cleared the cloud, eh?'

He turned to smile benevolently at Sophie.

'Your pardon, miss, I didn't mean to interrupt, and my Flo will be giving *me* a trouncing if I leave her much longer. A pleasure to meet you, and look after the boy, eh? Turns out he needs it.'

Then he wrung her hand with such a broad grin that Sophie decided she liked him twice as much as she already did, before he disappeared into the crowd. She drew a deep breath and looked at Lord Rotherby, who regarded her warily.

'Did you leave London because of some kind of *gambling* scandal?' she ventured, recalling his feverish words when she nursed him.

'Roseby and O'Sullivan are JPs ... Sir Giles and Weston too strait-laced ... it's a damnable matter ... marked during the game ... it has to be one of us.'

She stared at his inscrutable expression, and knew at once she was right. It was just the sort of scandal that could destroy a nobleman's life, let alone his pride. And she wasn't naive when it came to matters of honour – her own father had gambled Phoebe's hand in marriage and left the instruction in his will – but this was worse. Marking cards during a game was cheating, and gentlemen shot each other for far less.

For a moment Lord Rotherby said nothing, then when he spoke, it was as though they were strangers again.

'As I have said before,' he replied tautly, 'my reason for leaving London are private, and I'd thank you not to inquire into matters that don't concern you. O'Reilly is a very old and loyal friend who knows me well. Unfortunately, as is often the way in life, not everyone shares the same degree of faith—'

'With good reason, sir! And I'd thank you to unhand my sister-in-law while your name is steeped in scandal!'

Sophie glanced up in sharp disbelief, certain her straining nerves had to be mistaken, but her flickers of hope expired instantly. The new gentleman was masked, but she would know his tall, distinctive profile anywhere, and he was glowering.

'Viscount Damerel!' she whispered, flushing to the roots of her ringlets. 'How ... fortunate to see you! But pray, where is my sister?'

'Phoebe awaits you at Madame Dupres's residence,' he replied tersely, 'because we were not informed of this excursion – as we have not been informed of many things, it appears. As a result, it has taken time to find you, and I am only here because half of Paris is in attendance at this debauched affair.' He turned to level a brooding glare at Rotherby. 'But now I can see, sir, that the rumours surrounding your departure must be correct, for not content with ruining yourself, it seems you must also drag my innocent sister into your scandal! Have you no honour at all?'

His tone was low but condemning, and any hope of a reasonable discussion died instantly. Sophie knew her brother-in-law well and every line of his body was taut with hostility, while his eyes glittered in a way she'd only ever seen once before ... when duelling with his brother.

'I beg your pardon, Damerel?' Lord Rotherby challenged in an ugly tone.

He stepped towards the viscount, his hand moving to his sword hilt, threateningly.

'I have in no way disgraced my name nor have I dragged your sister into anything – though Lord knows she has provoked me beyond all endurance!' he added, his eyes glittering.

'Charmed, I'm sure, when you're forever trying to coerce me,' Sophie shot back.

'If that's true I ought to cut your liver out right here!' Viscount Damerel growled.

'No, what I meant was—'

'Be my guest. Many have tried!' Rotherby replied glacially. 'But even you should know her fate was sealed the moment she chose to meet me outside Rotherby House.'

'It wasn't my finest decision,' Sophie agreed swiftly, 'but I still think this can be resolved another w—'

'You, sir, are a cad and a rogue!' Damerel snarled. 'I demand satisfaction, and will free Miss Fairfax from all obligation. Choose your weapon!'

'I really think Phoebe would not be at all happy—' Sophie tried again, glaring at her brother-in-law.

'Is that a challenge?' Rotherby hissed.

'It is a promise, sir!'

Sophie swung her gaze from Viscount Damerel to Lord Rotherby and back to the viscount in utter disbelief. Each was eyeing the other with such a murderous expression that she would have been tempted to laugh, had they not been wholly serious.

And this was only compounded by the fact that the fireworks in the gardens were beginning to pale beside the drama in the room. Whispers began to echo through the large hall, as guests turned away from the windows and towards the tense scenes unfolding behind them.

'Then let us dispense with the formalities and get on with it!' Damerel hissed, drawing his sword so swiftly that for a moment it seemed to be over before it had begun.

But Lord Rotherby was more than ready, and met his advance with a stinging defence that made the entire room gasp.

'With pleasure!' he ground out, forcing Damerel back with a series of menacing strikes that made several of the ladies swoon instantly.

Sophie scowled at their drooping forms, wondering if they knew what a disservice they were doing to the rest of their sex.

'Ten francs on the scarlet domino!' a gentleman called from the back of the crowd, prompting a flurry of similar wagers.

She glowered at the watching crowd, before spinning to cast an imploring look at the duellers, yet they seemed to have forgotten her existence already.

She bristled furiously. So much for protecting her reputation, they were intent on making her the talk of Paris! And yet, they were already halfway along the Hall of Mirrors, their feints and parries drawing a chorus of gasps and heckles from the mesmerised crowd.

Several times, a lunge nearly found its target, and several more times a lightning manoeuvre deflected it, prompting the crowd to acknowledge their skill appreciatively. Then a series of furious strikes drove Damerel backwards, forcing him over a drinks table and knocking a champagne bowl into the arms of a nearby footman. The whole room gasped as Rotherby snatched up the ice tongs and used them to deflect Damerel's sword, before they, too, were thrust into the arms of the gaping footman. And then they were back to it, driving each other harder than ever.

Sophie clenched every muscle she possessed as she followed their glinting blades in the candlelight. It was just like Damerel to defend her honour whether she liked it or not, and just like Rotherby to choose swords over reason. She scowled harder, wracking her brain for a way to stop the fight that didn't involve throwing herself between them.

'For I may be a Fairfax, but I have never pretended to be Phoebe!' she muttered savagely beneath her breath.

'*Le combat est trop serre!*' one lady moaned. 'It is too close ... they will die!'

Seconds later, several crowd members began chorusing their support, glaring at Sophie as though she had the power to stop it, and yet the duellists' fevered brows and unrelenting strikes said very differently.

Frantically, she cast her gaze around the room, but there was nothing but suspicious stares and judgement. Rotherby and Damerel were intent on murdering one another, the crowd were pointing and whispering, and by breakfast her name would be just as synonymous with scandal in Paris, as London too.

In truth, she could think of only one very sensible and proper person who could possibly make a difference now. Gritting her teeth, Sophie picked up her skirts and spun, cursing all gentlemen and their vainglorious ideas to eternity.

Chapter Nineteen

COMBAT AND DISHONOUR

Two minutes later

Sophie sprinted as only a debutante on the verge of becoming a murderess knows how.

'I heard you had to skip London because of some damned faro nonsense ... refused to believe any of it of course ... and then you turn up here like the devil himself...'

'Not content with ruining yourself, it seems you must also drag my innocent sister into your scandal! Have you no honour at all...?'

She scowled intently as her thoughts darkened. She'd always known Lord Rotherby was a rake, and that he was running from a scandal too, but to hear he was most likely a common cheat who'd skipped town felt far worse. A wave of intense disappointment flooded her veins, exacerbated by the viscount's accusations. And if he was capable of acting dishonourably with gentlemen, of what was he capable with ladies? Had she really, despite all her protestations, fallen for a skilled libertine?

'For while a libertine is a scoundrel, there is always a chance of redemption with a rake...'

Even Aurelia had known the score. And all his efforts to marry her, all his protestations about honour and reputation, had they been merely to ameliorate his own scandal? Or worse? Had he hoped to trap a wife before he became known as the most villainous lord abroad?

Sophie's spiralling thoughts worsened by the second until she was quite convinced she'd been as ignorant as any debutante could be, despite every warning about his character. And how she could have ever had a shred of doubt about dear, kind Sir Weston, who'd only ever tried to help her, felt like an injustice of the highest order.

Swiftly, she hurried through the connecting apartments from the Hall of Mirrors, scanning every flickering shadow with fresh zeal. Masked faces loomed out of every corner, while drunken, cajoling voices attempted to sway her in her progress. Yet all she could think was to find Sir Weston and entreat him to stop the fight. Damerel's arrival at Versailles could make him cry off their own assignation, but the thought of leaving the duellists to murder one another was unthinkable. Her chest pounded as she ran on, praying Sir Weston's tall, quiet personage would set him apart from so many drunken revellers. Yet there were just too many rooms, and guests determined to slow her progress. Then, finally, just as she was retrieving her hand from a cavalier who seemed determined to misquote Byron, she spied a familiar dress.

'Lu Lu?' Sophie panted into the shadowy alcove, certain she would know her friend's expensive silk anywhere. 'Where have you been? I really need to tell you something—'

'*Ma chérie!*' Lu Lu exclaimed, stumbling forward, her glossy hair dishevelled. 'I am so happy to see you! But please… I must introduce one of my oldest friends who I had no idea would be at Versailles tonight. Isn't it a happy coincidence?'

She flailed flamboyantly at her elegant companion who stepped forward in a duck-egg blue satin dress with matching mask, and a cloak suspiciously like the one in Madame Montmartre's window.

Yet Sophie would know her china-doll eyes anywhere.

'Aurelia!' she exclaimed in shock, feeling the world tilt on its axis again.

Of course they might know one another – ladies of the ton always did. Sophie's gaze swung between them as a wave of fresh questions flooded her thoughts.

Was this how Aurelia had known she would be at the Palais des Tuileries? Had she also known she was staying with Lu Lu when accusing her of enjoying 'life as a courtesan'?

'Ah, my least favourite Fairfax,' Aurelia said, placing an arm around Lu Lu's swaying form, 'and you've had considerable competition too! As dearest Lu Lu and I were just saying,' she continued, 'if you're going to play games on the marriage mart, you really should know your rakes from your libertines, otherwise you can end up looking rather *notorious* yourself.'

Lu Lu blinked in a haze of semi-consciousness, as Sophie's eyes narrowed, realising Aurelia was quite determined to ruin her, no matter the truth. And suddenly, she no longer cared.

'In truth, I'd rather be *notorious* than a pitiful, vengeful creature without one ounce of self-respect!' she hissed, snatching up a half-drunk glass of champagne and emptying it in Aurelia's face.

Then she grabbed Lu Lu's hand and pulled her away.

Sophie didn't look back, the extent of Aurelia's vengeance driving her pace and fuelling her search, until the rooms grew quieter and colder. Only then did she slow enough to take in the pitted walls and blackened gilt decor, lit by lone, flickering candles. It was an eerie sight, and briefly, she imagined Queen Marie-Antoinette running through, with a baying crowd at the gates. She shivered as a pair of burning torches came into sight, and was relieved to find they silhouetted an exit at last.

'Have you seen Sir Weston tonight, Lu Lu?' she said urgently as they stepped outside.

Swiftly, she scanned the *Cour d'Honneur* courtyard, which now looked as though it was lit by a thousand tiny stars that had fallen from the night sky. They shimmered to the faint strain of Mozart that rose from the gardens as she tried to catch her breath.

'You really should know your rakes from your libertines, otherwise you can end up looking rather notorious yourself.'

Aurelia's parting barb reached through her as she stared down at her friend, resting half-asleep against her shoulder.

'And why Aurelia, of all people?' Sophie added in a whisper, wondering if she'd been blind all along.

'Were you looking for your ... temptation?' she hazarded.

'*Oui*,' Lu Lu slurred in a forlorn voice, 'but I found a great *stupide* instead! Aurelia says not all gentlemen are made equally; some are more honourable than others. Thank heavens *mes chéries* do not suffer with the same malady...'

Immediately, Sophie pictured Rotherby and Damerel,

duelling in her honour at that very moment, and suppressed a rise of fresh fear. She could only hope Weston's very good sense would send him outside, once he realised the challenge of identifying anyone inside the palace.

'And you have become quite a favourite.'

Sophie gazed down at Lu Lu's drooping form, and knew then that whatever friendship she shared with Aurelia, she'd not intended to be disloyal. And now it seemed she had been let down as well. A flare of protectiveness flew through her as she wondered if she could possibly be the worst friend, as well as the worst sister, in the world.

'Miss Fairfax?'

Sophie started as a masked figure loomed towards them out of the shadows.

'Sir Weston?' she inquired incredulously, wondering if her stars could possibly have aligned at last. 'Is that really you?'

'It is, and I'm delighted you had the presence of mind to wait in the Cour d'honneur,' he replied. 'I was not expecting half of Paris to be here,' he paused to frown, 'as I was not expecting Madame Dupres to be with you. Is she quite well?'

Sophie thought rapidly. There was no way she could abandon Lu Lu, and every passing second could make the difference in the duel.

'She is fatigued, and not well at all,' Sophie replied, hoping he was too proper to consider the possibility of a noblewoman being drunk.

'I see,' he said with a swift nod. 'We will escort her away then. I have also brought a carriage as promised, with supplies,' he continued, as though midnight flights from the Palace of Versailles were the most commonplace occurrence.

'And, as far as I know, Rotherby's pastor still waits in Chartres. I believe it would be fairly simple to persuade him of our attachment, if you have reconsidered at all? I concede our hearts are not engaged, Miss Fairfax, but I'm certain that with friendship and time, they could be.'

Sophie inhaled deeply, briefly wondering how one gentleman could be so selfless, while others so stubborn they would rather endanger their own lives than concede, and yet there was no more time left.

'I thank you for your kindness Sir Weston, truly, but I have not changed my mind and there is an urgent matter—'

'*Le combat! Le combat!*'

Sophie felt the colour drain from her face as the faint shouting interrupted them. Swiftly, she glanced across to one of the entrances of the palace, which had spilled open to reveal two swordsmen silhouetted in flickering torchlight. Crowds of drunken guests had followed them, drowning out the musicians with their slurred carousing, while harassed footmen attempted to retrieve their ice buckets of champagne in vain.

For a second she could only stare, aghast, as the clashing of steel filled the night air. Rotherby was on the attack, his high brow creased in concentration, while Damerel was deftly parrying every thrust thrown his way. Then Damerel feinted a high attack before switching to a lunge that narrowly missed Rotherby's thigh, while the watching crowd groaned. Sophie caught her breath and tried to control her thumping chest, though she was conscious of Sir Weston's watchful gaze too.

'I would say your brother-in-law has this matter well in

hand,' Sir Weston offered calmly, 'and it is time for us to take our leave, Miss Fairfax.'

'But, we can't leave just yet!' Sophie protested, her voice betraying her fear.

He frowned as she gathered her skirts in her hand.

'This is all my fault!' she added guiltily, 'and while I am certain they are thinking of their *own* honour before mine – they do seem quite determined to keep going until one of them is murdered too! Please Sir Weston, we have to stop them!'

'On the contrary, Sophie,' Sir Weston replied unexpectedly, his hand closing over her gloved wrist. 'Much as I commend your instincts, their duel has actually created the perfect opportunity for our exit. The distraction will ensure our head start, and by the time they realise we're gone, we'll be halfway to Rouen – which is best for everyone, isn't it?' He paused to smile faintly. 'And besides, there is also your friend Madame Dupres to consider for she does, indeed, look most unwell.'

Sophie glanced down at Sir Weston's hand, as his use of her first name echoed around her head. She blinked. Sir Weston was her trusted friend, and any lapse in formality had to be attributed to the situation.

'Miss Sophie?'

She glanced up, suddenly so grateful to see Horace's familiar figure emerge from the darkness, swinging his gaze between her and the duel in the grand Versailles courtyard.

'What 'appened, miss?' he asked with his usual disgruntled expression. 'Why's the guvnor lookin' fit to murder the fancy gent?'

Sophie thought rapidly, realising Rotherby's fiercely loyal groom could be her last hope.

'I believe it may have something to do with a *game of faro*, Horace?' she replied urgently.

Horace's expression hardened, as Sir Weston looked on intently.

'Does it now. Well, I hope the guvnor trounces him good'n proper then, for he deserves it!' Horace said.

'I'm sure you're right,' Sophie agreed swiftly, 'though I think perhaps if he were *my* guvnor, I might try to *stop* the duel?'

'Stop it, miss?' Horace replied in horror. 'But it's a matter of honour, miss! You must know his lordship won't thank me for getting in the way.'

'I do know,' Sophie frowned anxiously, 'but the viscount's skill should not be underestimated, and his lordship *is* a little worse for wear, which hardly makes it fair, given his recent injury…'

Horace's eyes darkened, before he nodded.

'Aye, t'is hardly fair miss,' he growled. 'Right you are, leave it with me miss!' Then he turned and disappeared back into the crowd, leaving Sophie to meet Sir Weston's curious gaze.

'The viscount is my brother-in-law, and I've no wish to add murderess to my list of crimes,' she offered, a flush creeping into her cheeks.

Sir Weston nodded as he helped Lu Lu to her feet.

'But of course, Miss Fairfax,' he replied, 'I wouldn't imagine anything else.'

Chapter Twenty

DENOUNCING ALL RAKES AND LIBERTINES

A few minutes later

Sophie watched the palace recede with a churn of new feelings: relief at having left the drunken crowds behind, but also a new and distinct unease. She stole a glance at her shadowy escort, seated opposite, and couldn't help but compare Lord Rotherby's warm chaise to his rather shabby and rattling affair, though she knew it was the least of her problems.

Briefly, she conjured an image of the two duellists silhouetted by the grand lanterns of Versailles, and closed her eyes, praying Horace was successful. She hadn't asked them to defend her honour but couldn't bear the thought of either being hurt either. The viscount was Phoebe's whole world and Lord Rotherby was...

Swallowing, Sophie turned her gaze towards the inky night and finally freed every thought about him: his carefree kiss, his wild driving, his rueful laugh, his fever, his rescue from the rogues, and his unguarded moment in the Tuileries when he kissed her again. And then there was the moment tonight, in the Hall of Mirrors, before the scandalous reason he left London became apparent.

She released her breath, the memory of his intense eyes sending a swift dart of *something* from her chest to her toes, where it tingled in a very lonely way. He was unlike anyone she'd ever known and sometimes, he almost seemed to know her better than she knew herself.

'We must escort Madame Dupres home swiftly,' she murmured, surfacing from her thoughts. 'It would be unfair to burden her with the consequences of our actions tonight, especially when she has been nothing but the kindest of hostesses.'

A new smile played around Sir Weston's lips, and for the first time Sophie noticed just how thin they were.

'Calm yourself my dear,' he replied. 'We really don't have time for such a diversion, and I think we both know Madame Dupres's lethargy has nothing to do with exhaustion or illness. Thankfully, she is not an unmarried debutante, like yourself, and will lend some respectability to the first leg of our journey. I will, of course, ensure she is put on a coach back to Paris as soon as we stop, and by that time, I suspect she will be happy to wish us well.'

Sophie stared as he spoke, aware he was changing the plan, and yet unable to deny his wisdom either. She already knew Phoebe waited at Madame Dupres's residence, and a large part of her was guilty of wishing for Lu Lu's company a little longer too. She swallowed uncomfortably and swung her gaze back to the murky night, wondering how she'd arrived at this point, leaving behind the world she knew just so no one else could be hurt.

'Try not to worry, my dear,' Sir Weston said suddenly, sliding across the coach seat until he was directly opposite her.

'I am fully aware of the faro debacle that forced Rotherby to flee London, and I cannot abide dishonour of any kind. With luck, your esteemed brother-in-law will teach him a long-awaited lesson, and no one need ever speak his name again.'

His tone was so odd that a shiver slid down her spine. She already knew of their ready dislike of one another, but there was a new edge to his voice tonight, and he seemed most unlike himself. She gazed at his unsmiling countenance, etched by the moonlight into something harder. He'd never looked less like Rotherby, and the thought only worsened the ache within her chest.

'What *did* happen in the faro game, Sir Weston?' Sophie asked carefully, watching a shadow flicker across his face.

There was a brief silence before he replied. 'Rotherby was on a winning spree until I realised his cards were marked. I called his bluff, and he didn't like it.' His smile gradually widened. 'But marked cards are hard to deny, no matter how many well-connected friends one has at White's. It was quite a moment, I can tell you, Rotherby was entirely exposed as a cheat, the one thing noblemen cannot abide! It is beyond all things dishonourable, and I believe he will find it very hard to return to London. Now, with any luck, Damerel will ensure the same is true of Paris.'

There was another silence while Sophie absorbed Sir Weston's account. It was every bit as scandalous as she'd feared, and yet she was more unnerved by the crow in

Weston's voice than by his allegations. He was too delighted with Rotherby's downfall, no matter the bad blood between them.

She shifted uncomfortably, recalling Rotherby's wrath in L'Auberge Notre-Dame. It was so much more understandable now she knew Weston had been the one to expose him in London.

'You are but a day away from safety,' Sir Weston assured her suddenly, as though he realised he'd said too much. 'I have instructed the driver to make all haste to Chartres, where we will break our journey.'

'Chartres?' Sophie exclaimed sharply. 'But what of putting Lu Lu on a coach? And why Chartres? Surely we can choose another stop on the way to Rouen?'

'Sophie,' Weston said cajolingly, dropping his voice. He smiled ingratiatingly and leaned forwards, trapping her hands between his. 'Come, come. Chartres is the only town on this road for miles, and you must see sense now. We are travelling together overnight and your reputation is already beyond repair – I can offer you complete protection as my wife and no one will ask any questions because I am far too well respected for that.'

Sophie stared as though caught in the wake of a very bad dream.

'I've already taken the precaution of writing to the pastor to explain you're an orphan from a respectable background,' he continued with a perfunctory smile, 'and on that note, Madame Dupres might actually serve some useful purpose.' He paused, a distinct gleam of triumph in his eyes. 'I do believe this story will be enough to appease even the most cautious of natures, though we may need to persuade him of our natural affection too…'

A strange shudder reached through her as his smile widened. Lord Rotherby's proximity had never felt so intrusive.

'You said our hearts are not engaged, Sophie,' he continued in a lower voice, 'but I beg to differ. I have always held a torch for you, ever since our first meeting. Don't you recall my defence of you at the archery party? And my daffodils? Your express appreciation of them at the exhibition only served to encourage my belief that, one day, you might return my regard too.'

Dazedly, Sophie recalled the exhibition and how she'd only mentioned his flowers to make a point to Lord Rotherby.

'In truth, I have long been aware of your many qualities and will consider myself the most fortunate of gentlemen when I can call you my wife.'

Then, before she could collect her scattered thoughts, he leant forwards and pulled her into a sudden embrace.

At first, Sophie was too shocked to do anything but let his lips press against hers, to feel his arms tighten around her and inhale his sickly-sweet scent. Then, with a surge of horror, she tried to recoil, only to find his embrace tighter than any Lord Rotherby had bestowed upon her, and his lips quite intent on leaving their mark.

'I never allowed myself to believe I might stand a chance in London,' he whispered, as his hand pushed inside her cloak.

'Sir Weston!' Sophie protested, struggling furiously.

'Especially since Rotherby's interest was as plain as a pikestaff.'

'Sir Weston!' she hissed again, making Lu Lu stir on the seat beside her.

'And I was in torment,' he continued, deaf to her entreaties, 'until I saw you in L'Auberge Notre-Dame when I realised just how much you needed my help, and that your protests about marrying for love were all that your good breeding and manners would allow. Why else would you have asked me to escort you? But now you can relax, my dear, because I have everything planned and I hope this will be all the evidence you need that my heart is *very much* engaged.'

He tailed off then to caress her earlobe in a way that conjured images of the bulging-eyed Duke Wellington, while his fingers began fumbling with her bodice. Her stomach lurched as the true horror of her predicament struck her. Not only had she entirely misjudged Sir Weston's character, but he seemed wholly intent on compromising her virtue too. Never once had Lord Rotherby insulted her so throughout the entire course of their entanglement, while Weston now appeared to be the biggest scoundrel of them all.

This thought was all the extra strength she needed and, with a valiant effort, she yanked an arm free and reached up to cuff Sir Weston's face. He recoiled instantly, nursing his afflicted cheek which looked satisfyingly rosy in the gloom.

'Sir Weston!' she threw furiously. 'Compose yourself! We are *not* married and, quite frankly, after the behaviour of *all* the gentlemen of my acquaintance this evening, I have no wish to be!'

Muttering a curse that would make Fred stare, she reached down and grasped her friend, who'd somehow managed to slide onto the floor. Yet Lu Lu only snorted and mumbled something incoherent before starting to snore again, blissfully unaware of the drama unfolding beside her.

'I believed better things of you, Sir Weston,' Sophie continued accusingly. 'You led me to believe…' She faltered, hardly able to say the words that seemed so foolish and naïve now.

Why hadn't she questioned his ready friendship? Why had she been so naïve as to assume Sir Weston would be the human embodiment of his damned coats?

Yet, he was already moving, catching her hand and pressing his lips against it, sending rivulets of revulsion through her veins.

'I led you to believe that we were friends?' he quizzed, his eyes gleaming. 'We are about to be wed my dear, we need not be friends. You must not worry so much. Our fates are entwined now, and neither of us can do anything but marry after this night's work – I just wish I could see Rotherby's face when he hears the news!'

He laughed then and reclined, regarding her in a way that made Sophie realise this wasn't about her at all. It was *all* about Rotherby; it always had been. She clenched her fists, wondering how she could ever have got it so wrong. She'd trusted him at a time when she'd trusted no one else, and he'd deceived her in the worst way possible – yet, dwelling would not do now.

Her thoughts rattled furiously as she assessed her new choices. She could raise the alarm once they reached Chartres, but who would take her word over the very proper Sir Weston? And he was right about one thing: even the Parisian ton would struggle to overlook a debutante spending two nights with two different gentlemen and failing to marry at least one of them!

She stared at his gloating expression, berating herself, and yet knowing there was something missing still. Her thoughts hardened.

'What *exactly* do you have against Lord Rotherby?' she demanded.

Sir Weston regarded her with a piercing gaze.

'Why do you wish to know?' he countered. 'I was under the impression that Lord Rotherby had insulted you beyond forgiveness, that he'd ruined your chances of making a respectable marriage, and that you'd shot him in self-defence.' Sophie scowled as he paraphrased her confidences. 'Don't worry,' he added with a smirk. 'It's not the first time I've wondered if you protested a little too much, but it matters not one jot to me, my dear, for I'm the one who will shortly be calling myself husband.'

'You presume too much, sir!' She hissed, suddenly recalling the crossbow Lord Rotherby had given her, secreted inside her cloak pocket. 'I never courted Lord Rotherby's attentions, any more than he has sought mine.' His dark eyes, shadowed in hurt, reached through her thoughts and she faltered briefly. 'And my departure from Versailles was my decision alone. But now, sir, what of my question? Why is it you and Rotherby detest each other so?'

Sophie crossed her fingers within the folds of her skirt, praying his desire to blacken Rotherby's name would loosen his tongue.

'Rotherby believes his own reputation,' he said scathingly.

'But that's not it, is it?' she replied sceptically, watching his expression intently. 'There is something else, something that runs deeper.'

She returned his stare, knowing she'd hit a nerve.

'Clever little Miss Fairfax. You really are quite perceptive, aren't you?' His mocking tone made her itch to slap him again. 'Yes, you can definitely say there's something else. But that sordid tale is not suitable for your delicate sensibilities. Console yourself with the thought that marriage to me will result in much less scandal for the Fairfax name, than marriage to a Rotherby! At least it will by the time I'm through with him,' he added caustically.

Sophie stared, chilled by the threat in his voice. What could prompt one man to wish the downfall of another in such a way?

'How did you *know* Rotherby was cheating?' she pressed, and even though it was dark, his expression changed immediately.

'His winning streak was too consistent,' he said, his eyes gleaming. 'It made me suspicious and so I watched him. It quickly became evident he was using marked cards, and all those playing agreed the marks were plain to see. I may have been the one to notice, but Rotherby brought shame on himself by lying and cheating. There is no greater dishonour among noblemen, and he would have used you to buffer his scandal.'

Sophie frowned. Weston's heated accusation creating fresh doubts in her mind.

'But why would he need to cheat?' she challenged. 'He's rich enough already ... surely the idea of his cheating is nonsensical!'

Sir Weston shrugged. 'Rotherby may be rich, but his

arrogance and conceit make him believe he can treat the world and everyone in it as he wishes – just like his father before him.'

There was a tense silence while Sophie stared, rapidly recalling everything Lord Rotherby had ever shared about his childhood.

'You knew his father?' she asked lightly, hardly daring to breathe.

'I did,' he replied caustically, 'and let's just say the apple never falls far—'

But the rest of his words were lost as a shrill cry split the night, prompting the horses to rear violently. Sophie gasped, reaching for Lu Lu as Weston thumped the coach roof, before she realised something had changed.

'Lu Lu?' she whispered furiously.

Chapter Twenty-One

FOOTPADS AND BREECHES

Moments later

'*Mais*, where is the champagne, *ma chérie*?' Lu Lu asked groggily as Sophie attempted to prop her up. 'And why is this chaise longue so short?! I understand Versailles could not be refurbished in quite the same style but *alors*, I think some of my hats have more padding!'

'Please accept my apologies,' Sir Weston muttered drily.

'Sir Weston!' Lu Lu exclaimed. Her eyes narrowed as she shook back her hedgerow hair. 'But, why are you here? I told you I—' She paused to pull her cloak tightly around her small person. 'I told you I would not be seen in your company anymore,' she pronounced sharply.

Sophie swung her gaze from Lu Lu to Sir Weston's smug indifference in disbelief. Could Sir Weston also be the dishonourable *stupide* at Versailles?

'Did you see Sir Weston at the ball, Lu Lu?' Sophie asked, scowling.

'Not all gentlemen are made equally. Some are more honourable than others.'

'I had the misfortune to do so, *oui*!' Lu Lu glared. 'And then I learned he had the manners of – what do you Fairfaxes call it? – a pigwidgeoned dunderhead!'

Sophie turned back to Sir Weston with rage snaking up from the pit of her stomach. How she could have ever believed him the most proper of gentleman was fast becoming a mystery of unknown proportions. He was the very opposite: a duplicitous libertine who thought nothing of deceiving and insulting others in the pursuit of his own ends – which, she was increasingly convinced, was Rotherby's ruin.

'How dare you insult my friend!' she accused.

'Oh come, come Sophie,' he wheedled. 'It was just a little kiss. It was Le Grand Bal Masqué de Versailles after all!'

'Oh is that all it was?' Lu Lu remonstrated, waving her fan in Weston's face so furiously that Sophie would have laughed in any other circumstances. 'You, sir, are *no* gentleman!'

'No, he is not,' Sophie seethed, feeling as though she had never seen the world so clearly.

'He is a cad and a trickster and a libertine! In fact, he is *all* the things he would have had me believe of Lord Rotherby.'

'Absolutement, *ma chérie*!' Lu Lu said emphatically.

Sophie withdrew the miniature crossbow from her pocket and levelled it at Sir Weston.

'I have *not* given you leave to use my given name, sir,' she challenged. 'And I do not require your escort or the protection of your name. Stop the carriage at once!'

'Why?' Sir Weston laughed. 'Because of that *toy*?'

'It is not a toy,' Lu Lu declared indignantly. 'She shot my

dear Dominic with it, and I sincerely hope she shoots you too. But, is that why we are here, *ma chérie*?' she added fretfully, turning back to Sophie. 'Because you wish to marry this ... toad? *Non, non, non!* You must not marry this one when it is as plain as a pikestaff you're already in love with my Dominic—'

'I said as much!' Sir Weston cut in savagely.

'I am not marrying *anyone*, Lu Lu!' Sophie countered forcibly. 'Particularly someone with the moral compass of the amphibian you describe. But mostly because noblemen seem only to choose marriage when faced with scandal or a vendetta – not because they are in love.'

They were words Sophie never expected to hear from her own mouth and, briefly, Lord Rotherby's voice reached through her thoughts.

'Even the strongest of attachments rarely last a lifetime.'

She swallowed, feeling a wave of intense sadness threaten to engulf her. Lord Rotherby might be a liar and a libertine, but he'd also been right. Whatever she'd expected from the marriage mart had been entirely nonsensical and had she but taken his advice at the start, she might have saved herself a mountain of heartache.

'I am not marrying anyone,' she repeated, levelling the crossbow with renewed intent. 'Stop the coach!'

'Do see sense, Sophie— I mean, Miss Fairfax,' Sir Weston amended hastily. 'Consider what you are saying. Think of your sisters and the Fairfax family name. You have no money, no prospects and no gentleman of honourable standing will take you now. I am your only hope for respectability. And Madame Dupres's company will be no salvation if you are not married to me before tomorrow is done. You will be considered damaged goods Sophie – a ladybird no less!'

'Well, I'd rather be a ladybird outside this coach,' Sophie growled, fumbling for the window latch, 'than a buffle-head within it!'

'Sophie! *Ma chérie!*' Lu Lu shrieked. 'You cannot mean to stop here. We are in the middle of nowhere, and consider my new primrose silk slippers. They were not made—'

'Hush, Lu Lu!' Sophie said crossly, just as another cry echoed through the night.

She paused, frowning.

'Yes, there is someone in pursuit,' Sir Weston smirked.

'If we stop now, you risk our lead, and either Lord Rotherby will be your husband, or Damerel will return you to your brother who, if I am to believe his reputation, will ensure your disappearance from polite society for good.' Sir Weston's eyes glittered. 'Surely, marriage to me is preferential to that?'

'Doubtful,' Lu Lu muttered.

Sophie drew a deep breath, determined not to let Sir Weston glimpse her inner turmoil. She knew he was speaking the truth; her fate would be unrequited love or Thomas's convent. She could not bear either, and yet remaining in the same space as him was impossible too.

With fresh determination, she forced the sash window open, letting in a blast of cold night air.

'*Arrêtez!*' she yelled at the driver, and had the satisfaction of feeling the coach lurch to a violent standstill.

'I choose me!' she exclaimed, wiping the smile from Sir Weston's face. 'And I hope you've a plausible story for whoever is in pursuit, because neither Rotherby nor Damerel are known for their restraint. Lu Lu?'

Sophie jumped out onto the lonely heathland roadside and turned to grasp Lu Lu's reluctant hand.

'*Eh non!* This road is not safe for a walk, *mademoiselle*,' the beleaguered coach driver said.

'*Ma chérie*, my slippers!' Lu Lu wailed.

'Consider the mistake you are making, Miss Fairfax!' Sir Weston hissed.

'On the contrary Sir Weston,' Sophie replied, '*you* are the only mistake here, and Madame Dupres will be far safer with the driver and me, than incarcerated with you for another second!'

'*Eh non!*' the coach driver repeated, sidling back. 'No ladies with me!'

Sophie drew herself up proudly.

'I am Miss Sophie Fairfax of Knightswood Manor in Devonshire, and I'll not travel another second inside your coach with a cad and libertine! Either we get out or he does, and he is most certainly not sitting with you.'

It was at this exact same moment that a barouche and pair emerged over the crest of the hill behind them.

'Regarde!' Lu Lu shrieked in profound relief. 'We are rescued, *ma chérie!* There is no need for you to be Gaspard Bouis or Dick Turpin with that ridiculous crossbow anymore.'

She shuddered and began waving a white lace kerchief at the barouche, which appeared to be bowling along at a great pace.

'We are *not* rescued,' Sophie hissed, grabbing Lu Lu's lace kerchief. 'For we do not need rescuing! Inside, now!' she ordered Sir Weston, who scowled before retreating into the coach. 'And you, sir, *will* make room for us on your seat,' Sophie instructed the coach driver, who cursed as she pushed Lu Lu up onto the seat and tucked a thick blanket around her. 'There,' she said consolingly to her friend, who already had the look of one facing the gallows, 'this will be so much better than travelling inside with that ... *person*!'

Then the driver called to his horses, which sprang forward with fresh purpose.

It became almost immediately clear that riding atop the Fairfax chaise around the grounds of Knightswood in broad daylight, was entirely different to riding atop the worst-sprung coach along the Chartres road at midnight, but Sophie was determined to make up for lost time. And even if Lu Lu was pressing her lace hanky to her mouth in a distinctly discouraging fashion, she was convinced the cool night air was far better for her than the stuffy coach with that lecherous libertine ogling their every move.

In truth, the more she thought about it, the more she was convinced she'd managed the whole odious situation quite credibly, and in the past minutes the chasing barouche had even fallen out of sight again.

She exhaled raggedly. She was so done with gentlemen masquerading as libertines, libertines masquerading as gentlemen, and everything in between. She'd ruined it all, and the only thing she could do to give those who remained a chance, was disappear. Her life ahead wouldn't be the one she dreamed of but, as Lord Rotherby had pointed out at the beginning, dreams only ended in disappointment anyway.

It was just as she was contemplating this likely fate as a

ruined debutante, doomed to haunt potted roads between medium-sized French towns forever, that a lone rider loomed out the darkness ahead of them.

'It's past midnight,' Sophie frowned, as the coach driver cursed colourfully.

'We are doomed, *ma chérie*,' Lu Lu moaned into her hanky, 'quite doomed! This road is haunted by revolutionaries. We will now face *la guillotine* with the rest of Versailles…'

'That was nearly thirty years ago, Lu Lu,' Sophie remonstrated, 'and we will not face *la guillotine* for a few pigwidgeoned dunderheads!'

She swallowed painfully. Somehow, using Matilda's favourite phrase made her chest ache all the harder.

And yet the rider did not move, forcing the coach driver to slow to a standstill on the deserted Chartres road, in the middle of the black night.

'You ladies had best leave this to me,' the coach driver said.

'I think not.' Sophie replied, gripping the crossbow beneath her domino. '*Bonsoir!*' she called.

'*Bonsoir*. You have come from Versailles, *non*?' the rider called out.

Sophie frowned at the lean figure, just visible in the gloom ahead.

'Versailles?' she challenged, wishing her sisters were there to witness her accent. '*Mais non*. We're just ordinary *sans-culottes*, escorting this ordinary coach and its ordinary passengers—'

'Somewhere warmer,' Lu Lu interjected, glaring at Sophie.

'Indeed?' the rider drawled, leaning forwards on the pommel of their saddle. 'And there I was thinking you might be ladies from Versailles who'd run into a spot of bother. But since you're so very *ordinary*…'

Sophie frowned, sure there was something familiar about the voice. Then the rider shrugged before swinging a burgundy silk-lined velvet cloak over their shoulder with such decided style that Sophie's suspicions were redoubled … before she realised.

'Madame Montmartre!' She gasped, her eyes as round as saucers. 'I'd recognise one of your exquisite cloaks anywhere!

'*Ah merci*, Mademoiselle Fairfax.' The petite modiste grinned. 'They are *trop* elegant for a common footpad, *n'est-ce pas*?'

Sophie gazed in admiration as the modiste trotted forward, while Lu Lu stared in silent shock. And yet now she'd identified her, the figure couldn't possibly be anyone else. From her dark, expressive eyes to the daring cut of her riding breeches, the lone rider was clearly the revolutionary modiste.

'But your *breeches*, Madame Montmartre!' Lu Lu half wailed, half exhaled in admiration.

The modiste inclined her head most graciously.

'I made them myself,' she said, 'for I do not see why the gentlemen need have all the trousers to themselves.'

Sophie briefly recalled Phoebe saying something quite similar.

'*Ma chérie*, those breeches are too divine!' Lu Lu said, elbowing the coach driver out of the way to get a closer look. 'And is that silk? Your shirt?'

'*Oui*. A silk shirt and woollen cloak – for the cooler nights,' the modiste clarified, only too happy to share the secrets of her outfit with a favoured customer.

'La, I must have my own,' Lu Lu replied longingly.

'I would be only too happy to oblige,' Madame Montmartre replied, her pearly teeth catching the moonlight. 'Which is the reason I am here.'

'To take our orders?' Lu Lu frowned doubtfully.

'Non, non, though I would be happy to another time,' she beamed. 'I came because I overheard the plot against Mademoiselle Fairfax, and I believe in freedom above all things. *Vive la révolution!*'

For a second, no one said a word.

'Do not attempt to negotiate,' came a muffled shout from within the coach. 'Revolutionaries are cunning criminals!'

'I think you have some great *stupide* inside, *oui*?' Madame Montmartre said. 'Maybe I should just shoot him.'

'A very kind offer,' Sophie said quickly, beginning to think she'd underestimated Madame Montmartre significantly, 'but we left two gentlemen in Versailles intent on committing murder in my name and I've no desire to add to the body count.'

Briefly, a memory of the duellists in the flickering lantern light reached through her thoughts, prompting a fresh surge of dread.

'Aha! Versailles! You see, it is exactly as I said,' Madame Montmartre replied, sitting up to show off her silk ruffle shirt to its fullest advantage and making Lu Lu stare. 'When you were in my shop,' the modiste continued conspiratorially, 'I thought to myself, this lady who does not wish to be married, she is giving me a message though her brilliant designs'—Sophie glanced at Lu Lu, aware things were starting to get a little awkward—'and then when I met your Lord Rotherby, who I could tell was not going to take *non* for an answer, I understood ... *et voilà*, here I am.'

Sophie blinked, feeling sure she'd missed something.

'Pardon?' she asked faintly.

'I am here, to rescue you.'

For a second, there was no sound other than the wind barrelling across the sparse heathland, and some muffled laughter from within the coach.

'*Et maintenant*, you do not have to marry your Lord Rotherby, no matter how handsome he is and how many filigree masks he buys – though that is always nice of course – for you can join *la révolution* with me.'

Sophie blinked, knowing she ought to say something, but failing entirely. It was one thing choosing life in a provincial town as a dressmaker, and quite another to be strong-armed into a band of fashionable revolutionaries.

Thankfully, at that same moment, the barouche pursuing them barrelled over the hill at what Fred would have called a spanking pace. Madame Montmartre responded immediately, rearing up on her horse while brandishing her pistol in the air.

'And now, I will show you what true *fraternité* looks like!' she exclaimed. 'I will intercept this murderous gentleman and find you again in Chartres, where *mes amis*, we will arrange everything, *oui*?'

Then she galloped past without a backward glance, while the driver cursed and urged his horses forward.

Chapter Twenty-Two

LADYBIRDS AND PEACOCKS

Several cold hours later

'You couldn't look less like a revolutionary if you tried!' Lu Lu said placatingly. 'Not that you wouldn't look divine in a pair of those revolutionary breeches, though,' she added through a layer of blanket.

Sophie nodded, cold reality far outweighing any thoughts of revolutionaries or their breeches. Dawn had brought the very sobering realisation that not only did she care very much about the outcome of the duel, she'd also kidnapped a monstrous gentleman and incited an excitable revolutionary to murder too. The sum of this was a stone-cold fear that not even a dawn glow over the fabled town of Chartres could appease.

She closed her eyes and tried to ignore the nausea that had arisen since she'd admitted the true likelihood of Horace's success when it came to his guvnor's duel. If Rotherby had won, and the viscount was killed, she would have lost a sister; and if Damerel had done as he'd sworn and run a sword through Rotherby... Sophie clutched the sides of her seat until her knuckles turned white.

Miserably, she watched as the tired horses pulled them towards the approaching town, acknowledging that leaving Versailles and leaving her guilt were two very different things entirely, and whether Rotherby possessed a heart or not, she had most certainly lost hers.

'We only know true love when we face its loss,' Lu Lu said mournfully, side-eyeing Sophie. 'But my Dominic knows he must not kill any of your family, so it is more likely he has let the viscount kill him, *non*?' she added, patting Sophie's hand.

Sophie responded with a very strange groan.

'But of course we must wait for news before thinking of our widow's weeds, *ma chérie*,' Lu Lu continued rapidly, 'And in the meantime, we must rid ourselves of the great *stupide* and eat, for everything is always better after coffee and pastries, *non*?'

Sophie tried to smile. It had been a long night for them all and Lu Lu hadn't once complained at having been dragged into an entirely fresh scandal not of her making.

'Try not to assume the worst, *ma chérie*,' she said, slipping her arm through Sophie's as the tired horses trotted past the impressive façade of the cathedral Notre-Dame de Chartres.

'We will return to Paris after *le petit déjeuner*, and face everything together, *oui*?'

Sophie nodded wanly, but the truth was that Sir Weston had been quite correct. Not only was Lu Lu a widow, and therefore not subject to the same rigorous standards as a debutante, there was also the fact that if there had been a duel to the death at Versailles, all of Paris would now hold her responsible. And the more she thought about a world without the scandalous Lord Rotherby, the more she felt like shooting both the lecherous Sir Weston and the rude coach driver, who'd been singing to himself for at least an hour now.

Sophie cast a look around the sleepy courtyard entrance to Chartres's Hotel de Montescot, the only hostelry open to travellers, before nodding at a sleepy young ostler.

'Thank you,' she murmured, climbing down as though she'd aged a hundred years since Versailles.

The pan-faced ostler nodded, though his round eyes said everything about the appearance of two grand Versailles ladies, atop a common hire coach, at dawn, at the Hotel de Montescot.

Inhaling deeply, Sophie yanked open the coach door and discovered Sir Weston sprawled across the seat, as though settled in for the week.

'Madame Dupres and I have bespoken a parlour for breakfast,' she threw coldly. 'What you do now is entirely up to you.'

Then she turned and stalked inside to warm herself by the comfortable parlour fire, only to find both the coach driver and Sir Weston at her door a few minutes later.

'The landlord has only this parlour available for breakfast guests,' the coach driver said in a wheedling tone, 'and there are no other hotels open.'

Sophie closed her eyes in disbelief, while Lu Lu scowled.

'Well, come in if you must, but sit over there, out of the way!' Lu Lu scolded, before planting herself at the pretty parlour table. 'And do not even *think* about touching the pastries, for I am quite famished!'

For a short while, Sophie drowned her thoughts in the bottom of a pretty coffee cup, while Lu Lu put pay to a good number of the aforementioned pastries. Then the faint sound of fresh wheels reached through the courtyard window.

She glanced up swiftly, her skin growing clammy with fresh fear, and wondered if it was the moment of truth. She'd only wanted to take care of her family the only way she had left, but instead of fixing everything, she'd made it far worse. Lord Rotherby's dark eyes surfaced amid her thoughts, glinting at her in the candlelight, and her chest ached intensely.

'There's no point in hiding, for I know you're both in there!'

Sophie looked across at Lu Lu, hardly trusting her ears as the imperious voice echoed along the corridor.

'Aurelia?' she said in disbelief, as the voice was followed by a sharp rap on the door, before it flew open to confirm the new arrival was indeed Lady Aurelia Carlisle.

For a second, no one said anything.

She was still dressed in her Versailles finery – an exuberant affair comprising the duck-egg blue satin gown, overlaid with numerous layers of net and lace until Sophie wasn't entirely sure where the dress stopped and Aurelia began. Yet, it was all painted with a fine spray of mud, while her pearl-netted curls were askew, her rouge streaked, and her china-blue eyes glinting murderously.

Sophie blinked as Lu Lu beamed.

'Aurelia!' Lu Lu exclaimed delightedly, 'have you come all the way from Versailles? Oh! And Madame Montmartre too?'

Sophie's gaze widened as the revolutionary modiste

suddenly appeared in the doorway, looking decidedly the worse for wear.

'How lovely to see you again, Madame Montmartre,' Sophie said in a rush, her brain whirling with a thousand possible excuses as to why she might not be quite ready to join *la révolution*. 'We were so anxious for you when you left ... and do excuse me, but are you quite well? It looks as though you may have been in a skirmish?'

Sophie cast her gaze up and down the volatile revolutionary, who was now dishevelled and muddied, as though she'd encountered some fierce loyalists along the way.

'Was it the barouche driver?' she asked with a frown.

'*Mais oui*. It was this *rude* barouche driver,' Madame Montmartre stormed in, gesticulating at Aurelia. 'I'd half a mind to run my sword through her, but it is the bodice, you see, it is very fine lace so I could not bring myself to do it. And she says she is a friend of yours so ... *voilà!*' She flung herself into a chair beside Sir Weston.

'Wait, so *you* were the barouche driver?' Sophie asked Aurelia in astonishment. 'And you drove all the way from Versailles – after us? But what of the viscount or...'

Sophie faltered, unable to say Rotherby's name on top of the sudden, intense fear seeping through her bones. Whether from comfort or vanity, she'd convinced herself one of them was in pursuit, and now she had to face the possibility that neither were able to do so.

Aurelia smiled contemptuously, before pulling an ivory-handled dagger from her skirts, prompting a series of gasps around the room.

'I have pursued you all the way from Versailles,' she said

dangerously, 'without so much as a change of undergarments, and all you can ask is, *where is Lord Rotherby?*' She brandished the dagger in the air. 'Hopefully he and the viscount are fully impaled on the end of each other's swords by now, for they are nothing to me!'

'Aurelia!' Lu Lu scolded reprovingly, as a second gasp rippled through the room.

'You are speaking of my own very dear Dominic, and Sophie's brother-in-law too. Pray, do not forget your manners, *ma chérie*!'

'I forgot my manners the night Miss Sophie Fairfax forgot hers and stole my plan, though how Lord Rotherby ever mistook her scheming face for mine I've no idea!' she snapped.

'It was dark!' Sophie protested.

'Well, there must have been thick fog in both your heads but I care not! I'm so over the Fairfaxes and your husband-thieving games. What I cannot forgive is that you think nothing of stealing my cherished friend, while running away with another half-wit! And don't deny it – I saw the two of you carry her to your coach.'

Sophie blinked as a faint memory stirred.

'I also have an old beloved friend in Paris who has much influence with Lord Rotherby…'

And in a rush, Sophie realised she'd been staying with the friend Aurelia had mentioned at the exhibition – a friend she actually appeared to care about far more than anyone knew.

'*Non, non, ma chérie*,' Lu Lu protested. 'Sophie did not steal me, and she was certainly not running away with that great *stupide*, that *imbécile*! How could you think so? In truth, I thought him my friend also, but now I know I'd rather remain a widow for the rest of my days than marry Sir Weston!' she exclaimed with a look of disgust.

'Well, I think that's a bit strong,' he muttered indignantly.

Sophie took a deep breath, now certain Lu Lu's loyalty had never been in question.

'Aurelia, you know, even if you can't admit it, that I never set out to *steal* anyone,' she said in a low tone. 'And I am quite aware that your plan to spread rumours about my life will be all the harder if it risks the reputation of your beloved friend.'

At this Aurelia stared sullenly, yet Sophie knew that her pursuit showed a chink in her armour; that there was hope for her too.

'And really, *ma chérie*, I am only here because the great *stupide* thought I added respectability to his folly,' Lu Lu said with great solemnity, 'which is altogether *très drôle*, is it not?'

'Hurry, boy!' A sudden pompous tone filtered along the corridor, halting Aurelia's response. 'I have a *very* important meeting about a *very* urgent matter, and as I am already two minutes late, I must make haste.'

Feeling as though this morning couldn't possibly get any worse, Sophie shot a glance at Sir Weston, who was reclining in his seat with the air of one very satisfied with himself. A wave of suspicion arose within her – and then she just knew. She scowled intently at his horribly smug expression. Of all the hotels in all the provincial towns in France, they had to break their fast in the same one in which Sir Weston had arranged to meet the pastor!

A thousand conflicting thoughts hurtled through Sophie's head, but uppermost in her mind was the fact that she now needed to defend herself to the infamous English pastor in a muddied Versailles gown and domino, amidst the oddest array of company. Cursing beneath her breath, she did her very best to shake out her flattened curls and crumpled skirt. She might be the most disgraced debutante ever to walk the earth, but she was determined to look respectable enough for the pastor to listen to her, and not Sir Weston.

Yet the moment the door opened, her brief flicker of hope guttered, for from the slick of his oiled hair to the silk tassel of his Hessian boots, stood a greater stuffed peacock she had ever to set eyes upon.

'Ahem,' he cleared his throat noisily. 'I am looking for Sir George Weston, but feel I may have been brought to the wrong room. Pray excuse my intrusion into your'—his supercilious gaze swept the room, taking in the varied array of persons and their even more varied array of bedraggled clothing—'gathering,' he concluded disparagingly.

He prepared to withdraw, just as Sir Weston got to his feet.

'I am the gentleman you seek,' he confirmed with one of his most proper bows, 'and I thank you for being so prompt, sir.'

'The lady I am betrothed to wed is that one – not the one wielding a dagger.' He gestured at Sophie smugly. 'You see, dearest, didn't I say the pastor could be counted upon?'

Sophie glowered as the pastor ran his gaze slowly over Sir Weston's crumpled coat, dangling Versailles mask and half-eaten pastry, before drawing a visible breath.

'Your letter,' he enunciated very deliberately, 'stated that you were quiet, respectable persons, wishful of a quiet, respectable wedding, however'—he swung his gaze between them with the look of someone who'd stumbled across a water closet that hadn't been emptied for several weeks—'I see nothing remotely quiet *or* respectable here. Your manner, sir, is presumptuous, there are crumbs about your person, and your company is very much less than'—he cast a deprecatory glance around the room before wrinkling his nose in distaste—'honourable.'

'Vous avez raison, monsieur,' the coach driver nodded traitorously through a mouthful of warm bread, 'c'est vrai. The English lady, she seized my coach.'

Sophie looked at her feet as the pastor blanched and swung his condescending gaze back to her.

'Seized?' he pronounced awfully, looking her up and down, 'And now I know I have wasted my time entirely! I do not perform marriage ceremonies for persons of dubious quality, and I certainly don't dally in low company. Does no one in this party have any sense of propriety?'

At this, the ladies gasped.

'Monsieur, that is an insult too far!' Madame Montmartre exclaimed, shaking out her silk-lined velvet cloak to its fullest advantage. 'I have the privilege of dressing most of the ladies present and not only are they very respectable, they know, unlike you, to avoid green puce under all circumstances! I can assure you, not all my customers are so insightful.'

She turned to smile at the ladies in question, well satisfied with herself.

'And you are?' the pastor enquired, reminding Sophie of a beleaguered trout.

'Madame Montmartre, Parisian modiste at your service,' she replied, sweeping a haughty bow.

'A modiste? Dressed like a revolutionary?' the pastor accused, his eyes narrowing.

'Bah!' she said dangerously, 'better a revolutionary than a stuffed English peacock!'

Sophie took a deep breath, feeling her every crease and displaced curl flood with a curious kind of exhaustion. Quite aside from being a murderess, she'd travelled all night, hadn't bathed in hours, had suffered the attentions of lecherous libertines, and then been subjected to Aurelia's accusations before this poppycock of a pastor had appeared. She should be furious – and she would be – if it weren't for the fact that his pompous nature had also provided her with an opportunity. She glanced at Sir Weston, inspiration brewing. Perhaps this would prove easier than she first thought.

'This is clearly a meeting place for vagrants and vagabonds,' the pastor continued, 'and you should be ashamed of yourself, sir, for luring a man of the cloth into such company. I will remove myself before my reputation is tarnished beyond redemption.'

'You really should,' Sophie agreed swiftly, feeling Aurelia's stare. 'It is well known that I have a penchant for befriending rakes, rogues and everyone in between, sir. And there is no telling what damage you may do – to your heavenly reputation, as well as your earthly one – simply by being in this room with us. It is certainly for the best that you remove your esteemed personage while you still can—'

'Mais non, ma chérie,' Lu Lu interrupted, 'you are *tres honourable!*'

'Do not listen to her, sir,' Sir Weston protested. 'Miss Fairfax is all things—'

'No, no I am not!' Sophie interrupted furiously. 'I am extremely dishonourable and dubious and there is absolutely nothing to be done about it – the pastor really must know the truth.'

'Well,' the pastor blustered, his eyes bulging, 'in all my years, I have never heard such a confession spoken so glibly. For my part, I cannot imagine anything *less* heavenly than a marital union between a tap-hackled ne'er-do-well and common adventuress! I bid you goodnight.'

'In truth, sir,' Sophie called after him, 'the relief is all ours!'

Then she turned back to face Sir Weston with a look of triumph, but the victory was short-lived for no sooner had the disapproving parson disappeared, than the yard filled with the sound of more horses and ostler calls. She swallowed, knowing the brightening morning would bring a flurry of visitors to the hotel, and with them the very distinct likelihood of real news.

'*Mon dieu!* Who now?' Madame Montmartre exclaimed, rushing to the window.

'I could guess at a few,' Aurelia said with a smirk.

A fresh wave of suspicion stirred with Sophie.

'Did you tell someone you were following us?' she demanded.

'Oh no, well … not exactly,' Aurelia replied, breaking a pastry apart. 'Although I suppose I *may* have dashed off a letter to your brother, Thomas, before I left England, to let him know you were Lord Rotherby's new *courtesan*. Come to think of it, he wrote back most promptly saying he'd been informed otherwise, but that he was making all haste to Paris, and if Rotherby didn't escort you down the aisle, he would take the greatest pleasure in persuading him to wed you at the tip of his own sword! La, what a thought! I'd give *all* my pin money to watch anyone try to force Dominic to do anything he didn't want. And, now I think of it, I may have left a message about your excursion to Chartres for the charming viscountess too. She's newly arrived in Paris and most keen to see you, as I understand it, so really it could be any one of your delightful brood. How exciting!' She popped a morsel of croissant in her mouth.

Sophie listened in disbelief, subtly aware that there was something new in her tone – a note of regret perhaps – yet what did it matter? She'd done everything she could to protect her family, all for Aurelia to bring them directly after her.

'How could you?' she accused shakily.

'And now the two English ones will kill one another,' Madame Montmartre pronounced in an awful voice.

'That would certainly change my plans,' Sir Weston said, just as a familiar voice filtered through the draughty window.

'Excuse me, but is there an English miss here? It's of the utmost importance I speak with her.'

'Phoebe!' Sophie whispered hoarsely, her head spinning.

Her sister sounded grave and alone, and suddenly the full horror of discovering whether she'd ruined Phoebe's life, as well as her own, was more than she could bear. She cast a stricken look around the room before rushing to the door. She could already hear Phoebe at the front entrance, talking to the landlord, and a wave of homesickness threatened to topple her. She wanted nothing more than to run towards her sister, to throw her arms around her and bury her face in her warmth and protection.

Except Phoebe might not offer her warmth and protection ever again – and she would rather live her whole life apart than spend a second watching her beloved sister's heart break.

Which left Rouen.

Her chest pounding, Sophie sprinted as though her life depended on it, through the corridor and steamy kitchen and out of the back door into the fresh spring air. Then she let herself out of a small yard, slipped down an alley and emerged onto a town road where, to her wretched relief, a public coach was boarding.

'Rouen?' she panted, just as the coach driver was closing up.

He frowned at her crumpled Versailles gown, before she proffered her gleaming crossbow fare, a question in her eyes.

'*Oui*,' he replied with a shrug, opening the door for her.

With a last big effort, Sophie climbed up and squeezed into a corner of the rickety contraption, beside an elderly farmer with a basket of goods.

'*Oignon?*' he offered kindly.

At which point, she thought only of Phoebe, and promptly burst into tears.

Chapter Twenty-Three

ONE CONSUMMATE ACTRESS

Several pot-holes later

Sophie very swiftly realised that the hideously overgrown road to Rouen was only partly responsible for her misery. That the greater part of her despondency stemmed from the realisation that, while leaving her sister behind was one of the hardest things she had ever done, facing her would have been even worse.

'*Actrice?*' a small boy with bright copper hair enquired.

She nodded faintly, drawing her cloak tighter around her muddied gown and bedraggled hair. He'd clearly spied her precious gold filigree mask which still hung around her neck on a cream ribbon and assumed she'd come from a stage. And in a way, she had.

She hadn't been herself from the moment she'd crossed paths with Lord Rotherby. Phoebe had tried to warn her, but she'd ignored her and not because she wanted to win the wager, or even because she was aware she liked him. It was so much bigger than that. She'd wanted to prove Lord Rotherby wrong in the most fundamental way possible: *she'd wanted him to fall in love with her.*

And she'd wanted him to do this, in spite of his protest that he didn't possess a heart.

The more she thought on it, the clearer it all became. It had started at Almack's when she'd accepted his wager, and then every decision she'd made since – attending the exhibition, interfering with Aurelia's plans, staying to nurse him, defending her freedom so fiercely – had all been back-lit by the vain hope that, at some point, he would realise he was entirely wrong about love.

She swallowed. It was the ultimate deception – and now, with a trail of murderous duels, lecherous libertines, fiery modistes and broken-hearted sisters behind her, she was the one learning the lesson. She'd been as guilty of trying to control love, as Rotherby was of denying it. And instead of falling for her, she'd lost everything – while she didn't even know if he lived or died.

Dominic's moss-green eyes swam before hers, and the burning inside her intensified until they were back in the vast, shimmering hall and its hundreds of mirrors, facing one another.

'Though I, for one, believe position and control can sometimes mask...'

Had he been about to declare himself, or prove he was the dishonourable libertine the world believed him to be? She would never know.

Sophie stared out at the passing French countryside, at the fields of violets interspersed with early cowslips and lily of the valley. Occasionally, there were copses of budding magnolia and cherry trees, and the early spring blossom made her long for Knightswood, with its haze of bluebells dancing in the light.

It was by no means certain she would ever see it again, and while the thought was bleaker than any other, she also knew there was no turning back now. As it stood, it would still take all Thomas's scheming, as well as Phoebe's connections, to ensure Josephine and Matilda received respectable offers. All while she watched from a provincial French town, wondering how she managed to fall so far in just a few short weeks.

It was with this dismal turn of mind that she at last arrived in Dreux, a small town with medieval influences and a large gothic church that one of her companions called L'Église Saint-Pierre. It had such a quaint atmosphere, compared with Versailles and Chartres, that Sophie felt almost relieved as she followed the coach party into a small, respectable inn. She had no coin, just one thing left in her possession to trade for food and lodgings until she made the last leg of her journey to Rouen.

Reluctantly, Sophie removed the Versailles mask Lord Rotherby had given her, and approached the antiquated reservations desk where a ruddy-faced landlord rubbed his hands and beamed.

'*Et bienvenue, mademoiselle,*' he boomed, his breath reeking of red wine and garlic.

'What can Le Lion D'or do for you? Your maid is bringing your bags, *non*? My ostlers can be a little lazy I know…'

He looked towards the open doorway, and Sophie felt a rush of chagrin. He'd glimpsed her gown and assumed her to be a member of the haute ton come to grace his establishment, when nothing could be further from the truth. She took a breath and willed her French good enough to reserve a bedchamber and a small meal, as she placed the mask on the desk.

'I have lost my purse, but I intend to sell this gold filigree mask to pay for my board,' she said quietly. 'If you are happy with this arrangement, I will recompense you handsomely in return.'

Sophie waited, the pain of parting with Lord Rotherby's precious gift far outweighing any shame she felt at begging for a room.

But it was the landlord's wife who came bustling forward.

'*Non, non, non!*' she blustered vehemently, pushing her husband out of the way. 'No maid, no money, no room. Le Lion D'or is not for the likes of you. If you have no francs, there is a boarding house for girls like you who will take payment *in kind* … that way!'

Sophie swallowed, feeling all the colour drain from her face as the landlady sneered and pointed back out into the street. Never had she been spoken to in such a way, and yet she suspected it was just a taste of what was to come now that she was truly on her own.

'Please, my name is Fairfax,' she rushed in English. 'And I need only a small room to refresh—'

'*Non!* Le Lion D'or is a respectable establishment, not for girls of *your*—'

'Excuse my interruption, Madame Bernard,' came a querulous voice from the shadows. 'But it isn't often that I hear my own tongue spoken in these parts, and I wonder if I might be of assistance?'

'*Mais, m-madame*...' the landlady stammered.

'You agree? Excellent!' the voice declared smoothly.

Sophie flushed as a stooped figure emerged from the dark corridor. Her years were advanced, but she had a pair of shrewd grey eyes, while her high-waisted dress and draped muslin skirt were stylish, but dated. Sophie lowered her gaze and pulled her domino tighter around her. She had no doubt she was a lady of quality, and waited for her inevitable condemnation once she spied her own bedraggled person.

Instead, there was only silence while the lady perused her figure, before turning back to the landlady.

'But what a mercy you didn't send this young lady elsewhere, Madame Bernard,' she said authoritatively. 'For I know her *very* respectable family, and they would be most disappointed were you not to provide hospitality as you would to one of your own.'

'*Mais, madame*, I cannot...' Madame Bernard began in a scandalised whisper.

'But of course, madame!' the landlord exclaimed, overriding his horrified wife, 'any friend of yours is a friend of ours. Won't you follow me, mademoiselle? We have a most pleasant bedchamber for you upstairs. It is small but warm, with a freshly made bed,' he continued. 'And after you have freshened up, perhaps you would care to come downstairs for some light refreshment?'

'She will take a tray in her room and enjoy a good rest before she joins me in my private parlour this evening,' the unknown lady stated firmly. 'And I will stand surety for her bill, so there is no need to hurry into town yet, mademoiselle. After all, you'll not get a fair price for a Versailles mask in Dreux, as I'm sure my friends here will testify.'

The landlord and landlady nodded in unison, though Sophie was sure it was through gritted teeth.

'*Bon, bon ... et maintenant*, if mademoiselle would follow me?' The landlord invited, beckoning her forwards.

Sophie knew she owed everything to her mysterious benefactor, but was too exhausted to do more than smile wanly before forcing her legs up the rickety wooden risers. And when the landlord opened a door at the end of a narrow landing, she found a bedchamber just as he'd described – small, snug and clean.

She turned to thank him, but he'd already departed to make way for a young maid with a tray bearing soup, crusty bread and thick slices of ham. It looked heavenly and with a grateful smile, she took the tray to the window, before enjoying the best meal she'd had for some time. Then she took off her muddied gown, crawled between the freshly made bedsheets, and finally fell into a deep and exhausted sleep.

Chapter Twenty-Four

SOUFFLÉ AND DRAMA

Several hours later

When she awoke, Sophie discovered that the magic had extended to a small warm bath, fresh undergarments and a gown of sensible sprig muslin. Quietly, she climbed into the steaming water, feeling as though she might never appreciate something so much again.

'For you are still a Fairfax, no matter what,' she whispered, rinsing her face in the vain hope of ridding her eyes of their pink rim.

She hadn't cried and knew she daren't start for fear of never stopping. Briefly, she recalled the last time she felt like doing the same in the squalid, shady streets of Paris, and drew in a ragged breath. Back then she'd told herself she never wanted to see Rotherby's face again, and now she wasn't sure how to face the future without it – libertine or not. A twist of pain darted through her as she recalled his burning kiss in the garden at the Tuileries, before his shadowed eyes in the Hall of

Mirrors. And now, in trying to protect her family from the ripples of her scandal, she was quite alone in the world, as she deserved.

She pinched her cheeks hard and stared at her pale reflection, willing it to look more hopeful. Then she coiled her hair into a neat bun, before pulling a few curls free to frame her face. It was one of the first hairstyles she'd adopted as a schoolgirl before abandoning it in favour of more sophisticated updos. Tonight, though, it felt oddly comforting as she stood back and checked her wan reflection. She still had no idea why the unknown lady had helped her at all, but if it was true and she knew the Fairfax family, then the very least she could do was behave like one of them. Phoebe would advise her to thank her benefactor, and promise to pay back every penny of what she owed, and it was with this sombre intention that she left her bedchamber and descended the stairs for dinner.

If Madame Bernard still nursed any hostility, there was no trace of it when she greeted Sophie and escorted her to a private parlour, where a roaring fire and well-dressed table awaited. Sophie eyed it nervously as she entered the room. Now that the moment of truth had come, she felt strangely shy of the sharp-eyed lady who'd taken charge of her affairs so swiftly.

Yet she had only moments to wait before the parlour entrance darkened once more.

'Good evening, I trust you have rested well?'

Sophie turned swiftly to greet her benefactor, who was standing in the doorway, eyeing her with the same piercing gaze she recalled.

'Yes, thank you ma'am,' she replied, sinking into her most modest curtsey.

She was determined to make a better impression now she was dressed appropriately; it felt like the very least she could do.

'Well, come here then, child, so I might inspect you,' the lady replied, leaning on an ebony walking stick as she made her way towards the table.

Instinctively, Sophie started forwards, just as she might to help Harriet or any of her elderly relatives only to find herself waved away. But when her benefactor sank into a chair, there was a softer gleam in her eyes.

'Yes, you have the look of your mother, God rest her soul,' she said, pouring herself a glass of claret.

Sophie frowned faintly, her head filling with a thousand questions, just as a knock at the door confirmed that dinner had arrived. She swallowed and nodded politely, realising her questions would have to wait a while yet.

In fairness, dinner turned out to be a most delicious affair comprising three full courses: a vegetable soup followed by platters of capons and quail, and Sophie's favourite, *soufflé au citron*, before the last of the serving staff finally left them alone.

She looked up tentatively, wondering how to even begin to thank her for such generosity.

'Now then, mademoiselle,' her benefactor said, settling back in her chair. 'You look and sound like a lady I once knew, who would be most concerned by her daughter's appearance in Le Lion D'or with naught but a masquerade outfit to her name. 'I wish to help, but require absolute honesty in return. Can you oblige me this much?'

Sophie smiled nervously, knowing that nothing but the whole truth would do for this perceptive lady – but that she wanted to tell her everything too. She drew a breath and then, haltingly at first, the whole story came tumbling out. She omitted nothing – knowing this wise and perceptive lady would somehow know if she did – and when finally she came to the end and lifted her gaze, she felt a hundred times lighter.

'But what a tangled web you have spun in the pursuit of a love wager, my dear,' her benefactor mused, swirling her claret. 'I can only hope that this spoiled lord you describe has learned his lesson.'

'If he is still alive,' Sophie said, sniffing dolefully, 'and if he is, it means I have consigned my sister to a lifetime of heartbreak.'

The kindly lady only smiled consolingly.

'If I know ought of the characters involved, my dear, they'll have come to their senses long before any bloodshed and realised that murder, in the name of honour, is rarely honourable at all. But your plan to remove to a provincial French town, despite numerous offers of marriage from undeserving puppy dogs? Now that has a truly noble ring to it! Tell me, does anyone else know of this plan of yours?'

Sophie shook her head doubtfully. It had been such a relief to unburden herself, but her own behaviour couldn't be further from noble.

'And your fashion designs have been influenced by the public exhibition in London, as well as your time in Paris, you say?'

Sophie nodded again, wondering why she was taking such an interest in the dismal plans of a likely murderess.

'Excellent! You remind me of someone else at your age in the way you've pursued your own path, and not bowed to societal pressure.'

'But that's just it,' Sophie protested. 'I was always the one most expected to make a good match, not *pursue my own path* or defy societal pressure – that's Phoebe … or Matilda.'

'You have Fairfax blood, Sophie,' the lady said with a smile. 'You have more fire than you realise – and sometimes our hearts know what we want, even when our heads don't agree.'

'Speaking of which, I believe we have company…'

Startled, Sophie pushed back her chair and jumped to her feet, as the sound of whinnying horses and tired ostlers reached through the small parlour window.

'They have followed me from Chartres,' she whispered, feeling the colour drain from her face. 'Please, they will force me to marry … or join a convent … or…'

'You have resisted them before,' her benefactor replied calmly, picking up her glass. 'And there is nothing to be gained by hiding, after all. We must face them and determine our fate without fear.'

'But you don't know the gentlemen involved! My brother and Sir Weston, they are determined—'

'I have more than thrice your years, child, and have navigated the world of gentlemen for as long. I know just what it is to feel the pressure of our position, and I never resolved anything by hiding. Trust me, we shall resolve the matter together, tonight, but not by running.'

Sophie stared in despair at the unruffled lady, who seemed unable to understand the severity of her situation and wondered if she'd thrown away her precious lead on a kind, but eccentric, stranger.

'Take the horses please, I'm in a hurry!'

Sophie felt the rise of nausea in her throat as a curt tone filtered through the open window. She gripped her chair.

'Sir Weston,' she whispered. 'He's the *real* libertine.'

'I've yet to meet a man who doesn't have the potential, given half the chance,' her benefactor observed drily.

Then there was only a low mutter, and swift footsteps in the corridor, before the door was flung open without ceremony.

'There you are!' Sir Weston growled, marching across the room, his sheen of good breeding entirely discarded. 'You spent the night in my company and by God, you'll marry me if it's the last thing you do! I'll not have *my* name dragged through—'

'I don't think your name warrants any interest whatsoever,' her benefactor cut in, 'but I anticipate one has just arrived who may beg to differ.'

Sophie spun with mounting horror, as the yard outside filled with the sound of more horses and new, urgent voices. At this fresh intrusion, Sir Weston shot a scowling glance in the lady's direction, before drawing his sword and turning back towards the door.

Then there were more harried conversations and impetuous footsteps, before the door flew open again to reveal not one but two riders gazing back at her. They were dishevelled, exhausted, and covered in mud, but unmistakable all the same.

'Viscount Damerel! … and Lord Rotherby,' Sophie

whispered hoarsely, unable to tear her gaze from Lord Rotherby's dirt-streaked face.

Her heart pounded: he lived. They both lived. She was not a murderess.

Yet, by the look on Weston's face, there was still time.

'Sophie, thank God! Please, let me explain properly—' Lord Rotherby began, ashen-faced.

'Thank goodness we have found you, Sophie. Phoebe is beside herself!' Damerel exclaimed.

'I'll thank you to choose your weapon, sir! We will finish this now!' Weston hissed, silencing them both.

'You!' Lord Rotherby snarled, pulling out his sword and advancing with such venom that Sophie felt it through her bones. 'You are correct that we will finish this now, sir, and you will feel my blade for this night's work!' he added furiously. 'God knows I've kept silent over the years, even though you have taken every opportunity to blacken my name! And I may not have yet proven that it was *you* who marked my cards in London, but the moment you involved Miss Fairfax, you crossed a line!'

Astonished, Sophie could only watch as Rotherby closed in on Weston, who brought his sword up so furiously that she knew at once they were evenly matched. She paled as she swung her gaze between the two men, reading hatred in every line of their bodies, while blood thrummed in her head.

'You chose the family feud, while I left it where it belonged,' Lord Rotherby accused with an ugly scowl. 'And while there has never been anything I could do to change history, you have sought to punish me our whole life long!'

'You knew his father? I did, and let's just say the apple never falls far from the tree.'

Weston's words reached through her panicked thoughts, as Viscount Damerel's gaze narrowed sharply. And she knew exactly why he stared. Their likeness had never been so obvious as now: it was in their murderous expressions, their proud stature and the flare of their tempers too. A chill chased through her as she locked eyes with her exhausted brother-in-law, never more certain their shared blood was the cause of their feud too.

'The family feud?' Sir Weston sneered angrily. 'How poetic that sounds! Yet in truth, our father was a blackguard who thought nothing of taking what he wanted while ruining the lives of others. My mother was honest with me about his ruthless pursuit – which sounds more than yours ever managed.'

'How dare you!' Lord Rotherby hissed, white-lipped and furious. 'You may have my commiserations on your blood, but my mother was beyond reproach and I will not have her name sullied. You will never speak her name again in my presence!'

He lunged then, though Sir Weston met him with a stinging defence, before following up with a series of powerful strikes.

'You must forgive me if I fail to be moved by your *tragic* childhood,' Sir Weston said, panting, 'because while your mother enjoyed every luxury, mine was condemned to a life of misery. She was forced to live a life of shame for your father's violation, while I grew up in the shadows – and all the while, I've watched you enjoy every privilege, knowing Rotherby blood ruined my life!'

'You sir, have no idea of what you speak!' Rotherby snarled

as he parried, before advancing again with furious strikes and a final lunge that saw his blade pass terrifyingly close to Weston's neck. In a heartbeat, Sophie snatched up a water jug and emptied the contents over the duellers, who paused, gasping for breath.

'Well played, Sophie!' the unknown lady said approvingly. 'If gentlemen behave like children, we must treat them as such. And I'd rather not ruin my soufflé with blood and drama if possible – cards is my preferred entertainment after dinner.'

Sophie glanced at her companion, who'd been watching from the shadows, and wondered again if she wasn't a little touched in the head. It was impossible to understand how she could be so calm unless she didn't grasp the full situation, after all.

Yet, to her utter astonishment, both gentlemen suddenly froze, before lowering their swords and turning towards her, their expressions a mixture of incredulity and fear.

'Tante Elizabeth!' Rotherby was the first to find his tongue, executing a deep and respectful bow.

Tante Elizabeth? Confusion flushed Sophie's veins as she swung her gaze back to her mysterious benefactor, who seemed just as serene and unmoved as ever – before she smiled.

Sophie clamped her hand to her mouth in horror.

Hadn't Aurelia mentioned an aunt who'd stood guardian through Rotherby's childhood? Could she have confessed her entire pitiful story to none other than Lord Rotherby's own Aunt Elizabeth? *Including a very plain account of Lord Rotherby's own misdoings too?*

It was inconceivable, and yet the only answer, too.

Flushing scarlet, Sophie recalled everything she'd relayed to Rotherby's aunt in painful detail.

'I'm so grateful you decided to come to Chartres, Aunt Elizabeth,' he continued, 'and can only thank the heavens that Sophie – Miss Fairfax – had the good fortune to fall in with your company. Perhaps now you perceive the charms I wrote to you about?'

Sophie's flush deepened.

If he'd written to his aunt about Chartres, she must have known about her fall from grace from the moment she'd shared her name.

'Yes, well, you can save those pretty compliments for one who will appreciate them. And, of course, I was on my way. You wrote that you'd lost your heart, boy – the nephew who claimed never to have one!' his aunt said, waving her glass of claret. Startled, Sophie stole a glance at Lord Rotherby's rueful smile. 'As for the rest, I *have* had the good fortune to enjoy Miss Fairfax's company this evening, and can fully understand the appeal, though why she might wish to give either of you a second glance, is quite beyond me.'

Sophie watched in astonishment as Elizabeth pushed herself to her feet and shuffled into the light, where there was no denying the resemblance in her proud profile at all.

'Now listen to me, all three of you,' she commanded, eyeballing the gentlemen, who looked more like recalcitrant schoolboys with every passing second. 'This is a most unfortunate business, and it is imperative you do not blemish this young lady's name further, though you haven't made things easy at all.'

She jabbed her cane as though it was a sword itself.

'Rotherby, you were ever the impetuous hothead! When will you learn you cannot inflict your will on the world? And didn't I say to find me if ever you were in a mess? You should have brought Miss Fairfax to me the moment you landed in France.

'Weston, you were dealt an unlucky hand, but that does not give you permission to scheme against my nephew. You, sir, will confess your wrongdoing in a witnessed letter before this night is done and I will not, no I will *not* hear another word against my sister, or I will run you through myself!

'And as for you, Damerel, you haven't helped matters at all with that entirely unnecessary show of heroics at Versailles! You were ever the same as a boy, far too free and easy with that sword of yours.'

'Apologies, my lady,' Viscount Damerel mumbled with a crest-fallen expression.

'In truth, I am furious to discover that between the three of you, you have managed to force the hand of this young lady so much that she had to flee across France with only a Versailles mask to her name. And so, it appears, I am left in a quandary.'

Elizabeth paused to assess each gentleman with her razor-sharp gaze, making them shrink visibly before Sophie's eyes.

'Miss Fairfax reminds me so much of myself at the same age, yet this world does not know what to do with women of our mould, does it, Sophie?'

Sophie shook her head speechlessly, feeling as though she'd agree with anything this marvellous lady might say just now.

'Clearly, in besmirching her name, you each bear a responsibility to clear it.' She eyed Rotherby and Weston with derision. 'And yet, I feel certain that between us, Damerel and I could concoct a tale plausible enough for the world to swallow, should she desire it ... which brings us back to you, Miss Fairfax. You have confided in me without shame or embellishment, and in return for your honesty, I offer you a choice.

'You may choose Rotherby, if you desire it, though I struggle to find a heartfelt recommendation just now, or you can tour the galleries and fashion exhibitions of Europe with me until such time that you deign to give him a second chance ... with your ridiculous brother-in-law's blessing of course.'

At this further condemnation, Viscount Damerel sunk his chin into the folds of his cravat.

'I am sure I have lived long enough to lend us both sufficient respectability while we put about an alternate narrative: that your sister the Viscountess was delayed in Europe while you were travelling to stay with her, and Rotherby gallantly offered to escort you to his aunt, an old family friend, with Madame Marie-Louisa Dupres in attendance. Above all, there need be no talk of marriage, unless you wish it.'

'But Tante Elizabeth,' Rotherby protested, a little flushed, 'Damerel and I duelled at Versailles. Any number of the ton will assume it was a matter of honour concerning Miss Fairfax.'

At this, Elizabeth drew in a deep breath, her eyes glinting.

'And you would be the first gentlemen to create a drama because *your* honour had suffered? Though you are correct in assuming that in thinking only of yourselves you have created further problems for the young lady you protest to care for so very much!'

Sophie stole a glance at Lord Rotherby's ruffled profile, feeling as though she'd been living in a darkened room these past few weeks.

Could he really have lost his heart, just like she had, at the start?

'You are fortunate indeed that my reputation is such that no one will dare say there was ever a different story!' Elizabeth said in a steely tone.

'We ladies of the ton are makers and breakers of reputation with a few well-chosen words, and it wouldn't be the first scandal to be *moulded* into something else – that part you must leave to me. Yet I will say I am disappointed, for I may have thrice your years, but I have a thousand times more sense in my little finger, than you gentlemen have all together!

'Now then, Miss Fairfax, the time has come. What do you choose?'

Silently, Sophie swung her gaze from a pale Lord Rotherby to a glowering Sir Weston, a sheepish Viscount Damerel, and finally back to Elizabeth's sharp, inquisitorial expression.

She lowered her eyes and drew a breath to speak, just as a low voice intervened.

'May I speak, Miss Fairfax?' Lord Rotherby asked urgently.

She glanced up and nodded faintly.

'I wish to say that I'm sorry…'

'No please, let me say this,' he entreated as Sophie tried to pause him.

'We both know that you would not be here if it were not for my wager that night in Almacks. I was arrogant and unfair on a young lady in her first season, and if I could go back now and change them, I would,' he paused to exhale, running his fingers through his unruly hair. 'You must understand that love has always seemed a *weakness* to me, something that rarely results in anything but unhappiness. It hurt everyone I knew when I was growing up, and I vowed never to be that vulnerable with anyone. I told myself that if I believed I had no heart, I could exist in a space where no one got hurt ... but what I did not understand was that we are never the authors of love, but rather the pages upon which it must be written—

He broke off to take a few unsteady breaths, and when he spoke again, his voice was shaking.

'Marry me, Miss Fairfax ... because I have never been in less doubt that I do, indeed, possess a very real heart – and it burns and yearns for you, most furiously.'

Sir Weston groaned audibly and the viscount flicked some imaginary dust from his sleeve while Sophie stared, stilled by a raw vulnerability where once there was only detachment. His face was so close to hers, his scent enveloping her, making her ache so intensely that she felt it reach through every limb.

'Touching though this display of sentimentality is—' Sir Weston began.

'I don't recall anyone giving you permission to speak!' Elizabeth said gloweringly, cutting him off. 'In fact, I believe you forswore the right to *anything* when you treated Miss Fairfax to a display of your less than gallant colours on the journey to Chartres. You'll be lucky if I don't share that particular tale with every respectable family on both sides of the Channel, if only to ensure no female ever has to put up with your insidious attentions ever again!'

It was Sir Weston's turn to pale, as both Rotherby and Damerel turned back to him, scowling.

'Which is not another invitation to behave like schoolboys!' Elizabeth exclaimed, before levelling a softer gaze on Sophie. 'Come, child, you've heard what my tiresome nephew has to say, and you need not worry that either your brother or the viscount will bring any view to the matter. You have me now, and few spar with Tante Elizabeth and emerge unscathed. So, what is it to be?'

Sophie inhaled raggedly, the events of the past twenty-four hours beginning to take their toll, and yet somehow making more sense than anything had in a long while.

'You owe me no apology,' she replied directly, looking at Lord Rotherby. 'I was the one who took it upon myself to prove I was right when in fact … neither of us were.' She paused to swallow, 'And you are correct when you say that we are not the authors of love, for it can be neither controlled nor denied when it is but a hope. You see, your wager has actually taught me a great deal.' She glanced at Sir Weston, who looked up hopefully. 'Including the *true* nature of a scoundrel!'

A fresh scowl settled on Sir Weston's face as she pulled her gaze back to Lord Rotherby.

'And when I said I would marry for love,' she continued, 'I never once imagined it would be to a rake with a reputation for scandal.' A shadow crept into Lord Rotherby's eyes, as she took a step towards him. 'Yet I've also learned that reputation is only ever a mask.' She paused, his eyes never leaving hers. 'And now your aunt offers me the most wonderful opportunity to study the galleries and fashion exhibitions of

Europe, which I have longed for my whole life and so I must choose ... Tante Elizabeth...'

Her voice faltered, as she placed her hand against his thumping heart.

'...Until such time that we tell the world of our engagement.'

He cursed then, and damning all propriety, pulled her into an ardent kiss.

'So long,' she chuckled breathlessly against his lips, 'as you concede the wager?'

'I concede every wager,' Lord Rotherby said through a million tiny kisses, 'I ever made, most readily.'

'It is well then,' she smiled tenderly, 'that a Fairfax *always* honours their word.'

Chapter Twenty-Five

KNIGHTSWOOD MANOR

Six months later

Lord Dominic Hugo Rotherby withdrew from his naked entanglement with his usual regret. His new wife was near impossible to leave, but he'd promised Damerel some help with the school.

Furthermore, there was Horace to consider – Horace, his feisty tiger who'd adored both his guvnor and the new Lady Rotherby right up until their wedding day, after which he'd morphed into the most difficult human being of their collective knowledge.

They'd offered him a position as Head Groom in the hope it might offset the wedding blow, but neither his new quarters, nor his eye-watering allowance, had raised so much as one condescending eyebrow. Sophie joked he was still affronted by the new lavender phaeton he was obliged to perch upon on occasion, but they both knew the truth – that he was afflicted by the much greater offence of having to share him.

Thoughtfully, Dominic surveyed her sleeping form, her hair fanned out like spilt honey across their tangled sheets. Despite making him wait far longer than he wanted, fully supported by his fierce aunt, the last six months had been the happiest of his life.

He'd thought he knew all there was to know about women – every curve caressed, every mystery uncovered – yet Lady Sophie Rotherby had taught him he was nothing more than a hapless schoolboy, naïve to the joy of body-and-soul-bewitching love. And now he was as much enchanted as he was married – even more so when Sophie announced that their distraction had resulted in a further distraction, forecast for late summer.

It was the news for which he never thought he'd hope, after spending so many years believing he'd never marry. And while he couldn't wait to meet a new Rotherby with Fairfax virtues, neither he nor Sophie had the stomach to tell their beloved Horace that his bad dream had just become a nightmare.

His smile spread as a low knock sounded at the door.

'Apologies for the disturbance, my lord,' Benson murmured quietly, looking a little flustered.

Rotherby surveyed his elderly butler with misgiving and, not for the first time, wondered if he'd done the right thing in bringing some of his household to Devon. He and Sophie had thought it a chance for them to consider retiring to the sleepy local village, yet retirement seemed to be the last thing on their minds.

Benson cleared his throat.

'Miss Matilda sends her best regards, my lord, and wonders

if you and Lady Rotherby might be available to attend a circus performance in the blue saloon, after luncheon? I have been instructed to inform you that there will be acrobatics, juggling and some fire-eating – apparently dependent on whether the Viscountess Damerel has hidden all the candles. She has also recruited the services of Miss Harriet Godminster to assist with costumes, as circus-performing requires an extensive wardrobe … apparently.'

Rotherby smiled. His elderly retainer was wearing an expression of long-suffering disapproval, yet there was a twinkle in his eye he'd not seen for a long while, and colour in his cheeks only Devon could have put there.

'So long as Harriet is willing, I have no objections,' Lord Rotherby replied.

'Miss Matilda was also keen to impress that she would brook no absences, sir,' Benson said, pan-faced. 'And I'm to tell you she has also invited Sir Thomas Fairfax, the Viscount Damerel, the Viscountess, Miss Josephine, Masters Edward and Henry—'

'Yes, yes,' Lord Rotherby intervened hastily. 'I understand the entire household has been invited, thank you—'

'But, and on this point she was quite particular, my lord,' Benson said emphatically, 'no *pigwidgeoned dunderheads*!'

'Ah, and do we know many of those, Benson?' Lord Rotherby replied, feeling rather bewildered.

'Apparently, Lady Sophie knows of a few my Lord, and Matilda wanted to remind everyone that only persons of *good* character are on the invitation list.'

'Well, that's a relief, thank—'

'Including Duke Wellington.'

'I see…'

'Who is to perform as well.'

Lord Rotherby waited, beginning to understand that his wife's youngest sister had Benson entirely wrapped around her little finger, and Benson was as much traumatised as he was captivated.

'Miss Godminster also asked me to mention there has been a delivery from Paris, which she believes may be a response to her ladyship's sketches.'

'Ah, well that is good news, Benson.'

'Though I'm not sure what a Parisian modiste can have to say to a lady in the Rotherby household after all,' Benson huffed.

'Quite,' Lord Rotherby agreed, trying to edge back through the doorway. 'But if she takes Paris by storm in the spring, no one will be prouder than me.'

'Of course, my lord,' Benson said, clearly not quite ready to leave. 'Mrs Farleigh was also wondering, my lord … that is, she asked if you'd like the, ahem … adjoining bedchamber opened now?' he added, coughing to cover his embarrassment. 'It's only on account of the length of time Lady Rotherby has occupied your lordship's bedchamber, my lord. She is a little concerned that you might not both be getting … enough rest.'

A grin broke out across Lord Rotherby's face, as he finally understood the question to which his elderly retainer had been building.

'Benson, please tell Mrs Farleigh that I appreciate her concern, but my answer is the same today as it was three months ago. Lady Rotherby and I are most content with our bedchamber arrangements, and will undoubtedly be so for some time. Perhaps, if Mrs Farleigh is so inclined, she might like to redirect her concern to Horace, who will be in need of considerable understanding for the foreseeable future?'

'Yes, my lord. I will let her know, my lord,' Benson said with a sigh, finally turning away.

Rotherby closed the door with an amused smile, before glancing at his sleeping wife. Then he set about collecting his scattered clothing, marvelling at how he, Lord Dominic Hugo Rotherby, notorious rake, sworn gambler, wager-maker and unrivalled darling of the ton, could ever have been brought to this state: a married father-to-be with more headstrong family, whimsical friends and cantankerous dependents than he ever would have believed.

And that he was really, quite scandalously, content.

Glossary

Addle-pated – air-headed
Adventuress – Regency slang for prostitute
Bag of moonshine – Regency slang for lot of nonsense
The British Institution – Founded by a group of aristocratic connoisseurs in 1805 and preceded the National Gallery (1824)
Buffle-headed – Regency slang for stupid and dull, confused
Dunderhead – Regency slang for dunce, numbskull
Gaspard Bouis (1757-1781) – French highwayman renowned in Provence for his donations to the poor
High-stepper – Regency slang for a horse trained to lift its feet high off the ground when walking or trotting
King's route (or Rotten Row) – a route for fast riders through Hyde Park
Ladybird – Regency slang for prostitute
Libertine – person devoid of most moral principles, a sense of responsibility, or sexual restraints, which they see as unnecessary

Glossary

Meddlesome tabby – Regency slang for interfering woman/spinster

Paris to Versailles – the great distance of 17km (10.5 miles) was covered by coaches travelling at the rattling speed of 8mph, hence the typical journey time was between 1-2 hours.

Pigwidgeoned – Regency slang for a contemptible or stupid person; small or petty

Pyrexia – also fever (historical)

Single-Shot Flintlock – Typical duelling pistol in 1821 which fires a lead ball

Tap-hackled – Regency slang for drunk

Tinker's damn – Regency slang for not give a care

Psyche knot – a loose, Roman-influenced Regency hair-bun often accented by a ribbon tied around the head

Tiger – a smartly liveried male acting as groom or footman, formerly provided with standing-room on a small platform behind the carriage, and a strap to hold on by; or an outdoor boy-servant. Not in popular usage until 1817

The Arrow & The Dasher – The first cross-channel steam packets run by the Post Office from 1821

Thunder an' turf! – Regency exclamation

Acknowledgments

Some of my happiest childhood memories are of being curled up with a Regency novel, making this series very much a full-circle moment. Phoebe and Sophie are the feisty heroines of my Regency dreams, and their band of unruly siblings, the characters I needed while growing up in my own large and chaotic family of eight.

Yet, while the Fairfax Sisters have been a joy to write, they've also felt like a challenge because of the legacy of the authors I've always loved, and their many readers. The result is this series: Regency stories with modern heroines and a big family heart.

I'd like to extend my special thanks to:

My editors, Charlotte Ledger and Helen Williams, for believing in my feisty heroines from the outset.

My illustrator, Chloe Quinn, for the most perfect covers – I will never be over those eyebrows!

My agent, Elizabeth Counsell, for all the belief and support.

My writing buddies Bex Hogan, Serena Molloy, Katharine Corr, Holly Race and the original Scribblers for solidarity and the journey.

All the readers and bloggers (especially Claire @bookishreadsandme) who've taken the time to read and review – so important and very much appreciated!

And finally, thanks to my Mum and Dad, who somehow raised a whole netball team (+ one reserve), and managed to make it look easy – my heroes, always.

You are cordially invited to fall in love with your favourite new Regency romance novel…

'I don't pretend to know the details of your private life, Miss Fairfax, but you might do better to embrace the fortunate position into which you were born, rather than regret the one that only exists between the covers of a novel'

Miss Phoebe Fairfax dreams of being as free as her four brothers. When she discovers she is to be wed to a repugnant earl who is old enough to be her grandfather, she decides to embark on a real adventure…

Enter the insufferable – and insufferably gorgeous – Viscount Damerel.

Available in paperback, ebook and audio!

The author and One More Chapter would like to thank everyone who contributed to the publication of this story…

Analytics
James Brackin
Abigail Fryer

Audio
Fionnuala Barrett
Ciara Briggs

Contracts
Laura Amos
Laura Evans

Design
Lucy Bennett
Fiona Greenway
Liane Payne
Dean Russell

Digital Sales
Laura Daley
Lydia Grainge
Hannah Lismore

eCommerce
Laura Carpenter
Madeline ODonovan
Charlotte Stevens
Christina Storey
Jo Surman
Rachel Ward

Editorial
Kara Daniel
Charlotte Ledger
Lydia Mason
Victoria Oundjian
Ajebowale Roberts
Jennie Rothwell
Sofia Salazar Studer
Caroline Scott-Bowden
Helen Williams

Harper360
Jennifer Dee
Emily Gerbner
Ariana Juarez
Jean Marie Kelly
emma sullivan
Sophia Wilhelm

International Sales
Peter Borcsok
Ruth Burrow
Colleen Simpson
Ben Wright

Inventory
Sarah Callaghan
Kirsty Norman

Marketing & Publicity
Chloe Cummings
Grace Edwards
Emma Petfield

Operations
Melissa Okusanya
Hannah Stamp

Production
Denis Manson
Simon Moore
Francesca Tuzzeo

Rights
Helena Font Brillas
Ashton Mucha
Zoe Shine
Aisling Smyth
Lucy Vanderbilt

Trade Marketing
Ben Hurd
Eleanor Slater

The HarperCollins Distribution Team

The HarperCollins Finance & Royalties Team

The HarperCollins Legal Team

The HarperCollins Technology Team

UK Sales
Isabel Coburn
Jay Cochrane
Sabina Lewis
Holly Martin
Harriet Williams
Leah Woods

And every other essential link in the chain from delivery drivers to booksellers to librarians and beyond!

One More Chapter is an award-winning global division of HarperCollins.

Subscribe to our newsletter to get our latest eBook deals and stay up to date with all our new releases!

signup.harpercollins.co.uk/join/signup-omc

Meet the team at
www.onemorechapter.com

Follow us!
@OneMoreChapter_
@onemorechapterhc
@onemorechapterhc
@onemorechapterhc

Do you write unputdownable fiction?
We love to hear from new voices.
Find out how to submit your novel at
www.onemorechapter.com/submissions